Triple Alliance

One of Scotland's best-loved authors, Nigel Tranter wrote over ninety novels on Scottish history. He died at the age of ninety in January 2000.

'Fishing and hawking, porridge and game, the smell of peat and bitter cold Highland nights: a page from any of Nigel Tranter's Scottish historical novels evokes the lie of the land better than a library of history books' *The Times*

'Through his imaginative dialogue, he provides a voice for Scotland's heroes' *Scotland on Sunday*

'He has a burning respect for the spirit of history and deploys his characters with mastery' *Observer*

'A magnificent teller of tales' *Glasgow Herald*

'Tranter's popularity lies in his knack of making historical events immediate and exciting' *Historical Novels Review*

Triple A

Nigel Tranter

CORONET BOOKS
Hodder & Stoughton

pyright © 2001 by the estate of Nigel Tranter

ublished in Great Britain in 2001 by Hodder and Stoughton
First published in Great Britain in paperback in 2002
by Hodder and Stoughton
A division of Hodder Headline
A Coronet paperback

2 4 6 8 10 9 7 5 3 1

A CIP catalogue record for this title
is available from the British Library

ISBN 0 340 77017 1

Printed and bound in Great Britain by
Mackays of Chatham plc, Chatham, Kent

Hodder & Stoughton
A division of Hodder Headline
338 Euston Road
London NW1 3BH

Principal Characters in order of appearance

General David Leslie: Covenanting commander.

Patrick Murray, 2nd Lord Elibank: Former Montrose campaigner.

George Hepburn of Monkrigg: Laird and physician.

Oliver Cromwell: Lord Protector of England and captain-general.

Colonel James Stanfield: Roundhead officer.

Lieutenant-General George Monk: Roundhead commander, later Duke of Albemarle.

Lady Elizabeth Stewart of Traquair: Wife of Lord Elibank.

John Hay, Master of Tweeddale: Later earl thereof.

Major-General Morgan: Roundhead commander.

Helen Swinton: Daughter of Swinton of that Ilk.

Lieutenant-General Middleton of that Ilk: Scots commander. Later earl.

Joanna Auchmutie: Sister of Lord Elibank. Widow.

Richard Cromwell: Son of Oliver. Successor as Lord Protector.

Lord Lintoun, Master of Traquair: Later earl thereof. Brother of Elizabeth.

Charles the Second: King of the United Kingdom.

James Maitland of Lethington, Earl of Lauderdale: Chancellor of Scotland.

John Leslie, Earl of Rothes: High Commissioner. Later duke thereof.

Robert Blackwood: Edinburgh merchant.

Peter Dalgleish: Shipmaster.

James, Duke of York: Brother of King Charles and heir to the throne.

Lady Stanfield: Wife of Colonel James.
Philip Stanfield: Son of above.
General Thomas Dalyell of the Binns: New commander of
    the Scots army.
Archbishop James Sharp of St Andrews: Scottish Primate.

FOREWORD

In this novel I have taken some liberties with dates and sequences, not my normal custom, this in order to be able to bring in a due understanding of the wealth of important details, effort and initiative, spread over a quite considerable extent of time by the three main characters, whose lives interlocked and were so productive, but each ending at different and undefined periods. Lord Elibank, for example, died well before all the relevant activities were completed. So rather than break up this triple alliance, I have had to adjust the dates somewhat. I hope that I will be excused. This is a novel, after all, not a historical treatise.

NIGEL TRANTER

Part One

1

It made a strange march indeed, two strange marches, of two armies all but alongside, and enemy armies: the Scots under General David Leslie, victor of Philiphaugh which saw the downfall of the great Marquis of Montrose five years before; and the English Ironsides under the Captain-General Oliver Cromwell, who had brought about the downfall of Montrose's monarch Charles the First. The Scots were advancing, if that was the right word, while the English were retreating after being repulsed at Edinburgh. The two were only about three miles apart, both hosts heading eastwards, parallel, and both led by most able and experienced generals. They were well aware of each other's presence, of course, but neither wanted a confrontation – not yet, at any rate. The English were following the direct route, as indeed they had come, for a return to their own country after an unsuccessful campaign in Scotland, unusual for Cromwell; having crossed the Gledsmuir to bypass Haddington town, they were proceeding on by Hailes, below the great Traprain Law of legendary fame, on the way to Dunbar. The Scots were taking a much slower and more difficult route, up and down and inevitably devious, well to the other, south side of the said Traprain, by the Lammermuir foothills approach also to Dunbar, near to Garvald, to pass Whittinghame and Stenton. Leslie aimed to trap Cromwell at a strategic location between the narrow coastal plain and the Doon Hill, where the enemy had to wheel southwards, round those shouldering Lammermuir Hills, for Berwick-upon-Tweed and their England. Inevitably the

3

English, entirely a horsed army, moved the faster, however weary and dispirited they might be.

The Scots were anything but dispirited, all but assured of victory; and moreover with Almighty God very much on their side, or so the clergy declared loudly. And the said clergy were notably present, indeed all but in command, the Covenanting present rulers of Scotland, with young Charles the Second forced to bow the knee to them and all but a prisoner up in Moray, where he had come from exile on the Continent after Montrose fell, he declaring that Presbyterianism was no religion for gentlemen. The very Commission of State of the Covenanters was present on this march, guiding General Leslie, by their way of it, the almighty's authority supreme. These did not enhance the speed of the Scots march, of horse and foot, over those awkward hilly miles. But at least this army was cutting a corner, and they were not weary physically.

The situation was strange in more than this parallel marching and divided guidance. For the Scots army was oddly composed, apart altogether from the dominant and numerous clergy. Present was another General Leslie, and a senior one, indeed a field-marshal of Gustavus Adolphus's Swedish army: Alexander, Earl of Leven, no relation, who had commanded the victorious Scots at many battles, including the great Marston Moor, but who had fallen out with the Presbyterian churchmen for accepting the title of earl from King Charles, allegedly, and had come along on this venture, with his namesake, as a private individual. David Leslie in decency could not accept that, and had named him lieutenant-general, to the other's amusement.

The earl was by no means the only peculiar volunteer of this array. Among others were two former high officers of the late Montrose's army who, despite being labelled sinners and apostates by the Covenant, had rallied to the national standard at this Cromwellian invasion, and were now serving as mere private soldiers, however senior they formerly had been. There were others like them, but these two were friends, and lairds of properties quite close at hand: Patrick Murray, second Lord Elibank, from Ballencrieff, and George Hepburn of Monkrigg, each only two miles to north and south of Haddington, the county town. The former had been a lieutenant-colonel under Montrose, the latter physician-in-chief with that renowned guerilla-warfare host, unusual in being a laird with medical training. Now they rode side by side, well back from the leadership group and the clergy. Frequently they raised eyebrows at the loud pronouncements of the Covenanting divines. Elibank was an Episcopalian and Hepburn a Catholic.

Leslie had scouts out, of course, and these reported that the English were presently passing Beil and crossing the Beil Water, this only about four miles from Dunbar, where the turn south would be made. This word did concern Sir David Leslie, for he did not want Cromwell to get past the Broxmouth area, two miles beyond and south-east of Dunbar, where he aimed not exactly to ambush the enemy but to challenge them between the Doon Hill and the sea, where was a narrow plain. His own force was now only near Pitcox, short of Spott village, and still four miles from this hill. The English must not get past that position, if it could be helped, where the hills drew back and would give the veteran Ironsides room to manoeuvre. He urged haste; but a strung-out army of over twenty thousand, only partly mounted and in rough country, was not easy to hasten.

Fortunately or otherwise it was nearly dusk of a dull and damp day of early September. It would be dark soon, and with a host to feed, and a weary one, Cromwell very probably would choose to halt for the night near Dunbar town, where they could gain food. If he did so, then the haste was not so important. But that could not be relied upon.

After Spott, they could just see the isolated Doon Hill

rising ahead of them vaguely in the gloom. It was no mountain, rising to less than six hundred feet above sea level; but because it rose abruptly out of the coastal plain it looked the more impressive. It was no peak either, having a flattish summit of quite a few acres, whereon had once been a Pictish fort, or dun, which gave the place its name. This was Leslie's present target.

The western slopes of the hill were much less steep than those facing east and the sea, and, with night upon them, they mounted the former. They could not see Dunbar or the enemy, but their scouts would keep Leslie posted.

Soon a couple of these did arrive to inform that, yes, the English had halted at Eweford just south of the town, and were obviously going to encamp there. So it seemed that the Scots were going to have to pass a wet night on this hilltop, however unpleasant. But at least they had a sufficiency of food and drink, although there would be no campfires.

The younger Leslie turned to the elder, and requested the earl to take, say, five thousand of their horsed men and ride back whence they had come, and round the hillfoot to the coast, at Broxmouth, there to wait, to be able to act as a deterrent and distraction for Cromwell in the morning. This was agreed, and a quarter of their force departed. Patrick Murray and George Hepburn had not known whether to go with the Earl of Leven, but, given no guidance, remained with the major grouping.

Uncomfortable as that night was, these two at least were used to such in their campaigning with Montrose, so largely in the Highland mountains. They settled down, wrapped in plaids, and slept better than some.

At dawn, grey, wet and miserable as it was, all were roused, and Leslie announced his strategy and his orders. About one-third of his force, dismounted, would go part way down that steep face of the hill to where it lessened notably, this to tempt Cromwell to attack them. If they all stayed on this summit the difficult ascent would almost certainly deter the enemy, as a major handicap, especially for cavalry, and, with Leven behind them, they might well elect to hasten on southwards, avoiding battle. This would be contrary to the Scots advantage.

So down that awkward descent went some four thousand men, dismounted, leaving the remainder, with the clergy and the horses, up on the top. Halfway down, where the incline levelled off somewhat, they halted, to form up and present a tempting quarry for the mounted Ironsides. If and when attacked, they were to retire again, uphill, this to give the English the daunting task of mounting that steep ascent on their horses, or else dismounting to pursue, and this while Leven's force was emerging to threaten their rear. The rest of Leslie's army would be hidden behind the hill-crest.

It all seemed to be sound tactics.

Descending to the stage where the hill became less steep, the four thousand or so went, slipping and sliding, inevitably in no sort of formation, there to draw up into as orderly ranks as was possible, and to await developments. Elibank and Hepburn remained above, with what was still the major part of the host, some eleven thousand, keeping well back from the edge so as to be unseen from the low ground.

There was no lengthy waiting involved that morning before the English army came into sight and drew level. Cromwell's scouts would probably have seen and reported the Leven contingent's descent and move on to Broxmouth; also the thousands halfway down the hill would now be entirely obvious. What would he do? Would he split his army, to tackle both Scots groups? His force would still outnumber these two, and were seasoned cavalry. Or would he elect to press on southwards, avoiding battle? His mounted troops, in that case, would be able far to outstrip the Scots pursuit, these having to reassemble and the horsemen remount. He might well see the score of miles to Berwick's defensive walls, where he could enter and withstand possible siege, with the added protection of that castle's cannon, as the answer, to await English reinforcements to arrive to his aid.

In the event, the Lord Protector did neither. He drew up his force beneath the hill, but not over-close to it, and divided his squadrons into two, not actually separated but back-to-back as it were, one to face north, the other south, and thus remained, waiting.

Leslie, viewing it all, was presented with a problem. He could order his two forward contingents to attack, one downhill and afoot, and the other, from Broxmouth, mounted. But he could not go to their aid with his cavalry, for the horses would not be able effectively to descend that difficult slope in any order, if at all. And if his folk went, dismounted, the Ironsides down there would have the advantage.

He chose otherwise, demonstrating his efficacy as a strategist. He would leave the situation as it was down there, meantime, and take his hidden main host back and down the western flanks of the hill, still out of sight of the enemy, and then turn southwards, so to reach a point, a mile or two ahead, there to form up and block the English route to Berwick. From there he could advance to the aid of his two lesser units if they were by then actually fighting, not just waiting for Cromwell's move.

This seemed excellent tactics to Patrick and George, when it was announced – but, unfortunately not to the massed clergy. Immediately uproar arose from the ministers. Here was folly! Worse, cowardice. Sin! Malignancy!

As Leslie and his troops, or the vast majority of them, stared, the shouts arose and continued.

"Down; Down! Smite the Amalekites! Smite them hip and thigh! Or God's eternal wrath and curse upon you all! Down! Down! All. Or be for ever damned!" And the divines surged forward to the edge of the slope.

The host stood, astounded. Sir David Leslie bit his lip, frowning. He began to protest.

8

But the clerics were utterly determined; and they were, in these days, the real rulers of Scotland, the Covenant supreme, the generals and soldiery under their orders.

"Onward! Chastise them! Scourge God's enemies – or He will scourge *you*! Down on the foe!" the cries resounded, with pointings and first-shakings.

It was complete chaos and indecision there on the hilltop, men gazing from the clergy to their general, some shouting back, for and against, most bewildered, those experienced in warfare appalled. Leslie could never let this happen . . .

But that man became set-faced, and not in determination to assert his authority. He knew well where, in fact, authority lay. It was with the Kirk. He was the Covenanters' military leader, but only that. The General Assembly governed Scotland, and these ministers represented it, that all-powerful body. He could not overrule them. He would be dismissed forthwith.

With the hot demands continuing – Death to the heretics! Down upon Anti-Christ – Leslie bowed to the inevitable. Grim of features, he gave the order to dismount and descend – but on the *east* side of the hill. His lieutenants repeated these throughout the host, however unhappily.

Patrick and George shook their heads in despair and resignation, and vacated their saddles.

All came to line up on the brink of the steep, swords drawn, some still with their lances, all eleven thousand of them, and all now in full view of the enemy below. At length, at a long blast on a horn, the descent commenced, the front ranks with due care.

Care, however, like ranks, promptly became irrelevant as men began to slip and slide and stumble on the wet earth, grass, on stones and rock, and, pushed on from behind by the great numbers, staggered and frequently fell. Now those lances were a menace, getting between legs, bringing down their bearers and others, even the drawn

9

swords a handicap. In little more than moments it was sheerest chaos, disarray, utter pandemonium, an army suddenly become a tumbling, sprawling, rolling cataract of yelling humanity plunging down hundreds of feet of slippery hill.

The two Haddingtonshire friends were no more able than others to keep on their feet, or approximately in control of their persons; but they did seek to keep together in it all, gripping each other on occasion, cursing and gasping like everyone else. Thousands of men hurtling downhill offered a sight to be seen indeed.

And Cromwell did not fail to see it and its consequences, and acted to fullest effect. Pointing forward with his sword, he led his disciplined troopers of the west-facing squadrons at a steady trot, to mount the lesser slopes of the Doon Hill, where their horses could still maintain their footing, to ride into the lowermost Scots grouping, now being crashed into by the first of their tumbling companions from above.

There followed massacre, sheer and unrelenting massacre, the Roundheads methodically slaying, few of the Scots in any condition to fight back, mostly now without weapons save perhaps dirks, swords and lances gone, like morale and leadership, Leslie and his aides remaining on high to observe. Thousands died, and in short time, on that hillside.

Patrick of Elibank and George Hepburn, veteran fighters although only in their early thirties, were better able than most to save themselves from being cut down, although scarcely to assail the mounted, armour-plated foe. Patrick had retained his sword somehow, although his friend had not. Now, seeing an outcrop of stone nearby of some size, he cast that weapon away deliberately, and grabbed his friend's arm, to point. Together they lurched for the rock, tripping over fallen bodies as they went, to reach their immediate objective. There they were able to crouch, lesser stones around the outcrop sufficient to keep horses' hooves away; anyway, the Ironsides had ample victims to slay without troubling over this awkward, hiding pair.

So they remained, unassailed, while the slaughter went on, unheroic perhaps, but no amount of heroism could have improved the situation. To try to climb back uphill to their horses again was impossible, hundreds of the enemy now barring the way.

For how long they crouched there amid the shambles they knew not, watching men die, hell on earth before them. But eventually the killing began to lessen, with Scots survivors seeking to surrender in their droves, and the Roundhead officers calling a halt, the hillside all but running with blood. When a couple of Cromwell's troopers looked over at the two at the outcrop, they rose to their feet, holding out empty hands in token of submission.

Their dress, dishevelled though it had become by now, distinguished them as other than the common soldiery, and the mounted men, scarlet-tipped lances raised, beckoned for them to come, imperiously. They did not seek to question that.

Bloody swords directing them, the couple were herded past other prisoners still having to push their way over corpses and moaning wounded. And presently they were brought to a Roundhead officer, a handsome man obviously of fairly senior rank, who, breaking off instructions to a junior, eyed them questioningly.

"Ah, gentlemen, I think," he said. "If unfortunate ones. Or perhaps it seems to be fortunate?" And he gestured towards the slain hundreds on the ground.

Neither answered that.

"Foolish fighters have to pay the price!" the other went on.

"We are not all fools," Hepburn asserted. "Only the saintly ones, who command in their God's name!"

"Is that the way of it? Then you have my sympathy." He

11

turned to the two troopers. "Take them to General Monk," he ordered. "These may have something of value to tell him."

They were led away to a slight eminence where a group of officers sat their mounts. To a heavy thick-set man of middle years among these their captors went. "Colonel Stanfield sends these, sir," one of them said. "He thinks that they might have their uses, Sir General."

"Indeed? Why that?" Not waiting for an answer, the officer, of whom the Scots had heard, turned to the prisoners. "What have you to tell me, sirrah?" he demanded.

"Nothing," Elibank said. "Save that you have won an unearned victory, thanks to our would-be prophets!"

"Watch your words, fool!" That was jerked out.

"It is truth, if you want truth. Our Leslie would have mastered you but for the folly of the so-called divines."

"Leslie? Which Leslie?"

"Sir David." Patrick looked uphill. "The other . . . ?" And shrugging, he glanced northwards.

"They are both here, then? Leven and this David. Which commands?"

"That is not for us to say."

"You are arrogant for a captive, man! If you know your best interests, you will speak to better effect. Or suffer! How many has Leslie up there? Still? And what support to come? Tell us."

"We know not," Hepburn said shortly.

"I think that you do. You are officers by your looks, are you not?"

"We are not. We have no authority."

"I say that you lie! You are not any common dragoons. As Stanfield judged, did he not?"

Patrick took a chance. "We *were* officers. But not in this army of the Covenant. We served with the great Marquis of Montrose."

"Ah! Montrose? Who fought against these rascally

12

priests, or whatever they call themselves. Until they executed him! Why, then, are you with this horde? And claim no command?"

"We are Scots," Patrick said simply. "When Scotland is invaded, we must fight."

The general looked at his fellow-officers. "Here are strange captives," he said. "Are they to be believed?" There were various responses to that.

He tried again. "If you were Montrose's men, what of his others? They were not all slain or executed, I swear. Are they still against these churchmen? Could they work with us?"

"Not with Englishmen invading Scotland, no," he was told.

"But if we, that is the Lord Protector, were to aid them? Put them in power here? Then leave. How then?"

There was no reply given.

"Speak you! We have the power to slay you. Or to release you."

Still he got no answer.

Snorting, General Monk waved to the troopers. "Take them back to the colonel. Let him see to them," he commanded.

The prisoners were led through the reassembling squadrons to Stanfield. Looking eastwards as they went, they saw no sign of any assault by the Earl of Leven's force. Presumably, from his hidden position by the Brox Burn's valley, he had seen the disaster and recognised that there was nothing that his detachment could do now to right matters to any effect. What he would see as his course, they knew not. Possibly he would circle back behind Dunbar to join the other Leslie on Doon Hill again, then retire to Edinburgh.

Colonel Stanfield considered them with raised eyebrows. "Was the general pleased with you?" he wondered.

"He judged us informants – which we are not!" George Hepburn declared.

13

"We told him that we had been officers with Montrose," Patrick added. "But that did not make us the less leal Scots. He gained nothing else from us. Nor will you."

"So – Montrose's men! *He* was a notable commander. Yet his own folk slew him."

"Some of them. Argyll and his like. Fanatical Calvinists. And jealous of him!"

"Aye. You fought long for him? Both of you?"

"For more than two hard years, yes. Better fighting than this!"

"No doubt . . ."

A junior officer came to him. "The Lieutenant-General Monk would speak with all colonels, sir," he was informed. "On orders of Captain-General Cromwell."

Leaving the two captives in the care of a captain-of-horse, he rode off. Everywhere order was being restored. Prisoners were being formed into great companies, thousands of prisoners, troopers boasting of ten thousand, although how they arrived at that figure was doubtful. Patrick and George expected to be herded in with the rest, but Stanfield's captain held them back meantime.

The colonel returned, giving orders to his squadron. He glanced over at the two captives.

"Since you were officers under Montrose, you are not to be marched off with all these. What were your ranks?"

"I was lieutenant-colonel," Patrick said. "And Monkrigg was physician-in-chief, ranking as major."

"Physician?" The other stared. "You are that, truly? A physician?"

Hepburn nodded. "I was trained as such."

"We could do with a physician, see you. There is much sickness among our men. A great problem. What it is, we know not. Some sort of plague . . ."

"You say so? You all entered Edinburgh, before you were . . . repulsed? There is much quhew in that city these weeks. The grip, it is called. And the infection spreads fast.

14

Fevers and chills. Pain in the muscles. Weakness. Is it such?"

"Yes, indeed. Hew, you say? And grip? I know not such names."

"Quhew. The medical word is influenza."

"So? We lack physicians in our host. Your name, sir? Monk . . . something? Like our lieutenant-general."

"Hepburn of Monkrigg. That is my lairdship. Near to Haddington. And my friend is Patrick Murray, Lord Elibank."

"A lord? Sakes, we have two notable captives here! See you, I will take you to the general again. This of the sickness. You could be very useful, I judge. See, mount you behind these troopers."

They were taken through the forming-up squadrons and the crowds of prisoners back to that eminence. But there it was said that Monk had gone to confer with Captain-General Cromwell. So they all rode further back, to where a group of officers was dismounted and being addressed by a stocky man in what looked like his early fifties, not handsome like Stanfield, stern of feature but with a great air of authority. Monk was among those listening.

The newcomers, dismounting also, were ignored.

Stanfield moved over to Monk, and whispered. They heard the speaker praising God for His goodness to His humble servants, among other remarks – which was all too familiar to the captives, save for the expressed humility.

A few last orders, and the captain-general waved a hand to disperse the group, and Monk took Stanfield to the stocky man. After a moment or two, the three of them came over to where the Scots stood.

They were considered, and the announcement made. "I am Cromwell, commanding here. I learn that one of you is a physician of the former Montrose's army. We could use a physician. You will aid us?"

Hepburn inclined his head. "I do not choose whom I shall seek to aid and whom not!" he declared.

"As is right, sir."

"The other is the Lord . . ." Stanfield went on. "I misremember the name. Another of Montrose's officers, General."

"Elibank." Patrick mustered a faint smile. "Only second lord, but fourteenth laird!"

Cromwell raised an eyebrow at that, but returned to Hepburn. "This sickness has hit us hard. Many men have fallen off, in poor shape, and have been left behind. They shiver, all weak. Cannot keep in the saddle."

"That is the quhew, I judge, yes. And it can be passed on to others, all too readily."

"Is it . . . fatal?"

"No, sir. Not usually. It can lead to trouble with the lungs. To pneumonia, if neglected. Or if men are weaker, otherwise."

"We have lacked a sufficiency of food when besieging Edinburgh. Feeding a large army is difficult, as you will know. We have been eating horseflesh. I have sent many of the sick to that Dunbar town. In this weather . . ."

"Most will recover in a week, ten days. Some less fortunate. Rest is required, not warfare and hard riding, General."

"Mmm. Well, that may be possible, now, as matters have turned out, with the good God's help. Colonel, have your captives taken to Dunbar to see to the sick there. And entreat them . . . kindly." Cromwell waved them off. They heard him add, "General Monk, we march back for Edinburgh. That city will not withstand us now with no army to aid them. We have no need to go on to Berwick."

As they rode pillion behind their troopers with Stanfield's squadron, in the rain, for Dunbar, the pair were not close enough to converse. But Patrick recognised how fortunate he was to have been in the company of his friend. They had become privileged captives. Otherwise, who knew what

16

unpleasant conditions he might have been undergoing. He wondered what was happening with Leslie and the clergy, who had remained there on the hilltop? And Leven? They were probably halfway back to Edinburgh by now, in ignominious flight — and probably would not halt there but make for Stirling and the north.

At Dunbar town they found a cowed population being ordered around by another squadron of Roundheads to provide food and shelter for the hundreds of sick men. Most of these were being accommodated in the large collegiate church and in a lodge of the Templars, not in the castle on its rock-stacks rising out of the sea, linked by bridges, no convenient shelter for shivering weak men. George was taken to inspect them in the church and lodge, Patrick, feeling useless, inadequate, accompanying him but unable to be of any help. Meanwhile, Stanfield ordered his disciplined Ironsides into occupation of the town.

In time, the colonel came back to the church, where he found himself as incompetent to deal with the sick as did Patrick. The pair of them, in fact, got on quite well together, two colonels, merely looking on, with much in common, the Englishman praising Montrose and expressing admiration for Cromwell, but a little doubtful as to the latter's reliance on God's direction, he a less strict Calvinist. He mentioned that the captain-general had ordered the 117th Psalm to be sung by the entire army as they waited for the Scots attack. Both agreed that religious fervour and battle did not always go together.

When George had done what he could for the quhew sufferers, Stanfield was faced with a problem. What to do now with the prisoners? Cromwell had said to treat them kindly. And obviously Hepburn should remain at Dunbar meantime with the many sick. But he and his squadron of Ironsides were part of the English army which was on its way to the Scots capital again, there to seek to do what it had failed to achieve previously, take over the city, this with the Scots army no longer a factor to reckon with.

17

They should be with Cromwell. In something of a quandary over his two conflicting duties, he came to a conclusion. If the two captives, as gentlemen, would give him their word not to engage in any acts inimical to Oliver Cromwell he would allow them to remain here at Dunbar for such time as Hepburn could usefully aid the sick, and then they could return to their own homes, nearby he understood. He took note of their lairdships of Ballencrieff and Monkrigg where, if the captain-general disapproved of his decision, they could be reached and dealt with. Was it accepted?

Needless to say, it was, and gratefully, promises given.

So they parted from their captor, actually with handshakes, a strange situation.

That early evening, both recognising that Patrick was playing no useful role there, it was agreed that he might as well depart. If he was needed, he could be sent for. So off home to Ballencrieff, a mere ten miles away, he went, where he had a wife and bairns who would be worrying about him. George would probably be able to do the same in a day or two, leaving instructions as to the treatment of the more sorely stricken, although most would recover their health in a short time.

Patrick borrowed a horse, albeit not so fine a one as he had left up on Doon Hill, from the town's provost, and set off westwards.

Still it rained.

18

2

Ballencrieff was quite a large property in the Vale of Peffer, just under three miles due north of the town of Haddington, itself in its valley of the Tyne, the modest green Garleton Hills separating the two dales. The lairdship had a fair-sized castle but no major stronghold, and in no particularly strong position but attractive surroundings. On one side lay the marshland of the Peffer Burn, this famous for the great Battle of Athelstaneford fought against invading Saxons eight hundred years before, when Scotland could be said to have been conceived, with the victory, and the cross of white cloud appearing in the blue sky giving the joint victors, Picts and Scots, the national flag thereafter, the saltire. And on the other side of the castle spread fertile land, corn riggs, meadows and pasture, rising up to the Garleton Hills. The Murrays of Blackbarony, in Peebles-shire, which had been their property for long, had obtained Ballencrieff two centuries earlier, and had then built the original tower, now extended to be a tall L-planned fortalice.

Arriving home, Patrick had some difficulty in gaining entrance, this because of the darkness, and all the gates and doors shut and barred, including that of the little gatehouse giving access to the courtyard. Once there had been a moat, its waters fed from the Peffer marshland, but this had long been filled in.

There were lights gleaming from three windows, however, and, after his shouts had had no effect, Patrick dismounted and had recourse to scooping up turf with his dirk and hurling lumps of this at one of the lit windows, that of the withdrawing-room off the great hall on the first floor, where presumably his wife was presently sitting. Although not all of his missiles found their mark, for it was quite a lengthy throw, some did, and presently resulted in the small wooden shutters below the fixed glass being opened.

"Liz!" he cried. "Liz! It is me, Patrick. Have them let me in, lass."

"Patrick! Oh, thank God!" a woman's voice sounded. "My dear! My dear!"

The shutters closed, he led his borrowed horse back round to the gatehouse arch.

He did not have long to wait before he heard the drawbars being pulled back and the heavy double doors creaking open, two servitors effecting it. Beside them a young woman stood, arms out, and came running to him.

"My heart! My love!" she exclaimed, and flung herself upon him, uncaring for those men's grins. Her husband was nowise backwards in receiving her, dropping the horse's reins, to pick her up off her feet and swing her round, to mutual if distinctly random kissing.

One of the servitors went for the horse.

The Lady Elizabeth set down, hand in hand they made for the tower doorway, the great gates being shut and barred again behind them.

"Oh, Patrick, I feared! I greatly feared!" she told him. "We heard of battle. Defeat. Many men, fugitives, fleeing past here. Defeat at Dunbar. Many, many dead, they said. Oh, my dearest, I feared! When you did not come. I prayed . . . !"

"Defeat, yes. Shameful defeat. A folly. But I was captured, with George Hepburn, lass. Unhurt. It was all disaster. Those Kirk ministers! I will tell you all. But I got away. Almost by a miracle! Maybe your prayers? Back to you, my sweet Liz. Heaven be praised!"

They climbed the twisting turnpike stair to the first floor, to pass through the great hall to the tapestry-hung withdrawing-room, where a fire burned brightly, and all was comfort and warmth to support and correspond with that of the young woman with her loving embraces. These two, although seven years married and with two children, were still very much in love, and apt to demonstrate it.

"Patrick, you will be starved, wearied, much fallen and distressed," she declared. "Wine, here. I will have meats brought . . ."

"I ate at Dunbar, in the town. That can wait. It is *you* that I want to consume, woman! Dear woman!" He gazed at her.

And Elizabeth Stewart was worth gazing at. Still in her later twenties, she was lovely of feature as she was of figure, fair of hair and looks, vivacious, lissome. Patrick never ceased to wonder how he had won her, for she had had many suitors. She was the daughter of the Earl of Traquair, former Lord High Treasurer of the realm, descended from the royal Stewarts. She came also from Peebles-shire, none so far from the other Murray seat of Blackbarony, where indeed lived Thomas, one of Patrick's two brothers, who had also wooed her.

Taking only a sip or two of the wine that she had poured for him, he took her over to the fire, there to enfold her in his arms again, busy hands running over her rounded but firm and enticing person, she gurgling with laughter now amid the kisses, stroking his hair and brow.

When, at length, Patrick remembered his duties as a father and enquired after the children, he was assured that they were both well, young Pate, now five, needing his sire's strong hand, and Beth, eighteen months younger, a roguish expert at getting her own way. They would have been asleep for a couple of hours by now.

As the Lady Elizabeth rang a bell for a maid to bring food for the master, Patrick told her the long story of the parallel march, the wet night on the hilltop's strong position, the absurd and wicked insistence of the clerics to leave this and go on the attack down the steep hill, the

21

appalling consequences, no battle in fact only a massacre, his and George's capture, and the blessing of the other's being a physician, and what that led to. That was to be thanked for his being here this night.

Shaking her fair head over it all, Liz declared that he should never have volunteered to join Leslie's Covenanting army; after all, his two brothers had not done so. And George's misguided cousin, Sir Adam Hepburn of Humbie, although he was a Covenanter, indeed Treasurer of the Army of the Covenant, had not done so either. So now – what was to happen? The English would be in control of Scotland, would they not? Cromwell master, not young King Charles. Would Patrick be able to lie low, avoid any more involvement in affairs? As he should have done ere this. This English colonel he spoke of – would he leave him alone and not come for him? He sounded a decent man.

Patrick just did not know. In theory, he supposed, he was still Stanfield's prisoner. But there were thousands of other prisoners. They could not detain them all, guard and feed them. But he was an officer, and a lord. So he might be considered worth the holding. It was to be hoped not; and especially that there would be no demand for a ransom! Moneys. He could not afford anything such. He was impoverished already, after having to pay those damnable Covenanting divines that twenty thousand merks' fine for his support of Montrose. The estate could not raise more siller – and nobody would be eager to buy land in the present state of the nation.

Putting all this of the future from them meantime, the couple went upstairs, hand in hand again, despite Patrick, lamp in the other hand, having to lead a step in advance owing to the narrow scope of that turnpike. On the third-floor landing they went first into the children's room, where they looked down affectionately on the two youngsters fast asleep in their cots, Patrick shaking his head. It was only two weeks since he had last seen them, when he went to join Leslie's army on the Burgh Muir of Edinburgh and how much had happened since then! Stroking small heads, but not sufficiently to waken them, the parents went out and into their own bedchamber, up a couple of steps.

A fire was lit here too, with a tub of steaming water beside it, the maids having been busy. The door shut and the lamp set down, they turned to eye each other. And Liz chortled.

"I know what to expect now!" she said.

"Ha! Am I too weary and dejected to disappoint you?" he wondered.

"I would be surprised . . ." She got no further, vocally at least, before being all but carried over to the fireside and there methodically but expertly and most appreciatively disrobed, she scarcely needing to aid him. Then it was her turn, Liz making something of a performance when dealing with his lower half, suggesting that part of him was deliberately obstructive, yet requiring careful handling.

Naked, as they considered each other, she declared that he probably needed a good washing after all his riding and masculine activities, and was prepared to assist him in this; but he said that could wait, while *he* could not. Plenty of time for such niceties later. She then accused him of impatience, saying that the water would cool, nevertheless not refusing to be led to the bed. She threw herself upon it, arms out to him.

He fell on her, no preliminary love-play sought, nor necessary. That too could wait. Patrick had had a sufficiency of waiting. Their prompt satisfaction with each other thereupon was intense, however brief of duration.

They lay side by side, hands not inactive, for no lengthy respite before Liz again suggested the washing. But he was all for priorities, and pulled her over on top of him. Slapping him, she bit his ear, but straddled him anything but reluctantly; and this time their linking lasted considerably longer, to mutual satisfaction, amid gasping endearments.

It was quite some time before those recommended ablutions were proceeded with, however tepid the temperature of the water now was compared with that of the bathers. They washed each other most thoroughly, as was necessary.

Thereafter Patrick was told, as they lay hand in hand, in however drowsy tones, of how Liz's father was still held captive, after the Battle of Preston two years earlier, in Warwick Castle; as was her brother, the Master of Traquair, Lord Lintoun, although none knew where. A large ransom was demanded for the earl's freedom; this over and above the enormous fine laid on him who had been Lord High Treasurer by the Covenanting divines for his support of Montrose. He would be an impoverished man hereafter. John, her brother, was desperately seeking moneys; and Patrick, despite his own fining and those of his friends — for the Covenant had done financially, shamefully, well out of Montrose's defeat — would do what he could, she knew. Her sister Anne's husband, Sir John Hamilton of Redhouse nearby, and her other sister Margaret's husband, the Earl of Queensberry, in far Dumfriesshire, along with the Earl of Southesk, were all contributing. In the state of the country, invaded, it was difficult indeed. She feared that her father would not be freed for some time yet. If he had not been an earl it would no doubt have been less expensive. These allies of God, as they called themselves, English as well as Scottish, were extraordinarily obsessed with worldly riches. She wondered what Christ Jesus, born in a stable and a carpenter to trade, ever advocating giving to the poor and laying up treasures in heaven, not on earth, thought of them all.

For his part, Patrick told her more of the military situation, how Cromwell, first repelled at Edinburgh, was now in a position to return there and capture that important city — although probably not its fortress-citadel without prolonged siege — and take over the rest of Lowland Scotland now open to him, a dire thought. Their land

24

had not been English-occupied since the days of Edward Plantagenet, Wallace and Bruce, almost four centuries before. What was in store for them was problematical, but hard times were certain. It was sad for their youngsters to have to grow up in such.

It might not last so very long, Liz suggested. Another Montrose might arise. And there was still much royalist favour in England. The Highlands here were, and would almost certainly remain, unconquered; and if the clans could be persuaded to stop fighting each other and unite to smite the common foe who knew what could be achieved, for they were notable warriors. Young King Charles might be able to rally both kingdoms. Patrick was doubtful about that. From what he had heard about Charles, and what he had seen of the Hielantmen in the Montrose campaigns, he judged clan feuding to be almost their only concern, Lowland troubles scarcely any concern of theirs.

Despite the importance of such matters, the couple dozed over presently, and for some indeterminate time, before Patrick wakened sufficiently refreshed to instigate a final gentle and protracted coupling, to quiet satisfaction. Even Liz afterwards did not propose further washing.

They slept soundly for what was left of the night.

When, by noon next day, George Hepburn had not called at Ballencrieff on his way back to Monkrigg, Patrick thought that he had better ride over to Dunbar again to discover what went on, in case the Ironsides there decided that he ought to be held prisoner, or at least remain with George. Liz was unhappy about this, needless to say, afraid that she would lose him again, and for who knew how long; but he judged that his friend might need him. Moreover, they were *Stanfield's* captives, and having given their word to the Roundhead colonel probably nobody there would be in a position to countermand his authority. The situation was an odd one, admittedly.

So, with repeated urgings to come back quickly and not

allow those Englishry to detain him, Patrick set off east-wards again, by Drem and Fenton and Prestonkirk to Dunbar. There he found George more or less kicking his heels, and declaring that there was really nothing more that he could do for the quhew sufferers, many of whom were already recovering. Rest, quiet and a little time were what was required now. One or two of the wounded had died, but most others would just have to be looked after by their colleagues, his own further attentions unnecessary.

A Roundhead captain seemed to have been left in charge here, and he did not take it upon himself to question Colonel Stanfield's orders anent the two important prison-ers. With only a short delay, and telling the captain where they could be found, the pair took their leave.

George was well content to accompany Patrick back to Ballencrieff for the night. Only his elderly father, a wi-dower, lived at Monkrigg, his married brothers Andrew, Patrick and William having their smaller properties. It was early dusk before they covered the ten miles, with Liz vastly relieved to see them, and welcoming George warmly. The children were not yet bedded down, Pate calling the visitor Uncle, although he was no relation.

They spent a pleasant evening, and Patrick another very fulfilling night.

In the morning, George was for home, and his friend decided to accompany him, to see the old man, and to discover whether any repercussions of the invasion had affected Monkrigg, which was not on any direct road to the east. The two lairdships were only about five miles apart.

They rode over the Garleton heights to come suddenly in sight of the town of Haddington, hidden deep in its Tyne valley, a formerly walled town although its defences were now mainly gone, its great cathedral-like church of St Mary dominating all, and many fine town-houses of the Lothian nobility in evidence, including that of George's late far-out kinsman, James Hepburn, fourth Earl of Bothwell, Mary, Queen of Scots' third husband.

26

They crossed Tyne here, and climbed south-eastwards past the castle of Lethington of that Ilk, whereafter a long line of the Lammermuir Hills now fronted them for scores of miles, the lofty barrier between Lothian and the Borderland, and the greatest sheep-rearing territory in all Scotland, source of much trade in wool with the Low Countries. Here they swung off to the left across grassy and wooded slopes, cattle-dotted, to reach Monkrigg, another mile.

This one was no ancient lairdship, the lands only passing from Holy Church at the Reformation, when this branch of the Hepburns of Waughton had gained them. So George's home was no castle or fortalice but a fairly modest hallhouse, not yet a century old, with two farms attached, Easter and Wester Monkriggs. Thus, among all the Haddingtonshire Hepburns, of Hailes, Waughton, Luffness, Smeaton, the Haugh, Gilmerton and the rest, George's sire was by no means the most prominent or prosperous, hence his son being trained as a physician. But he did own valuable land along the Tyne close to Haddington, where mills were sited, and brought useful revenues. They saw no sign of devastation nor trouble as they approached.

George's father, another Patrick, was only in his mid-sixties but looked older, a frail, bent man, and short-sighted, but friendly, looked after by a grieve from Easter Monkrigg and his buxom wife. He welcomed his son's return thankfully, having been wondering whether he would ever see him again. The word reaching him had been of nothing but catastrophe, defeat and death, but details deficient, only that the man Cromwell would now be the ruler of Scotland. He thanked God that he would be unlikely to live long to endure such shame! That the Stewart line was ending in such feeble monarchs was tragedy, tragedy!

On the information that his eldest son was now a captive, on parole as it were, the old man wagged his grey head and

27

collapsed into a chair. What did this mean? Further imprisonment? Or ransom? Where would they find siller, if the last? Perhaps they could sell one of the mills at Haddington? Someone *might* buy that.

Patrick Murray said that he could be faced with the same problem, as, no doubt, would be many another. This was no time to try to sell land.

George asked after his brothers, to learn that they were lying low in their Lammermuir foothills sheep-farms, thankful that they had not volunteered to join Leslie's army, wiser than George!

The two friends wondered what was happening at Edinburgh and further north. Presumably the city would have fallen, for who could defend it? Certainly not the Covenanting ministers, however vocal they might be about the need; they would all be safely elsewhere. Where were all the thousands of Scots prisoners? These would be only a handicap to Cromwell. Would he just turn them loose, disarmed? The common soldiers, at least. The officers and gentry would be detained somewhere, almost certainly. Possibly many of the others might be sent back to Dunbar to bury the dead?

And how soon would they be hearing from Stanfield? And to what effect? Time would tell, undoubtedly; meanwhile all they could do was to wait, abiding in their places and by their given word.

Patrick returned to Ballencrieff. He had a mill, like every other barony, where his tenants had to have their grain ground, this on a dammed-up burn flowing down from the Garletons called Standalane. Would he have to sell that for ransom moneys? It would be a sore loss . . .

3

In the event thereafter, as days passed into weeks and weeks into months, Patrick, with Liz, and George Hepburn also, began almost to forget that they were less than free men, as no word came from Colonel Stanfield, and warfare and battle seemed quite to pass them by, however active were the forces opposed to each other elsewhere, with Scotland in a turmoil. But there, in eastern Lothian, all such appeared to be fairly distant, however dramatic and nation-shaking, apart from two smallish incidents, which did not affect the captives-in-name. They had to keep reminding themselves of their sworn promises and peculiar positions; and that one day they would almost certainly be called to account for their odd part in the Battle of Dunbar of 3 September 1650.

The news of what was happening elsewhere, not always entirely accurate or in detail, did reach them fairly regularly, some of it close enough to be readily confirmed. For instance, from Edinburgh, which fell to Cromwell almost without a blow struck – although its great rock-top fortress did not, its artillery strong enough to keep the New Model army's at bay – they heard that a lieutenant-general called Lambert had been sent with a small force, with cannon, back to these parts to bombard and capture Dirleton Castle, only five miles from Ballencrieff, and from where they could hear the gunfire resounding. This castle appeared to have held out against the English, as it had done many times in the past, strongly sited, this time occupied by a Sir James Maxwell. However the Cromwellian artillery did what others had been unable to achieve, and it fell,

Maxwell being hanged by Lambert, and the fortalice thereafter largely demolished. Patrick felt grievously unhappy and irrelevant, having to sit nearby and do nothing – but he had given his word.

The same situation was reported from Borthwick Castle, in Midlothian, another very strong place a dozen miles to the south-west, this where the Protestant Lords of the Congregation had failed to reduce it and capture Mary, Queen of Scots after her defeat at Carberry Hill. Once again superior English artillery won the day.

They heard that the captain-general had left Edinburgh Castle besieged, and moved on north-westwards to Linlithgow, this in October. From there he sent the efficient Lambert again south to Hamilton, in Lanarkshire, there to take the palace, seat of the duke thereof beheaded by Cromwell's regime in England a year before, after the Battle of Preston, this on a ridiculous charge of treason because he also held an English title. His brother, the next duke, a Covenant supporter, it seemed was belatedly assembling forces from those parts to resist the English invasion. Hamilton Palace fell, like the others, and the duke fled to the Isle of Arran, for which he held the title of earl.

And so on. One by one the strongholds of the Scots lords fell to the irresistible Ironsides and their powerful cannon.

In November the Estates of Parliament met at Perth, and had to disperse when Cromwell sent a squadron under Monk to try to capture the members. Before fleeing, they ordered General David Leslie to assemble all possible strength, including Highland clansmen if he could so persuade such, to defend the crossing-place of the Forth, at Stirling, as had been done so many times down the centuries. Leslie was said to be basing himself in the wide cover of the great Tor Wood, near to Bannockburn.

That Yuletide was one of the grimmest that Scotland had ever had to endure, with Cromwell still at Linlithgow and most of the land south of there under stern Ironside rule, the Roundheads seeking to prevent loyal men from heading to join Leslie. There was much of trial, imprisonment and hanging.

At Ballencrieff some semblance of Christmas cheer was attempted, for the sake of the youngsters, George Hepburn joining them. But it was, inevitably, a somewhat superficial celebration. Still no word came from Stanfield, wherever he was.

Then extraordinary news stirred the nation two weeks later. On the first day of 1651, young King Charles the Second, having accepted the Covenant, however reluctantly, up in the north of the land, in Moray, had been brought south by the Earl of Argyll, Montrose's executioner, and other Covenant leaders, and duly crowned at Scone, near Perth, the ancient coronation seat of the realm's monarchs, Campbell of Argyll himself placing the crown on his head. Now, all but a prisoner of these lords and the divines, he was to act as figurehead for a uniting of all Scottish forces against the invaders, the Earl of Loudoun, another Campbell, being sent to Leslie in Stirling's Tor Wood to command, of all things, an armed sally down through south-western Scotland and into England, hopefully to distract and draw Cromwell back to his own country. This seemed almost beyond belief to Patrick and George; but at least it did indicate some Scottish initiative and a semblance of unity so sorely needed.

The two friends wished that they could have joined in this venture, however much they disliked and distrusted the Campbell chiefs. If only they had not been captured at Dunbar . . .

Cromwell, however, was not easily distracted. He did send orders for any Scots descent on western England to be firmly countered, but he himself, with Monk and Lambert, remained in personal control of southern Scotland, consolidating his hold. He moved from Linlithgow to Hamilton Palace, there to ensure that the areas of Lanarkshire, Ayrshire, Dumfries-shire and Galloway were under

31

his rigorous control. And this move of his south-west-wards had its interesting side effects for at least some frustrated Scots, for who should then come down to Haddington but Colonel James Stanfield, sent as commander or governor for the area east of Edinburgh. And within a day or two of his arrival Patrick and George found themselves summoned to the county town to meet their captor.

They went together, with mixed feelings, to the Bothwell town-house which the colonel had made his headquarters. Now what? How were they to be treated under present circumstances? Why had Stanfield been appointed to take charge here? It could hardly have anything to do with themselves, an ineffective pair as they now were. Were they to be used in some measure? If it was against Scotland's true interests, could they effectively refuse? Questions!

Stanfield was not present when they arrived, but appeared fairly soon afterwards – and at least some of their many questions were promptly answered. For the colonel greeted them with a smile and handshakes, almost as though he were pleased to see them, offering them refreshments, and with no show of being the conquering master. Indeed, he expressed himself as well pleased that they had held to their word and not involved themselves in any hostile activities during his absence.

He was not long, however, in making it clear what he expected of them. They were prominent men in these parts, and no doubt with many friends and kinsfolk also of influence. His being sent here by the captain-general was in order to ensure peace and a return to normal living conditions in the area, not in any way to repress and dominate. Scotland was to be incorporated with England into a single unity – that was Cromwell's and the English parliament's decision – and the more peacefully it could be effected the better. They, his friends – and he called them that – might well not approve of this conception; but they

32

would recognise the blessing of peace and tranquillity, the renewal of trade and customary activities meanwhile. He was not asking them to engage in any hostilities nor positive acts against this newly crowned young monarch, foolish as that position was, only to help him, Stanfield, to govern this county well and effectively, for the benefit of all. There had been trouble enough. Now let them have peace and prosperity, here at least in Lothian.

To say that his former captives were relieved was to put it mildly, all this infinitely better than they had expected and feared. The colonel had, from the first, given the impression of being an honest and reliable man, and they could not feel that he was being misleading and devious in all this.

Patrick had the temerity to ask why he, the colonel, had been selected to govern this Haddingtonshire area? Was it just by chance, or had there been some especial reason?

The other smiled again. "Well may you ask, my lord. The captain-general is a wise statesman as well as a notable soldier. He believes that people's welfare should be the true objective of all warfare, not just victorious gain, and he is concerned for the Scottish people as well as the English. So he sent me, because I had spoken well of you and the physician here and had got him to attend on his sick and wounded after Dunbar. He saw me as being able, he hoped, to reach the landed folk hereabouts through you two. And I seek to do so without in any way committing you to the English cause, but trust that you will aid me in ensuring peace here."

His two hearers eyed each other. "That seems fair enough, Colonel," Hepburn declared, Patrick nodding.

"So be it, friends. And I have a task for you forthwith! There is some trouble brewing at the town of North Berwick, where some of the younger citizens have taken possession of the empty, part-ruined castle of Tantallon, a former Douglas stronghold, this in the name of King Charles. And after Lambert had reduced the nearby castle

33

of Dirleton. It is a strongly sited place, I am told, however derelict, and I have no cannon to reduce it. So, unless it is vacated by these foolish townspeople, I will have to send for artillery, possibly Lambert again, to evict them. And if that is done there could follow much bloodshed and hangings, there in North Berwick, for they could not possibly hold the castle. And our cannoneers are no gentle warriors! Will you come with me to try to persuade these citizens, unwise however patriotic, to leave Tantallon? This to prevent unnecessary suffering and vengeance on the town. I promise that if they heed us there will be no punishments enacted against them, or the town."

Once again the pair exchanged glances. Here was a prompt call upon their loyalties and judgment. Both knew Tantallon well, of course, on its jutting headland, one of the greatest landmarks and strongholds in Lothian, which even King James the Fifth and his whole army had failed to take. But improved artillery could almost certainly batter it into submission; indeed a dozen years before, the Covenanters had punished the Marquis of Douglas for making a stand in it for Charles the First, and had managed to reduce it, leaving it part-ruined. And Lambert had proved what could be done, at Dirleton and Hamilton. Young men from North Berwick could nowise hold it, even for an hour, against Cromwellian cannon. And the price they and their townsfolk would pay would be grim.

They both nodded, unspeaking.

"Good!" Stanfield said. "But first, let us have a meal. Then – North Berwick."

Thus, swiftly, did conditions change for them.

Thereafter the two former officers of Montrose's army had the odd experience of riding at the head of a half-squadron of Cromwell's Ironsides, alongside their colonel, both feeling distinctly unsure of themselves, although they agreed that their mission that day was a wise and worthy one, and not in any way against Scotland's best interests.

This taking and seeking to hold Tantallon Castle, however well meant, was folly for inexperienced young men, and to get them out of it would be of benefit to all.

They rode almost due north, passing not far from Ballencrieff to reach Dirleton, where they considered the badly damaged castle overlooking the village green, noting what Lambert's cannon could do. And so on to North Berwick town, Stanfield and his officers exclaiming over the dramatic isolated green pyramid of the law rising above the town; and then still more impressed by the sight of the astonishing mighty rock-stack of the Craig of Bass, rising out of the waves at the entrance to the Forth estuary, a mile from the shore, with its sheer cliffs soaring to a summit plateau, white with bird droppings under a screaming halo of thousands of solan geese.

At Patrick's suggestion, in the town itself they called upon the provost of the burgh, who proved to be a saddler working in his premises on the main street, and who was most alarmed to be so visited, the troopers blocking the narrow causeway. But he knew of Lord Elibank, and learning of their mission and something of the conse-quences if it was not successful, agreed to accompany them to Tantallon, admitting that he and many of the townsfolk had been against their young men going to take over the castle in the first place. He was named Wright, it seemed.

They mounted him behind one of the troopers and rode on eastwards for about two miles.

They saw Tantallon's tall towers rearing ahead of them against the infinity of the Norse Sea, red stone against blue waters, a challenging prospect, its semi-ruinous state not evident at that range. As they drew nearer, they were faced with a series of deep ditches or moats and ramparts thrown up between to keep cannon at a distance, effective in the past but no longer so. Beyond, the red walls soared high, oddly with a doocot for pigeons built not far out from the main drum towers.

Basically, they could recognise the fortress — for it was more than any mere fortalice — consisted of an enormous lofty wall sealing off a jutting headland of sheer cliffs, this some fifty feet high, topped by a parapet and wall-walk, with high square towers at each end, some five hundred feet of it, and with the two central drum towers forming a keep and supporting the portcullis and drawbridge over the final moat. Closer, they could see the damage done by the Covenanters' cannon those years before, gaps in the stonework, corbels displaced, the parapet broken here and there. But the Saltire banner flew above the keep, and the drawbridge was up and the iron portcullis down.

Their approach, of course, would have been evident, and as they drew near, crossing those ditches and grassy ramparts, two shots rang out to welcome them — but musket-shots not cannon. Out of range they did no harm, but indicated defiance.

Stanfield halted his men at a safe distance, and he and Patrick and George, with Provost Wright, dismounted.

"I think that we shall go forward, alone," the colonel decided. "They will not have many hand-pieces, nor shot therefor. If only four of us approach to hail them they will not fire on us, I judge. You, my lord, should speak first. Then this mayor, or provost. They will know and heed you both. That is best, no? Tell them that if they march out they will be free, unopposed. But if not, what will happen thereafter."

"Think you that they will shoot at us?" Hepburn wondered. "It is a chance we must take."

"They'll no' shoot *me*!" the provost said. "They'll ken me. It's nae sae far . . ."

"Very well." Patrick and his three companions moved forward to within hailing distance. There was no reaction from the castle, no shots, but no shouting either.

Patrick raised voice. "You in this castle. Men from North Berwick. I, Lord Elibank, speak. With Hepburn of Monkrigg and your Provost Wright. Do you hear me?"

A few shouts came over to them.

"Here, also, is Colonel Stanfield, of the English army. Sent by General Cromwell to govern this county. He offers you good, generous terms. You have taken over Tantallon. But you cannot hold it. Perhaps you could against the Ironside horsemen. But not again Cromwell's cannon. If you resist, the cannon will be brought. You know what their Lambert did to Dirleton. It will be the same here. The castle will fall, and quickly. Then you will hang! Lambert hanged Maxwell at Dirleton, and others. Think you that you will escape? And your folk in North Berwick? It will be bloody ruin. And for what cause? You cannot do aught for Scotland here. Cromwell rules the land, whether we like it or not. Our time will come, I say – but not now." He paused. This shouting was tiring on the voice.

George took it up. "Colonel Stanfield promises no hurt to you and your folk if you yield now. Walk off free men. If not, he will send for General Lambert. And you have heard what that means! Here is your provost."

"Aye, then," the older man called, less strong of lungs. "It's nae guid, lads. You'll no' can hud oot against yon cannons. And you'll suffer. We'll a' suffer, in the toon, like he said. Heed you me, lads, for a' oor sakes."

Silence from the castle.

"Wha's in chairge, there? Is it Dod Henderson? Tell him tae heed me. I'm no' going to hae ruin on the toon."

Patrick added, "You can trust Colonel Stanfield, I promise you. I, Elibank, swear it. I am not for the English. But I want no bloodshed here or in North Berwick, to no advantage to Scotland."

"My lord speaks truth." That was the colonel. "Walk out, free men. Or be prepared to hang!"

They waited.

At length a voice sounded. "When? When do you want us oot?" That sounded hopeful, at least.

"Now!" Stanfield called. "We wait here until you come.

37

Pack you, and come. I will give you one hour." And turning, he strode back to his troopers, whom he ordered to dismount. The other three followed him.

They did not have long to wait before a creaking and clanking noise from between the drum towers intimated the raising of the iron portcullis and the lowering of the drawbridge. No one emerged for a while, and Stanfield forbore to order his Ironsides to go and enter the castle. Then men began to appear, most laden with baggage and gear. It became a steady stream, nearly all young, in their twenties, and some youths.

Provost Wright went over to meet them. He shook hands with the leaders; and turning to wave back towards the trio he had left, he began to lead the procession the couple of miles westwards to North Berwick.

So fell Tantallon in the least bloody fashion in all its long and colourful history.

"Methinks, friends, we will have a look round this hold while we are here," Stanfield said. And he called forward some of his officers, to lead the way to the castle.

Over the lowered drawbridge they went, and through a high arched entry passage beneath the keep, this flanked by porters' lodges, and then out into a wide airy space, a strange feature for any fortalice, for it was not really a courtyard, merely a rock platform of the headland, this walled off by the great line of curtain walls and towers. There was a chapel and some subsidiary buildings on its west side, but otherwise it lay open to the cliff edge above the sea. A deep well was positioned in the middle.

Exclaiming over it all, the Englishmen went exploring, to gaze over to the waves breaking far below, to climb the various stairs up into the towers and keep and parapet-walk, and to find their way down into the dungeons and pits excavated in the rock. All agreed that it made a quite extraordinary fortress, and recognised that it could be supplied by ship in event of siege. Stanfield said that he would keep his eye on it hereafter. He added that he was

38

grateful for his two friends' help in the peaceful outcome of this mission. He would not forget that.

Patrick and George judged that they had done the right thing in this.

4

The colonel's next task for his two associates was to have them arrange a meeting with the magnates and landholders of the county for him to address on his attitude to the governing thereof, and his hopes of their co-operation in ensuring a peaceful and prosperous situation as far as national conditions allowed. He saw his duty as, in a way, to act the friend, not the dominant figure nor oppressor, and sought the help of all of influence in the area. He judged that his two collaborators thus far would be heeded in summoning such a gathering, all but a conference, he hoped.

The pair saw this as by no means prejudicing their positions as loyal Scots. Patrick suggested that the meeting would be best held, not in Stanfield's headquarters in Haddington but in a laird's house, his own Ballencrieff perhaps, larger than Monkrigg, this seeming less of an authoritative summons and governor's command. This was accepted.

So the couple set off on a round of visits to their lairdly neighbours, kinsfolk and friends. They were in a good position so to do, especially George, for the various branches of the Hepburn family were probably the most numerous in the county, although the Douglases, Hays, Hamiltons and Lethingtons were prominent also.

On the whole they were well received, although some doubts were expressed at seeming to deal with the Auld Enemy's invaders, all declaring that this of a proposed unity of England and Scotland in a single Commonwealth was totally unacceptable, their visitors in entire agreement with this attitude. But Patrick and George were in a good position to advocate such a meeting and discussion with Stanfield, for, after all, they had been volunteers with Leslie's army and had suffered therefor. And they had also been active with Montrose. So they were commendable to both Covenant and royalist supporters.

A meeting, then, was duly arranged at Ballencrieff, and Liz would have to act hostess to a large company. As the Earl of Traquair's daughter, and of the ancient royal Stewart line, she was a respected figure in these parts.

But before the gathering could take place, all learned that Cromwell had managed to outflank the defenders of the strategically placed Stirling crossing of Forth by ferrying his troops across the estuary to the east in a fleet of captured vessels, fishing-boats, barges, scows and the like, and so had been able to assail and capture Perth, which gave him a toehold into the north. He was now aiming at the city of Dundee. And if that was taken, he would control everything south and east of the Highland Line. There seemed to be no stopping the captain-general.

The meeting at Ballencrieff proved to be a success. Stanfield came early, and made a notable impression on Liz, who found him, in both his looks and behaviour, to be to her taste. When all the lairds and lords arrived, he greeted them in friendly fashion, and commended their hostess's hospitality, declaring himself as much her guest as them all.

This attitude created a good atmosphere for what had to follow. The colonel's opening address was comparatively brief, he emphasising that he considered his duty to be that of peacemaker and encourager of friendship, rather than supremacy. Perhaps the captain-general's armies had gained the reputation of harsh soldiering and stern conquering, but that was not Oliver Cromwell's wish. He had indeed punished some of his officers for violence and savageries in Ireland, and was determined not to have the like happen in Scotland. So he, James Stanfield, was concerned for the welfare and prosperity of the people of Haddingtonshire; and he hoped that all present would agree to work with him to that end. He asked for no commitment to the English cause, recognising that they all had their own loyalties and beliefs, whether towards the Covenanters or the royalists, or neither.

He scanned the faces before him, brows raised.

The first to speak was John Hay, Master of Tweeddale, heir to the aged earl thereof. "Sir, this talk of making Scotland and England one — which would become but greater England! English kings have been seeking this down all the centuries. Think you that we will agree to that because it is proposed by your Cromwell, not a king! Are *you* in favour of it?"

Stanfield shrugged. "For myself, I do not see it as important. So long as we are at peace, the two nations. But parliament has so ordered."

"Your parliament, not ours!" Hay had assisted at the recent coronation of young King Charles.

There were murmurs of support and approval on all hands.

"If we work with you here, as you suggest, we will seem to be agreeing to this folly." That was Sir Adam Hepburn of Humbie, former Treasurer of the Covenant.

"When I report to the captain-general, as I will have to do on occasion, I will tell him of this, of your concern and opposition. And that I consider it an unwise course. That it will turn all Scotland hostile. Pray that he heeds me."

"Will he?"

"He is a sound man. He has his own wisdom. And the parliament in London must pay heed to him, for he holds the power."

"You may be a good and fair governor for the county of Haddington," Hay went on. "But what of other counties? I hold the office of Sheriff of Peebles-shire. I have lands there. Who is to be governor there, if such there is to be? And if I deal with you here, and *he* is harsh, I may seem to

42

support him. Which I would not. The same could apply to other shires. All your Ironsides are not for peace and wellbeing, we know well. That Lambert! And Monk. And others."

"They are all under the captain-general's command. He will not have misbehaviour in those under him. I know him. Those in Ireland paid the price for their misdeeds."

"What would you have us to do?" Hamilton of Redhouse, Patrick's brother-in-law, asked. "King Charles has been crowned, here in Scotland. We are become his leal subjects. If he called on us for aid, how can we support an English governor?"

"That is for your own decision. But I say that you can aid *me* in building peace and fair living and trade here, without hurt to your cause. I ask no more of you. But I would remind you – I am no weakling! Where necessary, I must act for the Commonwealth's good. Pray remember it."

After that, there was no more debate. Patrick signed to Liz, and she, who had been listening throughout with her sister, the Lady Anne Hamilton, announced that there would be provision for all brought up from the kitchens. Meanwhile, wines were here for them. All to feel most welcome guests.

As they partook, the colonel circulated among all, chatting affably, and most responded suitably. The meal thereafter was excellent, and helped to generate a warm and congenial atmosphere. There were no speeches, but lively conversation, in which Stanfield joined.

When eventually he made his departure, he did so to no sour looks, and with not a few handshakes. As Patrick saw him off for Haddington, he expressed himself as well pleased with the evening, and of his gratitude to his hostess. George chose to accompany him, on his way back to Monkrigg, and the Master of Tweeddale to Yester at Gifford, also south of Haddington. Few lingered long thereafter, with some having quite long distances to ride.

Liz, with her sister and brother-in-law, agreed with her husband that it had all been very worth while, an occasion to remember – and hopefully of some lasting benefit to their people. Patrick declared that he would have to watch his wife hereafter with that Stanfield, whom she had sat beside at table, her appreciation of his company all too evident!

It was only three days later that they heard that Dundee had fallen, and that Cromwell was proceeding on northwards towards Aberdeen, leaving Monk in command of the former city. But, shortly afterwards, the news was that the captain-general had suddenly changed course, and in quite the opposite direction, this because young King Charles, with General David Leslie – not the Earl of Leven, who had been captured at the fall of Dundee and sent prisoner to London – were now well on their way southwards and through the West March of the borders, to cross into Cumberland and so cut the Roundhead army off from its homeland, and thus arouse the English royalists to rise in arms against the common foe. Cromwell evidently considered this move to be sufficiently dangerous for him to take personal counter-action.

So now it was all waiting and wondering and hoping for so many in Scotland, the invading forces at something of a standstill meantime, Monk presumably left in command but with a reduced army. Was there opportunity for a national uprising? So much would depend on the reaction of the English royalists and Cavaliers. If they rose in large numbers, Monk might well have to go to the assistance of his superior; and the Scots, however leaderless and lacking any experienced general – it was to be hoped, without the urgings and misguidance of the clerics – could possibly rally to rid the land of the remaining invaders, and then go to assist their young monarch in his attempt to recover his English throne.

Colonel Stanfield, very much on the alert needless to

say, had to wait like everyone else; but he kept his fears and wonderings to himself, and maintained his command of Haddingtonshire as firm and trouble-free as ever.

As the weeks passed, tidings from England were scanty, and the activities of both Leslie, with Charles, and Cromwell were little heard of, although there was a rumour that the latter was having difficulty with his parliamentarians, and was more apt to be in London than hunting for the Scots invaders. But news from the north was firmer and more encouraging – save for Stanfield. The lords and chiefs up in Angus, Atholl and Mar were stirring themselves, led by the Earls of Crawford and Airlie and sundry lesser magnates to, as it were, erect a barrier across the width of the land, to prevent Monk and Lambert making any further advance beyond Dundee and Perth. And the Catholic Gordon, Earl of Huntly, was mobilising forces up in Aberdeenshire and seeking to arouse the Highland clans, which had hitherto largely remained all but uninterested in what went on in the Lowlands, save for Argyll and the Campbells, although Maclean of Duart had somehow become involved, and fought well. And as well as this heartening news there was continuing word of bickering and enmity among the Covenanting hierarchy itself, which seemed to have split into three distinct parties, separate enough to have taken names for themselves: those led by the said Argyll, Johnston of Warriston, the Convenor of the Parliamentary Committee, and the fiery Reverend Rutherford calling themselves the Protesters; others backing Leslie and Charles, known as the Engagers; and a third group styled the Resolutioners whose aims were uncertain, save that they allegedly sought to unite the others. The Scots had ever had a fatal tendency to fight among themselves rather than against the common foe, and this was now being strikingly exemplified.

Patrick and George and their friends discussed it all, and wondered where their duty was going to lie, and when it was going to be made clear. Meanwhile, a kind of peace reigned in Haddingtonshire, much to Liz's approval and relief.

But this could not last, of course, not in the prevailing circumstances. The so-effective Cromwell triumphed, managing to locate, corner and defeat Leslie and Charles at Worcester, in the English west none so far from the Welsh border, that autumn, the king escaping somehow but Leslie being captured and sent to join his namesake, Leven, in the Tower of London. The army was shattered and dispersed, none seemingly knowing where the young monarch was now, his royalist supporters in England having largely failed to rise for him.

So Monk and Lambert were established as firmly in control of all Scotland south of Dundee and Perth, although Cromwell himself remained in England, at odds with the parliament there and indeed dismissing it, so powerful had he become. But Crawford, Airlie and Huntly maintained the barrier to the north. Stanfield was left almost in limbo in Haddington, whatever was happening elsewhere, this while Monk announced, presumably with Cromwell's acceptance, that members of the Scots parliament could send representatives to a new parliament being set up in London, as part of the uniting of the Commonwealth. There appeared to be no volunteers.

Patrick and George saw a lot of the colonel, he being a frequent guest at Ballencrieff. It was at one of these visits that Liz gained from him something that they had not realised hitherto, namely that he was a married man with a wife and son. Somehow, this had never occurred to them, no hint of matters matrimonial ever having been dropped. But apparently he was squire of two properties in the English shires, in one of which he had bred sheep and established a woollen mill to spin the fleeces, this before he had joined Cromwell's Ironsides. He had done this last at the urging of his father, who had been a military man, indeed had served in the celebrated army of Gustavus Adolphus of Sweden in the religious wars against the emperor and overweening Catholicism, he approving of Cromwell's aims.

This information led George Hepburn to enlarge on the fame of his own cousin, a son of George Hepburn of Athelstaneford nearby, the renowned Sir John Hepburn, who also had fought for Gustavus Adolphus, had proved himself a notable commander, and had transferred his military abilities to France and the Low Countries, still opposing the emperor, and had won many victories. He formed a band of fellow-Scots into what the French named the Regiment d'Hebron, but which he preferred to call the Royal Scots. He became a Marshal of France before being killed at the siege of Lorraine in 1636.

Stanfield was very interested in this, saying that he had heard of the Regiment d'Hebron but never connected it with the name of Hepburn. George should be very proud of his kinsman.

So passed 1651 in Scotland, Haddingtonshire something of a haven of tranquillity, however anxious about the future some of its folk.

5

George's ailing father died early in the following spring, and he became Laird of Monkrigg, which indeed he had been acting as for these last years when not in military activities. Now he made some changes in the property, especially in the Lammermuir foothills area, where he sought to rival his brothers in sheep-rearing – this to the interest of James Stanfield. Monkrigg owned extensive uplands flanking those of Hay, Earl of Tweeddale, east of Yester and Gifford in what had formerly been part of Dunbar Common, however far from that town; and George took this period of freedom to increase the profitability, enlarging flocks and employing more shepherds. It made an odd situation to have a Roundhead colonel quite frequently accompanying him on his surveys and inspections; but Stanfield found this to his taste, and concern for his own lands. Patrick did ride into the hills on occasion with them, sometimes accompanied by Liz, for they both enjoyed the feelings of freedom and space and farflung vistas up on the heather-clad heights, from which, in clear weather, they could see as far as the Highland Line, where they wondered what went on between its defenders and the Roundheads. If the colonel wondered similarly, he did not remark on it. Patrick's own lands, low-lying in the Vale of Peffer, were more fertile, suitable for cattle-rearing rather than sheep, although he sometimes wintered some of George's breeding ewes and gimmers on his Garleton slopes.

Sometimes the two friends wondered whether Stanfield had been all but forgotten by Monk and Lambert, for he never seemed to be summoned north to report to them. Presumably his governorship proving so successful and trouble-free, they were well content to leave him to it. He had sent most of his squadron of Ironsides over to join the two lieutenant-generals long since, rather than have them idling around Haddington, North Berwick and Dunbar. And he seemed well content to remain so employed rather than involved in actual military service.

It so happened, however, that there was some contact with the Roundhead leadership in the early summer. Stanfield had a visit from a Major-General Morgan, a Welshman, sent south from Dundee to arrange the removal of the Scots regalia, the royal crown, sceptres and sword of state, presently kept in Edinburgh Castle, which was held by an English garrison. Cromwell, it seemed, had ordered that it should be sent to London, as indication of the conquest of Scotland and the ineffectiveness of Charles's coronation, sovereignty nullified. This was to be sent south by ship, in order to avoid any possible attempts to save it on the way down through the Scots Borderland by the wild mosstroopers of those parts, noted for their fierce and ungovernable behaviour. This Morgan had come by a suitable ship from the Tay to Leith, the port of Edinburgh, and now visited Stanfield to borrow his troopers to act as a strong guard for the regalia being taken from the fortress-citadel down to the vessel, en route for the Thames.

Word of all this greatly upset them at Haddington, needless to say, an outrage, the debasement of a nation. But Stanfield could by no means refuse the use of his half-squadron of horse to a superior officer, and the troopers were sent off.

Anger and resentment continued to be expressed over this decision to remove the historic and revered symbols of what was claimed to be the most ancient kingdom in Christendom. Even the colonel admitted that he thought that Cromwell had shown misjudgment in this.

But when, two days later, the Ironsides returned from Edinburgh, Morgan not with them, it was with an astonishing story. It seemed that the city rang with it. The regalia was removed from the castle, yes – but not by Morgan. And it had gone, not southwards but northwards, and by ship indeed. Involved was no less than Edinburgh's former Lord Provost, reputed to be the wealthiest man in Scotland, Sir William Dick of Braid, amazingly with his wife Anne, the Lord Gray and a young man called Ramsay, son of the Laird of Bamff, none so far from Dundee. These four, hearing of the decision to remove the precious Honours to England, had acted, and swiftly. They had gained the co-operation of the wood merchant who supplied Edinburgh Castle's garrison with fuel, and hiding themselves, Lady Dick included, under the tarpaulin covering a load of timber in the usual cart, had thereby gained access to the fortress, and managed to win their way into the very tower where the regalia was kept, with wood for its fires; and thereafter smuggled the crown, sceptres and sword out in the empty fuel sacks. And all hidden again under their cover in the empty cart, got out with it past the guards at the gatehouse, and so back to the woodyard. And now all was on its way, allegedly, up to the all-but-impregnable castle of Dunnottar, on its isolated rock-stack south of Stonehaven and Aberdeen, where it would be secure from the invaders, it was hoped.

Great was the rejoicing at this news, even the colonel conceding that here was a most notable achievement, although he was sorry for General Morgan, whom it appeared he liked well, and whom he had asked to appeal to Monk to allow him, Stanfield, a brief period of leave from Haddington to go south to visit his wife and son, whom he had not seen for three years, and give some small attention to his properties. Whether this would be granted remained to be seen, especially in present circumstances.

It proved to be so, for two weeks later the permission arrived from Dundee, and was brought by none other than

Major-General Morgan himself, who, it seemed, was to act governor of the area for ten days while Stanfield was absent.

So the colonel took his leave, and the Welshman took over meantime. All concerned were thankful that there seemed to be no suggestion that this was anything more than a very temporary arrangement, and that Stanfield would return to resume his command.

There was no word as to the regalia. Presumably it had reached its due destination safely.

Morgan proved to be no despot, a quite reasonable man, his Welsh accent finding approval at Haddington as not unlike their Scots lilting Highland speech; and there, for only a very short period, he did not seek to make any different regime or change of attitudes. Stanfield's friends recognised that they were fortunate.

The colonel came back two days earlier than expected, which surprised all. Was this of some significance, it was wondered? It would have been thought that so brief a leave, after so long a period of duty, would have been made the most of. But no questions were in order, and no explanations offered, at least to the Scots, whatever Stanfield said to Morgan. That man took his departure the day following.

So conditions were back to normal, at least as far as Haddingtonshire was concerned.

It was soon heard that normalcy did not apply everywhere else. The word came that Monk himself was marching north, with a strong force, to seek to regain the regalia from this Dunnottar Castle, a Keith seat of the Earl Marischal of Scotland. He was thus taking the risk of being outflanked by Crawford and Airlie on the west and Huntly and the Marischal to the north. But it must be on Cromwell's orders.

Hepburn of Smeaton, who had northern connections and knew that area, said that Dunnottar Castle would not

51

be taken save by lengthy siege, starving its people out, for it was so placed that artillery could not be brought within sufficient effective range; not only that, but its rock-top height ensured that cannon barrels could not be elevated to a lofty enough angle from the low ground to aim at the walling. Those saviours of the regalia knew what they were at.

Stanfield was able to tell them something of the dramatic happenings in England. Cromwell was completely master there now. He had dismissed what was left of the so-called Long Parliament, this known as the Rump, and appointed a selection of his own nominees, which was being termed the Barebones Parliament. But in fact these assemblies were merely façades, all real power resting on the shoulders of the Commonwealth's army commander, he who was to be called the Lord Protector, and who now wielded considerably more authority than had the monarchy he had put down, a strange situation. And he had declared England and Scotland now one nation, something many kings of England had sought to do. Not that anyone accepted that in Scotland.

No information came from the north as to the fate of the regalia. If it *had* been recovered by Monk, the whole land would have heard, undoubtedly.

What they did hear of was the emergence of a new figure of note on the Scottish scene, one John Middleton. The name meant nothing to anyone at Haddington save, oddly enough, George Hepburn, who had heard of him through family connections. He was a laird from Kincardineshire, none so far from Dunnottar, son of Middleton of that Ilk; and as a young man, with a taste for things military like so many another young Scot, he had joined as a pikeman in the regiment of King Gustavus Adolphus of Sweden commanded by Sir John Hepburn, and in due course proceeded to France with Hepburn and become an officer in the Garde Ecossais or Regiment d'Hebron. He appeared to be a great survivor, for he had been captured and escaped many times, from different foes, including Roundheads when he had fought with the Cavaliers for Charles the First. He had been exiled to Holland, returned to Scotland with Charles the Second, been wounded at Worcester but escaped abroad with Charles, and apparently was now back somewhere in the Highlands, allegedly with the rank of lieutenant-general, and seeking to co-operate with Huntly, announcing that he would lead Scotland back to independence.

However doubtful many were about the arrival of this character, George and Patrick were interested enough to discuss what he might be able to achieve in the north. Would Crawford and Airlie, Huntly and the Earl Marischal be prepared to serve with or under this newcomer? And even if they were, would their forces be in any way strong enough, however well led, to challenge the might of the invaders? So far, there was no one south of Perth and Dundee of sufficient military ability and experience to replace the captive Leslie generals; and such would be essential before any concerted rising could be attempted with any hope of success. Scotland's military leadership had been decimated at the Battles of Preston, Dunbar and Worcester. They needed another Montrose. This Middleton . . . ? So often Patrick and George debated the situation, and their own position. They had military experience, both of them, although not in any high command. They could and ought to join in any major and unified uprising, Stanfield notwithstanding.

It was George who raised the subject of the Borderers, those unruly, mosstrooping freebooters, all but brigands in the eyes of most Scots, these occupying all the breadth of the land between Tweed and Solway, the East, Middle and West Marches. These had taken no noticeable part in the failed defence of the realm, their concerns being cross-border raiding and reiving, cattle-lifting and ravishing, or so it was held. Yet Monk had been sufficiently afraid of them to order that regalia to be sent to London by ship rather than risk its passage through their territory. Their fighting abilities must be notable. If they could become involved in the national cause . . .

Patrick wondered who were the effective leaders – if there were any such? The Homes and Swintons on the East March; the Kerrs, Douglases and Elliots on the Middle March; and all the Maxwells, Johnstones, Armstrongs and Grahams on the West March, these the most notorious ones. Admittedly, if they could be induced to come together, act together, they would certainly make a force to be reckoned with, and all horsemen. But they would require accepted leaders, not just local chieftains but important men, sufficiently prominent to guide and control them, and with military skills other than just at border reiving.

The pair wondered whether here was something that they could do. Might they go and find leaders who might be willing and able to muster a large host of riders and mosstroopers capable of making a challenge to the Ironsides in the south? They did not know any such border magnates; but they, one a lord and with Peebles-shire property at Blackbarony, and both having fought for Montrose, might be heeded.

Liz, who was not enthusiastic about them getting involved in possible action and warfare again, did suggest that they could visit the Swintons of that Ilk. The recent head of that ancient borders line, Sir Alexander, twenty-second chief, had died only the year before. He had been a friend of her father's, and Sheriff of Berwickshire. He had been succeeded by his eldest son, John, who was a royalist supporter and had fought but been captured at Worcester, with two of his five brothers dying there. But there were three others, one a judge of the High Court of Session, Lord Mersington. He would not be likely to be of much use in this of warfare, a lawyer based on Edinburgh; but the other two brothers at Swinton could be helpful. *They* would know all the Borderland chiefs.

54

Go and see the Swintons, then? The colonel could hardly be told of their objective, but would have to be offered some reason for their going off southwards, on this parole as they were. Patrick thought that he could claim to require to visit Blackbarony, near Peebles. This was not in the Swinton direction, just on the northern edge of the Middle March; but from there they could ride down Tweed into the Merse and Swinton, some forty-five miles admittedly.

Stanfield made no objection to this request, declaring that as far as he was concerned they were free men – it was only his superiors who could think differently. The askers both felt a little uncomfortable about deceiving him.

So they rode off, to Liz's cautionings, south-west, by Humbie and Soutra, then over to the Gala Water valley by Gilston to Heriot, and through the Morthwaite Hills to Blackbarony, north of Peebles. There they spent the night in the tower-house tenanted by Patrick's uncle, Walter Murray, a typical square, battlemented keep within a curtain wall, which George had never visited. They found all well there, and with nothing to delay them. Uncle Walter, sympathetic towards their mission, said that Kerr, Earl of Lothian, might well be the individual they were looking for.

Next day it was down Tweed, by Innerleithen and Clovenfords and St Boswells to Kelso, where they headed north-east for another dozen miles. They were very much in the steel-bonnet country of the Borderland here; indeed they passed close to Smailholm Tower of the Kerrs and the lofty Home Castle. But although they were eyed watchfully by various other horsemen, they were only challenged once, when they asked the way at Eccles; but their destination, Swinton, gained them passage. They had not seen a Roundhead since they left Haddington, this they did not fail to remark upon. Were these parts immune from the invaders? Or did Cromwell and Monk consider the English garrisons at Berwick-upon-Tweed, Norham and Wark a sufficient safeguard?

They reached Swinton in late afternoon, set in rolling country of gentle braes and many streams, a village with a quite large green and ancient market cross and a worthy church. The Swinton family seat was a fine hallhouse rather than a castle, as though they had no need for defence, they one of the most ancient and renowned in all the Borderland, although not large as to numbers.

On arrival they were greeted by a young woman of attractive appearance and easy friendliness, who said that her name was Helen and that her brothers George and David were presently at Leetholm, but would be back shortly for the evening meal. She declared that she had heard of the Lord Elibank: was he not married to a daughter of the Earl of Traquair, whose brother they knew? And was Doctor Hepburn some kin to the Earls of Bothwell's line? This one was knowledgeable about families, and cheerful company.

They were kindly entertained until, in due course, the Swinton brothers arrived, both men in their thirties and far from notably clad. Apparently they had been attending to one of the barony's mills, at Leetholm, where the mill-wheel had broken down, damaged by a flash flood bringing down a tree-trunk in the Leet Water.

When these two had washed and dressed themselves more suitably, and they all sat down at table to a very worthy meal, the guests explained the object of their visit, the possibility of finding a borderline leader of sufficient renown and military experience to persuade an army of mosstroopers to rise against the invaders. This was received doubtfully by the brothers but applauded by their sister. She immediately said that she would have suggested the Earl of Home, who had supported the late King Charles and been colonel of the Berwickshire Regiment which had joined in the attempt to rescue that monarch in 1648. But he was now in England, not exactly a prisoner, but in the care and custody of the Earl of Dorset, whose daughter his son had married. It might be hard, if not

56

impossible, to persuade him to contrive a return to Scotland to head this venture. So what of the Kerr, Earl of Lothian? He had fought for Montrose had he not?

Both Patrick and George knew Lothian, to be sure, but said that they believed him presently to be at Breda in the Netherlands with the exiled Charles the Second, with whom he had managed to escape from the Battle of Worcester. The Swinton brothers agreed that they understood that he had not come back to Scotland.

Not to be discouraged, Helen, admitting that she could think of no other suitable character in the East and Middle Marches, while eyeing her brothers with raised eyebrows, said that the West March lords were a wild lot, but always eager for fight, and some of *them* might well be prepared to raise the banner. How about the Lord Herries? Had he not also fought for Montrose? And been excommunicated by the General Assembly of the Kirk?

Her guests were aware of this also, and had fought alongside the Maxwell Lord Herries, a dashing individual. But they had thought that he had been held prisoner in England, one of the many, and exempted from pardon for aiding the executed monarch.

The Swintons however said that the word was that he had been either released or had escaped, and was back at Terregles, in Dumfries-shire. As well as eighth Lord Herries, John Maxwell was heir to the other Maxwell line, Earls of Nithsdale. Would *he* serve?

Of all the West March lairds, and riding-captains as they were called, the Maxwells of Caerlaverock and Terregles were probably the strongest and the most influential. If anyone could captain the mosstroopers and steel-bonnets, Herries probably could. Whether he would agree, and be able to persuade the Middle and East March riders, was of course to be discovered. But it was at least possible.

Helen Swinton clapped her hands at this recognition. If this one had been born a male, her guests might well not have had to look further afield on their quest!

57

It must be Terregles, then, near to Dumfries, for them next day, a long journey, not far off one hundred miles, they reckoned, across the width of southern Scotland, and hills most of the way, two days' riding. They got the impression that Helen Swinton would almost have wished to accompany them, so enthusiastic was she over their project. She did insist that when they returned northwards they should do so by Swinton, and report.

The pair made an early start of it, without demur at the hour by their hosts. They headed back by Kelso and then up Teviot, not Tweed, to Hawick, and thereafter commenced their climbing into the high hills, by Teviothead, and onward south over the watershed, and downhill now towards Eskdale, to spend the night at the little town of Langholm, a major ride. But they reminded themselves that the courageous but unfortunate Mary, Queen of Scots had done it, from Jedburgh right to Hermitage Castle in Liddesdale and then back again, all in one day, this to visit her wounded husband, Hepburn, Earl of Bothwell, an epic feat.

From Langholm they swung due westwards, still through hills, to cross the Kirtle Water to reach Lockerbie in Annandale, and on to Lochmaben, where some claimed that Robert the Bruce had been born, then over to Dumfries in Nithsdale.

In that town, where Bruce had slain the Red Comyn, they asked where was Terregles, the Herries seat, and were directed some three miles westwards, into fine country of more gentle slopes and green pastures, where they quickly learned that they were now in mosstrooping country, for, after passing through the hamlet of Kirkland, they were very soon galloped after by a group of rough-looking riders, who surrounded them and demanded who they were and why they entered Maxwell territory without due permission. They said that they sought the Lord Herries, with whom they had served in the Montrose campaigns, and this gained them a suspicious escort for the remaining mile or so to Terregles Castle.

There they were handed over to a young man, who proved to be no Maxwell but the Viscount of Kenmure, a nephew of the Lady Herries, who told them that she and her husband were presently visiting neighbours at Terraughtie, but were expected to return in the evening.

The visitors were somewhat doubtful about this Kenmure connection, although the young man seemed friendly enough, for his mother was known to have been a daughter of the hated Earl of Argyll, Montrose's enemy and slayer. Yet Herries himself had been Montrose's man.

When John, Lord Herries and his lady got home, their surprise at seeing the pair from the east was considerable, but they were not unwelcoming. The Maxwell remembered them, of course, and forbore to ask them what had brought them all this way from Lothian. He was a man in his forties, brisk of manner, of square build, square features and squarish manners, one who gave the impression of making a bad enemy. Young Kenmure was obviously in awe of him. The Lady Elizabeth, on the other hand, was quietly serene.

Patrick did not delay unduly in broaching the subject of their visit. "What think you, my lord, of the Roundhead invasion of our land, and the man Cromwell's claim to have incorporated Scotland and England into one Commonwealth?"

Herries's snort was sufficient answer to that.

"Ought we Scots not be seeking to do something about it?"

"Leslie and young Charles so sought, at Worcester. And achieved nothing. *Their* swords were not so sharp as Cromwell's! As was shown at Dunbar also."

"We know that. We were at Dunbar. Captured. Thanks to the folly of the Kirkmen."

"The folly of Leslie, who heeded them! Whom did he heed at Worcester?" Herries all but spat.

"We could do better," George agreed. "Some in the north, Crawford, Huntly and the others, are showing the way. Should not we do the like?"

The other eyed him, silent.

"You in this Borderland are notable fighters, my lord, are you not? Yet have not risen, as yet. If you united, to form a hard-riding host, you could make the Ironsides sore troubled. With others of us, to be sure. Who need a leader, leaders."

"Such as yourselves?"

"We are not . . . sufficiently prominent," Patrick said. "We fought for Montrose, yes. But not in any high command. *You* could lead to better effect with your mosstroopers. And those of the other lines, Johnstones, Armstrongs, Grahams and the like. And with the March-men of the Middle and East – Kerrs, Homes, Turnbulls and others."

"Why come to me? Others nearer to you, in Lothian."

"Would your Marchmen heed *them*?"

Herries took a step or two up and down that chamber, brows furrowed.

"I will consider," he said at length. That was brief.

They necessarily left it so.

At the meal that followed, the subject was not raised again directly, although there was, of course, talk of the troubles, the follies, the divided state of the nation, and the price they all were paying for it. The name of Argyll was not mentioned, with young Kenmure present, his grand-sire.

The guests were given a bedroom to share, thereafter. They slept, George more hopeful than Patrick.

At breakfast, Herries in his abrupt way told them that he would speak with Johnstone of Lochwood, the Arm-strongs of Mangerton and Gilnockie, and Elliot of Thirl-shope. That was all. No further commitment. The pair were not asked to accompany him on these approaches.

Was it all sufficient to make their long journey worth the

while? They could not tell, only hope. At least Herries had heeded them enough to put the issue before others. And those he had named were notable and active chieftains.

No suggestion was forthcoming that the visitors should linger at Terregles. They took their departure on the assumption that they would hear further from the Lord Herries in due course.

Had they anything of worth to tell Helen Swinton?

On the way back, it occurred to them to call in at Smailholm Tower, which they must pass, to test out the Kerr laird as to their project. After all, he was by heredity and situation one of the key figures in the established Marches alarm-system, responsible for lighting a beacon on his tower-top in the event of any large-scale enemy crossing of the borderline. When invasion occurred, down the years, certain castles and towers in prominent positions had the duty to light their beacons, smokes by day and fires by night, in a lengthy chain right across the land, their men always on the look-out, so that, lit up in turn, in a matter of mere minutes the entire Borderland learned of it and could unite to take the necessary action. If they could work together thus over mere raiding, how much more they should unite against national invasion.

Smailholm, a typical tall border tower set on a lofty ridge of rock above a small lochan, and visible for miles around, they found to be in the keeping of a far-out kinsman of the Earl of Lothian, the Kerr chief, a young man of hearty disposition, who declared himself all in favour of a borders rising against Cromwell's wretched underlings, and thought that the Kerrs might play a part effectively. He was somewhat doubtful about Herries, or other West March character, in command, but had no alternative to suggest.

They left him encouraged.

At Swinton they were well received, especially by the sister, who was eager to hear of the reactions to their

61

mission. She said that she was sure that something would come of it, that if the Maxwells led, others would not be far behind, rivalry ensuring that. She thought that Herries would make a good leader. Her brothers, without being quite so enthusiastic, agreed that they could provide a troop of perhaps seventy men. They had evidently been calculating numbers, no doubt at Helen's urging.

A quite lively evening was passed after the meal, with David proving to be adept with the fiddle and the young woman clearly fond of dancing, enough to summon one of the maids from the kitchen to partner her other brother, herself skipping between George and Patrick. They both appreciated her attentions and frank pleasure in the occasion, George in especial showing his enjoyment of her uninhibited personal zest and relish. Without being in any way immodest she was stimulating to masculinity, with just a hint of the provocative. Patrick, while nowise backward in esteeming her kindnesses, was interested to observe his friend's reaction, for George had never been notably a ladies' man, although Liz said that he could flirt on occasion; but now he was clearly enjoying himself.

When it came to bedtime, and they were shown to their room by their hostess, and she went in to check that all was in order there, fire blazing, water warm and wine by the bedsides, it was George who escorted Helen back to the door, and followed her out on to the landing, from which he took a little time to return. Patrick smiled, but forbore to comment.

In the morning, when they set off northwards, all three Swintons accompanied them a little way on their journey in kindly fashion, as far as the Blackadder river-crossing; and at the parting, both guests received an unexpected kiss, as further demonstration of hospitality, however brief coming from the saddle, with instructions to haste them back. George's assurance to that effect was entirely positive.

Back at Haddington that evening they reported their

return to the colonel, without detailing their activities, although they did mention that they had come back by the Merse and Swinton, just in case the word got out. They had been gone six days, but Stanfield asked no questions.

Lady Elibank was otherwise. She demanded to hear of all that had transpired, said not to get too hopeful over those West March freebooters, and was much interested to learn of Helen Swinton and George's evident admiration for her, wanting details as to that young woman – and expressing alleged concern that her own spouse was perhaps all too knowledgeable about this – but delighted if George had indeed found a suitable and possible partner. He needed a woman in his life. Would this one serve? Although she need hardly ask that, from Patrick's glowing description!

Their love-making that night at least proved that Liz's professed fears were groundless.

6

There was dire word from the north, although the siege of Dunnottar Castle was still going on, Lambert's cannon clearly useless. But elsewhere all was gloom for Scotland. Monk had received an additional twenty thousand men, sent by Cromwell, and with this enhanced force advanced to take Aberdeen, then on to the Spey, where he defeated Huntly, who fled with Crawford's son, Lord Balcarres, into the Highland mountains. Inverness fell to the invaders, and from there Monk issued stern announcements. All authority in Scotland not deriving from the English parliament was abolished forthwith. All persons holding appointments not given by Monk were dismissed. English judges were to take over in Scottish courts.

Save for the Highland fastnesses, the land lay totally under the heels, or hooves, of the Ironsides.

It was scarcely an encouraging time for the Marchmen to stage a rising.

Thereafter there was surprising news, and which indeed might just offer some small hope for the Scots. Monk himself had been summoned south by Cromwell to take part in the war at sea, which had developed greatly, with the Netherlands. He was to be one of three generals who were to act admiral and take charge of the English fleets. The Low Countries had risen in anger over Cromwell's order that all English trade, and trade with England, was to be carried only in English ships, this a serious blow to the Dutch, who were the greatest trading people in Christendom. Van Tromp, their High Admiral, was sailing the seas with whips at ships' mastheads to indicate his intentions, his vessels even entering the Thames estuary. Cromwell retaliated by affixing brooms to the English fleets, to show who would sweep the waters. In this connection it was worthy of remark that, although Scotland was now allegedly part of the English Commonwealth, Scots ships were not allowed to trade with England.

Even Stanfield shook his head over much of all this. He greatly admired Oliver Cromwell, but wondered if he was beginning to lose his good judgment.

His fears were perhaps substantiated shortly thereafter, when the tidings were that in Monk's absence Morgan and Lambert, left in charge in Scotland, had made a serious error in strategy. In their efforts to subdue the Highlands they had despatched three separate expeditions into the mountains. One with a General Dean, from Perth, north-westwards into Strathtay and Glengarry; one under a Colonel Lilburn west from Inverness to head for Lochaber; and the third, oddly, commanded by a Colonel Overton, going by ships from Ayr to land in Kintyre and Argyll – this last hardly wise, for it infuriated the Earl of Argyll, and caused him to rally the entire Campbell clan against them.

The other Highland clans were not to be outdone by the hated Campbells. They rose in their thousands under their chiefs, Lochiel, Glengarry, Fraser of Lovat, the Mackintosh, Clunie Macpherson and the rest. And these knew how to make the land fight for them, the upheaved and watery land with its narrow passes and lofty ridges, its bogs and lochs and rushing torrents, where horsemen, however well trained in warfare, were at a great disadvantage, and Highlanders on foot were at home. All three expeditions failed ignominiously, and were driven out of the mountains.

Further good news was that although Dunnottar's garrison had at last been forced to surrender, owing to lack of food – they had been existing on fish caught from their seabound rock for weeks – the regalia had been secretly

65

smuggled out beforehand, with the help of the local minister's wife and other women, even the sword of state disguised as a distaff, and the crown concealed under clothing to make one woman look pregnant to the unsuspecting Morgan, who took the surrender. The Honours were now hidden somewhere unspecified.

More personal matters had their developments also. George Hepburn approached Stanfield to ask permission to pay a brief visit to friends in the Merse, which was granted without enquiries, Swinton not being mentioned. And when George returned, after three days, it was to announce, although not to the colonel, that Herries and a force of his steel-bonnets had made a raid across the Esk into Cumberland, over Lyne and Irthing, to assail and take Corby Castle on the Eden, east of Carlisle, a worthy gesture which, it was to be hoped, would be but the beginning of a series of attacks along the borderline, which ought further to distract and worry Monk's successors. So the journey to Terregles had not been fruitless.

George also intimated, although privately and in a by-the-way fashion, that the Swintons had again been kind, more especially Helen. He did not go into any great detail, but admitted a growing fondness, which he believed was reciprocated in some measure. Liz, pressing for rather more information, got out of him enough to indicate that matters had got beyond a mere friendly kiss or two, and that George had reached the stage of wondering whether he might presume to progress to a permanent relationship – which was one way for a modest man, even a physician, to describe love and possible marriage. At any rate, he had promised to return to Swinton fairly shortly. Would Stanfield allow it?

Liz shook her head over him.

Patrick did rather better than that. He went over to see the colonel at Haddington, and declared that his friend had become enamoured of this lady at Swinton, and was, needless to say, desirous to visit her frequently, a man who could do with a wife.

The other declared himself as happy for Hepburn, who must feel free to go to Swinton as often as he desired. He wished the couple well.

Stanfield himself, however, was a somewhat worried man at this stage of affairs in Scotland. The lack of Monk's strong hand on the helm, transferred to that of shipping far-away; the failure of those three attempts to subdue the Highlands; and the fact that Cromwell was said to be sick with what was being called an ague, were all concerning him. And he had heard of Lord Herries's assault over into Cumberland, which meant that troops would probably have to be sent to those parts, which had hitherto been more or less trouble-free. He hoped that he might not be called upon to go and deal with this matter, as probably one of the nearest area governors. There was also news that the Cunningham Earl of Glencairn, from Ayrshire, had risen in what he called revolt, and this might well require dealing with. Altogether he felt that the sooner General Monk's duties against the Dutch were over and he could return to Scotland the better. He did not expect his friends to feel the same way, of course, however politely they listened to him.

When, in a couple of weeks, George announced that he thought he should visit Swinton again, Patrick decided to accompany him, to try to discover the situation as to the Marchmen. The colonel offered no objection, especially when Lady Elibank declared that she would like to go along also, to meet this Helen Swinton.

So the trio rode off southwards, directly now with no need for strategic diversions, the thirty or so miles through the Lammermuir Hills by Cranshaws to Duns in mid-Merse, to pass Kimmerghame, another Swinton property on the Blackadder. Liz was a good horsewoman, and enjoyed the ride, in fair weather. She did not hold up the menfolk to any degree.

At Swinton they learned that they must have passed near to the brothers, at Duns, where they were attending the late autumn sales when the sheep stock from the Lammermuirs were brought down to reduce the numbers on the high ground for winter grazing.

Helen, welcoming the visitors, eyed Liz speculatively, and Patrick warmly with a kiss, although a slightly less lingering one than she gave George, seeming in no way put about by their unexpected arrival. Liz herself did some assessing, however inconspicuously.

When, after some refreshment and talk, and some instructions to a housemaid, Helen conducted them all upstairs, the room situation presented itself, Patrick coming to recognise it. Hitherto the two men had shared a bedchamber, but now they were shown into two rooms, husband and wife into one, George into that which they had previously occupied. Water to wash in was already steaming in tubs. Left alone for the moment, Liz smiled to Patrick.

"This was one, just one, of my reasons for coming with you," she mentioned. "I wanted to meet this Helen, yes – and she seems to be . . . not unsuitable! But now George will have better opportunity, will he not? To find out. At bed-going!"

Her husband wagged his head. "You women!" he said.

Downstairs again, they had not long to wait before a great baaing heralded the brothers and their shepherds with a flock of sheep from the sale. The two visitors went out to help in the dividing and penning process in the infields and out-fields, prior to distribution over to further pasture-land, which took some time, themselves used to similar activities. When they got back, it was to find the two women equally busy, and apparently in close co-operation, superintending the hanging of new tapestries, which Helen had just completed, on the walling of the great hall, which demanded some repositioning of sundry family portraits and ancient banners. The men, shrugging, left them to it.

Over the repast that followed, it was Liz who announced that Helen had told her that, only the day before, they had heard that there had been another raid over the border, this time from the Middle March, at Carter Bar and the Redeswire, south of Jedburgh, and down into Redesdale, to assail the castle of Rochester, this presumably led by Herries but no doubt with Kerr and other Middle March support. Perhaps it would be the East March's turn next? This must be alarming the Roundheads. Patrick agreed that it was concerning Colonel Stanfield, who might well be called upon to mount some counter-action.

The Swinton brothers looked less than happy about this.

Later, there was dancing again, no maid having to be brought in to partner the other George this time, Liz more than adequate, although she deliberately stole their own George from Helen on occasion, vying with her in flirtatious by-play, all in a good cause no doubt. Some of the dances were of the purely Scottish variety, reels, strathspeys and the like, in which all mingled and circled together. Liz declared that it was a shame that David, doing the fiddling, was unable to take part. She volunteered to chant a rhythmic melody for them, for she had a fine singing voice, and this was accepted with acclaim. After a while of it, David himself, complaining that he had not had opportunity to dance with Liz, suggested that they all contribute and hum and sing as best they could, while they danced, however tuneless might be some of them. This was agreed to with laughter and, Liz leading off, distinctly chaotic, tripping and breathless cantrips followed until, exhausted, all were ready to collapse around the table in the hall and sip wine to ease their throats and revive their persons. There was not a little appreciative demonstration of congratulation and affection.

Altogether it made a lively and memorable evening for all.

When it was bed-going, Liz heedfully led Patrick off first, this to ensure that George and Helen were able to make their way upstairs alone, and to indulge in whatever demonstrations of affection they felt inclined for. Liz guessed that Helen would lead the way up, in more ways than one.

These two visitors themselves were not too tired with all the dancing and merriment to leave all the fondnesses to others.

They spent another rewarding day at Swinton hawking along the verges of the Blackadder for mallard, teal and other wildfowl; and a second enjoyable evening of high spirits and jollity, with late retirement.

In the morning it was back to Lothian, with George, on the way, informing that he and Helen had now become betrothed. And he would wish to marry as soon as possible, but admitted that circumstances might make an early wedding inadvisable. How thought his companions?

His friends, by no means surprised, saw no point in any delay. He might wait long enough for conditions to improve in any major fashion. If Stanfield did have to take action against the Marchmen, he would not be likely to involve them in any degree in that. Why wait? Liz thought that Helen would certainly agree with them. And if her brothers did join in any East March rising, she would be better at Monkrigg with George.

At Haddington they found the colonel to be still further concerned. It seemed that a colleague whom he had known for long, a Colonel Kidd, governor of Stirling Castle, had heard that the Earl of Glencairn had mustered a force none so far west of there, at Aberfoyle, just within the Highland Line, and Kidd had gone to deal with this, with two squadrons of horse. And, like those other three Roundhead officers, unused to fighting in mountain conditions, he had been trapped in the narrows, which amounted to a pass, near Loch Achray and been defeated, with serious losses, eighty Ironsides dead, before they could extricate themselves and get back to Stirling. This of the Highlands was proving to be the heel of Achilles for the Commonwealth in Scotland.

One item that Stanfield mentioned in the by-going and which greatly interested his hearers was that one of Glencairn's lieutenants, who had apparently been prominent in the fighting, was a Viscount of Kenmure. So that young man whom they had met at Terregles had elected to follow Herries's example and take to arms, but had evidently gone north not south. Kenmure Castle was in Galloway, none so far from Glencairn's Ayrshire seat, so there might be a connection there, even relationship?

Morgan and Lambert were not having a very happy time of it in Monk's absence.

George took the opportunity to inform the distinctly distracted colonel that he was contemplating marriage with Helen Swinton. Would there be any objection to this under their parole situation? None was voiced, at any rate; indeed Stanfield wished him well.

7

George Hepburn was not long in hastening back to Swinton with his news and proposal for an early wedding. He returned to announce that Helen was nowise reluctant, and she was suggesting a day two weeks hence at Swinton Kirk, a speedy reaction, but by no means too soon for the bridegroom-to-be. Her brothers were making no objection. So there was much activity at Monkrigg, with considerable tidying up and refurbishing to see to, in order to make that rather neglected hallhouse into a fit state to welcome a new bride.

As they waited for the happy day, the friends learned of a rather extraordinary happening. A former Cavalier colonel, Wogan by name, had raised a couple of troops of royalists and ridden north with them through the English counties, claiming that they were Commonwealth troops, this in the west, encouraged by Herries's raiding. They had crossed the border near Carlisle, and promptly reverted to being royalists. Whether or not they had consulted with Herries or other Marchmen was not known, but they had continued their progress northwards, to join the victorious Glencairn behind the Highland Line, the first adherence of Englishmen to the Scots cause for many a year. It made cheering news.

The wedding party duly set off for Swinton, clad in their best, scarcely suitable garb for riding through the Lammermuirs perhaps, among the sheep and heather, the croaking grouse and loping hares. The custom of the bridegroom not seeing the bride on the day of the wedding before the nuptials had to be observed, and they repaired to the parish minister's manse in the village, where they waited until they were given the signal to move over to the church.

It was a fair-sized building, very old, its pre-Reformation character still being evident however Protestant its incumbent, an elderly man of notably grave appearance. The church was already all but full, all the villagers having turned out, as well as Swintons from near and far. The minister led them up to the front row of pews, where he sat Lady Elibank, and then George, with Patrick to act as groomsman, to be left standing alone at the chancel steps, the pair feeling somehow awkwardly conspicuous.

George's avoidance of seeing his loved one before the ceremony was not the only tradition to be observed that day, the bride arriving late, despite the short distance to come from Swinton House, this entailing a fidgeting wait by the two at the steps. But when Helen did appear, escorted by both brothers, she was worth the waiting for, looking radiant indeed, a picture of confident loveliness, clad to do justice to the occasion, and to her rounded, superb figure. Murmurs from the congregation greeted her progress up the aisle. Whether he was supposed to turn round and greet her, or not, George did so, beaming, and having to restrain himself from going forward to take her in his arms, unease forgotten.

The minister emerged again from the vestry, on cue, and eyed all there somewhat after the manner of a stern but patient father. George, a Catholic, would have expected a choir of singing boys, but here there was nothing such, only a precentor with a tuning-fork, which, at a nod from the divine, he tapped on the lectern to produce a melodious note, this enabling him to lead off with the first words of a psalm, the congregation duly joining in with what developed into a chanting enthusiasm, however uncertain as to the words was the bridegroom.

Thereafter the marriage ceremony, simple and telling, went ahead, and comparatively brief, save for the address to the newly-weds, and indeed to all married folk in the assembly, that followed, not quite a sermon but getting on for such, on the sins and wickedness of marital infidelity, and the duties of spouses, with the dire punishments which the Almighty could visit upon all such backsliders and transgressors. Standing just behind the couple now, Patrick saw Helen turn and make a face at her new husband.

All presently followed bride and groom out of the church, to congratulations and well-wishing, and it was back to the hallhouse, the Reverend Denholm, with his wife and with changed demeanour, among the guests, feasting to follow. George would have wished to set off for Monkrigg forthwith, which they could still reach before the early October darkness, but the customary banquet had to be provided and attended, and it would not be acceptable, however generous, without the presence of the newly-weds.

The notable repast went on and on.

The hall at Swinton was insufficiently large for all the great numbers of guests to dance thereafter, so entertainment was provided of a different sort: dancing, yes, but by a troupe of gypsies from Yetholm, with their especial skills, attitudes and dress, men and women appropriately challenging in the offerings and demands. They had also brought a wild boar captured apparently as a swinelet and reared tame, this to parade around in salute to the Swintons, who had gained their name, repute and lands six centuries before as boar-slayers, these then a menace to the countryside. There was singing to David's fiddling, and border-ballad reciting.

But as the evening wore on, with much wine consumed, there was an ever-growing demand for the bed-going ritual, this a quite frequent procedure on wedding nights, when the guests escorted the bridal couple to their bedchamber and ensured that they coupled as effectively as they were able, the women present traditionally undressing the groom and the men the bride, this with much appreciation and good advice given. But on this occasion Helen disappointed many, although not her husband. When eventually she rose to announce that all present could go on enjoying the evening for as long as they wished and were able, she and her loved one had others matters to attend to that night. Despite kind offers to assist by many, however, they were perfectly capable of achieving this desired end without guidance, and intended so to do with, they hoped, well-wishing from all. Lord and Lady Elibank, who had been the means of bringing them together in the first place, would accompany them upstairs, they hoped, representing all, for a final blessing.

There were murmurs of dissent, even protests, at this declaration, however smilingly Helen had made it, and no applause – save by the Reverend Denholm, who clearly disapproved of such ongoings. Patrick and Liz rose, well pleased for their part, and George sighed with relief.

So to varied expressions of scolding and remonstrance, the four of them left the company, to climb the stairs, Liz congratulating their hostess on her decision.

At Helen's bedchamber she led them within, declaring with a laugh that this room was not entirely new to George, although he might just possibly be inexperienced in what was to follow? She doubted however whether he would require Patrick's guidance, any more than she would Liz's! That couple proclaimed themselves as nowise essential guides, and well content to depart to their own room and their own ways of dealing with a bridal situation.

However, Helen saw the occasion as one to be marked by some small gesture of appreciation and reward for the groomsman's help and support, and she moved over to the fireplace, and there held out her arms to Patrick.

Bowing, with something of a flourish, that man went over to embrace her, receiving a warm kiss, and having her bridal gown's bodice pulled open for him to slip the silken material back over white shoulders, and the splendid bosom below made evident and available. He thereupon planted two kisses of his own.

Not to be outdone, Liz turned to George who, grinning, began to unbutton his doublet. She helped him to slip it off and declared that she liked men with hairy chests, and gave him a kiss on the lips in turn.

Then, wishing their friends well indeed, they left them for their own nearby chamber, not returning to the hall below, tradition adequately celebrated.

In the morning there was much packing-up of woman's clothing and gear before the desired start for Monkrigg could be made, Liz assisting. Without going into details, it was indicated that the bridal night had been rewarding in every sense, and future developments could be looked forward to.

Eventually the four of them set off northwards, the Swinton brothers seeing them on their way.

At Monkrigg they found all in order that afternoon, with Liz saying that she had helped George to improve things, but that no doubt Helen would see much that could be bettered and rearranged. Any aid required would be forthcoming from Ballencrieff. And there, needless to say, she would always be more than welcome, George having for long made it a sort of second home.

At Haddington they called on James Stanfield to acquaint him of their return. There they learned from him that General Monk had arrived back in Scotland, to his relief if not theirs. Van Tromp had been defeated at a sea battle off Calais; indeed he had been killed in another affray at Scheveningen. Now they could expect to see a very different situation in this part of the Commonwealth, Monk quite the ablest commander in the field after Cromwell himself. Middleton was reported to have taken over from Glencairn in the north, with rumours of a dispute. The Scots apparently could always be relied upon to fight among themselves. Patrick could not deny that. But was not something of the same apt to apply in England? What of royalists and republican? Cavaliers and Roundheads? Cromwell dismissing one parliament after another amid accusations of failure to agree? The colonel could not deny this, shaking his head over mankind. But this of Glencairn and Middleton seemed to have been folly indeed. One of Middleton's officers was said to have declared that Glencairn's Highlandmen were but a pack of thieves and robbers, this man Sir George Munro. He would show them all a different sort of fighters. Glencairn had called him a liar, and Munro challenged him to a duel, on horseback. They had sought to unseat each other with lances, and when this was indeterminate, fired pistols, neither scoring a hit, and then with swords, with Munro hit on the head so that he could not see. This was considered a win by the earl; but Middleton had him arrested for some reason, whereupon Glencairn departed, leaving the army, and went back to his own Ayrshire. Had they ever heard the like?

Patrick said that there was always apt to be this rift between Highlanders and Lowlanders, although Glencairn was himself a Lowlander, but commanding a mainly Highland force. He agreed that it did not say a lot for Scottish generalship. Nor did it give him any great respect for this Middleton, if he was to be the king's representative in Scotland.

They left it at that.

8

Stanfield's assertion that Scotland would see major
changes with Monk's return was quickly substantiated.
That general marched a large force northwards without
delay. But he was not going to have his Ironsides trapped
in Highland defiles, sunk in peat-bogs or cut down at
rushing river-crossings. He learned that Middleton had
left Easter Ross and the Dornoch area, and moved south-
westwards down Loch Ness-side into the mountains of
Glengarry's country, where he was summoning the clans
to rally to his banner, despite the attitudes of that Sir
George Munro. So although Monk led his horsed host
thither, he took the precaution of sending out scouts to spy
out the land well in advance. These discovered that Glengarry, opening westwards off the Great Glen, held a long
narrow loch, seven miles of it, with a road along only the
north side of it, the southern side all but impassable for
horsemen, with steep and broken banks and many cascad-
ing torrents. Highlanders on foot could probably traverse
this, if Monk's troopers could not. So, learning that
Middleton's force was massed at the west end of the loch,
he lured the Scots along that south shore by seeming to
send his Roundheads along the northern road, but only a
section of them, keeping his main host at the open ground
at the loch-foot, where they could deploy effectively on
horseback. The decoy squadrons had, halfway along the
loch, turned northwards up a minor incoming valley and
so round and back to their comrades. This strategy had
worked. Half of Middleton's force had come down the
south side of Loch Garry, intending to get behind the

invaders, who they thought were strung out along the north shore road, and would thus be cut off, trapped on that narrow track, the Scots facing them on both east and west. Instead, of course, they found Monk's army awaiting them on the firm meadowland at the loch-foot, where horsemen had all the advantages, and had there been cut to pieces. The western half of Middleton's force, when it heard of this disaster, had discreetly dispersed into the empty clan mountains.

So that Scots royalist threat was cancelled out, and Monk was securely established again as master of the northern kingdom.

Patrick was duly impressed.

From England the information was that Cromwell was a sick man now, but lacking nothing in drive; as Lord Protector he had appointed major-generals to govern all the shires of that land, and was giving his officers properties in Ireland confiscated from the Catholic landowners, indeed acting more autocratically than the monarchy he had put down. One of his parliaments had in fact offered him the crown itself, whether or not entitled to do so, but he had scornfully turned it down as a republican. However this stance made him no less of a despot.

Patrick and Liz arranged a party at Ballencrieff to introduce Helen to friends, kinsfolk and neighbours; and it occurred to them that since James Stanfield had, as it were, blessed the marriage with his permission and good wishes, he might be invited also, whatever some of the other guests thought of having to share the entertainment with the English governor. In the event none expressed nor demonstrated any objections, and the colonel got on well, paying not only Helen Swinton but all the other ladies courteous attentions, particularly one of Patrick's two sisters, Joanna. She had been married to Auchmutie of nearby Gosford, but had been fairly recently widowed, with a small son, and was in a somewhat depressed state, always rather shy and reserved; and here she was the only single woman present. Presumably recognising this, the colonel spoke with her more than with others. A little embarrassed at first, she quite quickly came to find his company acceptable. Liz did not fail to notice it, and was amused at one stage to hear her sister-in-law seeking to correct the governor's pronunciation of her married name from Okmoodie to *Auch*mutie, and telling him that Auchmutie of that Ilk was, like Swinton, a small but very ancient Scots family, Auchmutie being over in Fife.

Helen made a major impression on the other guests, with her looks and her liveliness, and it was recognised that she would be a social asset to the neighbourhood.

They made a successful evening of it, with music and dancing, although scarcely of the hilarious sort that had developed at Swinton. Stanfield was the first to leave, and when he thanked Patrick and bade him farewell, he said that it all had been good for the image he wanted to present, not that of a stern overseer but of a friendly and accessible guardian, who would make the Commonwealth regime more acceptable. He also saw the new lady of Monkrigg as quite a character, and he judged her husband would have to keep an eye on her! He ended by asking where Gosford was, or was it Gooseford? He was told that it was an estate lying less than a couple of miles from this Ballencrieff, westwards, between the villages of Aberlady and Llanniddry, famous for its ponds, these a succession of artificial lochans which had been created when the marshy ground of a burn entering Gosford Bay was drained, and being at sea level the water had been difficult to make flow to the beach. These ponds had proved to be the answer. They were notable as a haunt of wildfowl, and so were an excellent and envied location for the sport of hawking.

When it came to Joanna's turn to depart, and Liz's sister and her husband, Sir John Hamilton of Redhouse, just south of Gosford, took her home, she said what a pleasant man was Colonel Stanfield. Smiling, Patrick warned her that he was a married man with a wife and son back somewhere in England.

Liz said that she was glad that they had asked the colonel. It would help to make conditions in Haddington-shire better for all concerned.

It was as well that Stanfield's rule in the area was indeed becoming ever more favoured by the population thereof, for elsewhere General Monk's hand was heavy, his author-ity strictly enforced. He would make up for what he judged was the weakness of his lieutenants. Whether the colonel received orders to that effect was not known. But if so, he did not alter his firm but all but benevolent behaviour.

He had become quite a frequent visitor at both Ballen-crieff and Monkrigg, Liz and Helen making him very welcome, and frankly admitting that he was a man that they liked as well as admired. On one occasion when he was visiting the former house he mentioned that it seemed a very long time since he had done any hawking, a pastime he enjoyed. Patrick had falcons. And had he not learned that there was an excellent place to practise the diversion, at that Gosford was it? Patrick agreed to arrange a day there with his sister Joanna.

This was not difficult to contrive, that youngish woman happy to co-operate, admitting that it was some time since there had been hawking at Gosford, and the company proposed would be welcome. George was invited also, and Helen, declaring that she enjoyed the sport, came along with him, which had Liz joining them. So one forenoon a party of five, with three falconers with the hawks, made their way westwards the short distance to the lesser bay which neighboured the great Aberlady one, where a medium-sized tower-house rose near the end of one of the ponds. Even as they rode up to this, a flight of duck squattered off over the water at the clip-clop of the horses' hooves.

Joanna, and her young son called John, joined them, so

it made rather a large party for hawking, with two of the Gosford men to act as tranters for the retrieving of the flown falcons and any prey that they managed to bring down. Joanna said that the sport was usually pursued on horseback, but here, with the close proximity of all the ponds and the fact that when the fowl rose at sight of them, they normally flew off only to one of the other lochans, these all within a short distance of each other, although hidden by trees and bushes. Sometimes they did flight out to the bay and salt water, but this was seldom. On foot, the hawkers would be less likely to scare away the birds than would be horses.

Joanna and young John led the way, round-about, to avoid the first pond already somewhat roused, and to approach the next one from cover, quietly, the colonel admitting that he had never gone hawking thus before. But it was an intriguing way of going about it, creeping up stealthily through the bushes to sight of the water and ready to unhood the falcons the moment the fowl were aware of them and rose to flight off.

There was, apparently, no lack of game, flocks of mallard and teal and a few widgeon proliferating, with heron and wild swans also apt to be there. In fact it was a heron that rose to flap slowly, deliberately, off as their first sighted prey, and Patrick, flicking off the hood that covered the head of the falcon sitting on his padded left arm, tossed the bird up, and it soared off forthwith. It went much higher than did the heron, and, circling, flew off to hover over the slower, larger bird for moments and then to stoop, or dive, plummeting down on its victim, to strike with a flurry of displaced feathers. Claws embedded, it and the heron dropped down, fortunately not on to the water of the pond but into nearby bushes, and a tranter ran off round the bank to collect them, to kill the heron if it was not already dead, and recapture the falcon before it could start major pecking at and eating the flesh.

This successful start produced its own side effects

however, one of the challenges of the sport here at Gosford. For the hawk-heron encounter did not go unnoticed by the other fowl of that pond, and occasioned arousal, some duck rising to fly off, some merely to patter away across the water, half paddling, to further reaches – for these ponds, although narrow, were lengthy. And this presented its demand on the sportsmen, for the hawk could be distracted from its original target and seek to drop on one of the flighting ducks, which would be seen as a failure. Also, sometimes a falcon would choose to stoop on one of the flapping fowl on the water itself, rather than one in the air, and this was, needless to say, to be frowned on, for the kill would be effected on the pond's surface and would inevitably present difficulties for the tranters in retrieving hawk and prey. There were rafts moored on each pond, Joanna told her guests, for this to be achieved, but it was an awkward, unseemly and delaying procedure.

On this first flight, all was well. And quickly thereafter other participants in the sport were unhooding their hawks at those flighting ducks, and mainly with success, so much so that Patrick and his nephew both changed their roles to that of tranters, to help retrieve. The score for that first pond was one heron, two mallard and a teal.

Avoiding the next pond as over-close and likely to be disturbed, Joanna took them round through the woodland to another, where, approaching quietly, they saw a couple of white swans swimming among rafts of duck. Swan's meat was much prized for dinner; but these were, of course, very large birds and not every hawk would or could tackle them. George released his falcon to try, but it, after a preliminary circling, chose to drop on a duck in preference. Liz followed suit, and her bird likewise stooped on a mallard. So Stanfield tried, and was rewarded by seeing his falcon make for one of the swans, these still swimming, not flying. There followed the astonishing sight of the two swans pattering off across the water to rise into slow flight, long necks outstretched, one with the falcon sitting firmly on its back and pecking, a problem indeed for any tranter. Had they lost that hawk? Normally these birds dropped on their prey with precision exactly to break the neck of the victim, and so slay it at once. But a swan, however long its neck, made a difficult target. All watched, wondering, as the three birds disappeared beyond trees, and Joanna expressed fears that they might never see any of these again, for the swans, plus their attacker, could well head off seawards, out into the Firth of Forth.

However, her concern proved groundless, for presently just the one swan came circling back over their heads, and this carrying no hawk. So almost certainly, she said, the other, with its assailant, had dropped somewhere beyond, for they would not have parted otherwise. So one of the tranters, and John, were sent off to search.

The hawkers returned to the central pond which they had hitherto avoided, and found it undisturbed and well populated with fowl. Four falcons were released here, and all made kills, although one with its prey fell into the water, which had Joanna herself, who knew where the required raft was moored, in the absence of a tranter going to launch and paddle it out to retrieve. But the colonel forbade it, declaring this quite unsuitable, and took the paddle to board and steer the unwieldy craft quite expertly out and bring back live hawk and dead fowl, to the cheers of the others. Helen's falcon had to be brought back otherwise, and proved to have killed an eider-duck, a seafowl which ought not to have been on this inland water, and was considered to be inedible anyway, to her chagrin.

All this had taken some considerable time, with much walking about involved, and everyone was well content to return to the modest castle for the promised midday meal, slightly late as it would be.

Washing and preparing for this, they were glad to hear that young John and his tranter had returned with swan and hawk, found eventually on the seashore.

After a worthy repast, they lingered for quite a while pleasantly. When departure was indicated, they all expressed their appreciation, especially Stanfield, who said that he had not enjoyed an occasion so much for long; and might he come back another day for the like? Joanna told him any time, any time. But why not return very soon, and help to consume his swan, which she would meantime keep fresh in her icehouse? He agreed that this was an excellent suggestion.

Three days later Patrick learned that the colonel had indeed gone to Gosford again, to eat his swan, and had presented Joanna with a jewelled brooch, which she was treasuring. He was just a little concerned about this, his sister and this married Englishman becoming so friendly, an association which could not come to any fruitful conclusion by the nature of things. But Liz said not to worry. Stanfield was an honourable man, almost certainly a Puritan, with high standards of behaviour, or he was unlikely to have become a colonel in Cromwell's army. And Joanna was a sensible soul. It was surely possible for a man and a woman, neither immature, to have a quite close relationship without going to bed with each other, this to the benefit of them both. No need to discourage it.

Patrick noted that the colonel had not suggested, or at least had not evidently been granted, another leave of absence from his duties to go south. Was that significant? His marriage could hardly be a satisfying one.

No further cross-border assaults by the Marchmen were reported. Perhaps Herries and his friends were deciding that they had done sufficient, in view of the now complete lack of any armed uprising elsewhere in Scotland. General Monk's abilities, successes and fame seemed to have produced quiescence in the land that was not noted for such. Where Middleton was now no one seemed to know.

In fact, Monk's rule, however strict, was effective, just as far as was possible, and more trouble-free than had been the case for long, indeed for many years before the Cromwellian invasion. From the Reformation onwards Scotland had been in turmoil: Protestant versus Catholic; the Lords of the Congregation against Mary, Queen of Scots; the Covenanting troubles and King Charles the First's attempts to impose bishops on the land; Montrose's campaigns; and the harsh dominance of Argyll. So a strong reign of peace, even by an English general, had its welcome aspects, however inimical were all Scots to the idea of the Commonwealth and the northern ancient kingdom being united with the southern. That must not be allowed to continue for long. But meantime this form of peace and order had its compensations.

In Haddingtonshire, James Stanfield successfully maintained a similar policy of rule.

So a new year was ushered in, with Helen announcing that she was pregnant, to George's joy.

9

They were not long into that year when they heard news that set tongues wagging. Cromwell was an ever more ailing man, and was now said to be schooling his son Richard to succeed him. So he might have refused the crown, but he seemed to be assuming a hereditary protectorship. Would this be acceptable in England, whatever the Scots thought of it? It was rumoured that there were murmurings.

Further tidings were that Middleton had left the north and gone to rejoin Charles Stewart at Breda, where he was said to be advocating that the young unseated monarch should seek French help to regain his throne, under the traditional Auld Alliance. Charles's mother, Henrietta Maria, was a sister of the King of France, who was paying his unfortunate nephew a pension and enabling him to keep up some sort of court. If Cromwell died . . . ?

Stanfield received a summons from Monk to attend a meeting at Dundee, which the latter still used as his headquarters, the first such to be held so far as the colonel knew. When he came back he did not announce what had been discussed, but seemed grave and preoccupied.

Oddly enough, it was Joanna who gave her brother some idea of what had gone on at Dundee. Stanfield had mentioned to her, at one of his visits to Gosford, that General Monk was worried about Cromwell's health and this of his son Richard being allegedly groomed to succeed him. He knew that young man, and did not admire him, considering him a weakling. The Commonwealth in his charge would be in a sorry state, he judged. He, Monk, desired all commanders in Scotland, and he hoped Cromwell's eleven major-generals in England also, to combine to urge the Lord Protector to make other arrangements.

Patrick for one wondered whether Monk himself deemed that he might make a worthy successor.

His sister also revealed that the Roundhead command was concerned over increasing reports of misbehaviour by Ironside troopers with Scots women, especially in the north, apparently; perhaps not to be wondered at for men so long parted from their own partners in England. All governors of shires and provinces were to act on this, and punish transgressors severely. Not that the colonel had apparently had complaints as to this in his area.

It was intriguing that James Stanfield had seemed to confide in Joanna. Possibly he needed someone such. To be military governor of a nominally hostile area, with no close associates other than the men under his command, must be a lonely and at times frustrating position. Someone, some person not involved in affairs, whom he could trust, especially a quiet, friendly woman, was probably a relief, all but a necessity.

Patrick and George sometimes felt quite sorry for their captor.

Despite Cromwell's illness, that man was clearly not abdicating from his responsibilities as yet, for it was reported that he had declared war on Spain, just why was uncertain, but possibly partly because Middleton was now said to be advocating Spanish help to gain Charles his throne of England, as well as French aid. Also, Catholic Spain was gaining vast wealth from the Americas, discovered by their Christopher Columbus to the envy of the rest of Christendom, and Cromwell needed money to help pay for his great armies, military rule being notoriously expensive. In addition Spain had now established peace with the Netherlands, and this could lead to renewed warfare with the Dutch. At any rate, he had despatched a large fleet under his favourite admiral, Robert Blake, to Cadiz and then westwards.

Monk, it seemed, was not too happy about this, seeing it as an unnecessary diversion which might weaken the Commonwealth situation at home. Also, if Blake was not successful, it would strengthen King Charles's position, he now being linked with Spain in some measure; indeed he was said to have appointed his brother James admiral of a joint fleet of English and Irish royalist exiles to help counter Cromwell's latest moves, presumably again on Middleton's guidance.

All waited to hear the outcome that spring and summer, whether favouring one side or the other.

But there were other concerns eagerly awaited by some in the Haddington vicinity in these months, as Helen's delivery drew near, George, needless to say, anxious, although Liz, and Helen herself, kept reminding him that giving birth was no unusual or normally dangerous event, as old as was mankind itself, however painful it could be, temporarily, for the mother-to-be. If the outcome was a boy, he was to be called Patrick, if a girl, Elizabeth, after their good friends.

At the end of May a son was duly born, after quite a long but not too grievous labour, and Patrick Hepburn entered this unsettled and challenging world. He was promptly nicknamed Pate. What would life hold in store for him? they wondered. George was as proud as though he had given birth himself.

They made a pleasant and uneventful summer of it, the highlight of which was a visit to Haddington by George Monk himself, who was making a round of the counties and their governors, checking up. He seemed well satisfied with *this* command, praising Stanfield in his rather curt fashion, for he was not a notably amiable man. He was, among other activities, taken to see the great and semi-ruinous Tantallon Castle, which he had viewed in rather different fashion those years before; and also taken on a hawking expedition to Gosford. He appeared to enjoy this, although the colonel deliberately did not emphasise his friendship with Patrick and George, in case the general did not approve of such.

Then, in the autumn, they heard that Admiral Blake had been successful in his assaults on the Spaniards, and his ships had captured Jamaica for the Commonwealth, which seemed to validate Cromwell's decision, whatever Monk thought. Also it indicated the failure of James Stewart's attempt to counter the English, and to bring Spain into the royalist cause, none of which greatly affected conditions in Scotland, which continued under a veneer of normality, whatever feelings, hopes and intentions lay beneath.

So winter came upon them, the sixth such of that realm's humiliation, with a Huntingdon squire of Welsh descent succeeding in doing what even Edward Plantagenet, Hammer of the Scots, and Henry the Eighth in his Rough Wooing had failed to achieve.

Lambert, in England, and now a full general, had become Cromwell's right-hand man, which did not appear to please Monk, jealousy undoubtedly involved. He was a staunch republican, and condemned the offer of the English throne to the Lord Protector, and frowned on this of Richard Cromwell's advancement – which ought to have pleased Monk. Morgan was now Monk's principal lieutenant in Scotland, a much less stern man. The friends wondered whether, if Monk found the Welshman too moderate and lenient, he might possibly have Stanfield replace him and be promoted to major-general? They hoped not, if that would mean that they would lose their good captor.

At Ballencrieff that autumn they had an unexpected visitor, none other that Liz's father, the Earl of Traquair, from England, where he had been a captive since the Battle of Preston those years before. Sick and growing old, he had been released, although his son, the Lord Lintoun, captured at the same battle, was still a prisoner. A sad figure, the earl came to his daughter and Patrick, homeless, for his Traquair House in Peebles-shire and other properties had been confiscated by Argyll's regime, and he had been fined an enormous sum by the extreme Covenanting rulers for his support of Charles the First, and his son's serving with Montrose. Now he was impoverished, indeed destitute. Yet he had been Lord High Treasurer of Scotland, Commissioner to the General Assembly of the Kirk in 1639, and opened parliament; but, at Montrose's defeat, he had fled to England, joined the royalist army there, with his son, and after Preston held prisoner in Warwick Castle, the mighty fallen indeed.

Liz had long been anxious for him, needless to say, and now welcomed him with thankfulness, however sorry a figure he cut, saying that he must make Ballencrieff his home now, Patrick glad to agree. Their son, another Patrick but known as Pate, now aged twelve, promptly took to his grandfather, and declared that he would look after him always, even though that always did not look likely to be of very long duration, sadly.

James Stanfield took a very real interest in the older man also, visiting him often; and of course his presence with them brought about more frequent visits from his other daughters, Anne from nearby Redhouse, and Margaret, Countess of Queensberry, who had to travel from far-away Drumlanrig in Nithsdale, and could come only seldom to Lothian.

The earl was, naturally, much worried over his son, Lintoun, like the others of his family. None knew where he was being held prisoner, possibly even in the dreaded Tower of London. Indeed, he might not be still alive. Stanfield said that he would make enquiries, and even would suggest that, if the young man gave his word not to engage in further action against the Commonwealth, he might be released to return to Scotland, this gratefully acknowledged by them all.

So passed 1657, with the next year awaited with much question, forecasting and apprehension. The way matters were going on the national and international scene, anything might happen.

10

Happen it did, and in a big way. Oliver Cromwell died on the third day of September, and much of Europe was plunged into uncertainty, not only England, Scotland and Ireland, but France, the Netherlands and Spain also, so great an impact had the demise of one man upon them. Many mourned, but not all.

Richard Cromwell forthwith declared himself to be Lord Protector of the Commonwealth; and immediately vehement voices were raised against this, including that of General Lambert, who now found himself more or less in command of the Ironside army, with not all the major-generals agreeing with him. Much uncertainty reigned.

In Scotland Monk issued no statement, but James Stanfield believed that he would agree with Lambert's attitude as regards Richard, if not in much else. He feared that there would be great turmoil over this issue. What the colonel's own position in it all would be he did not volunteer. But there was a surge of hope among the Scots. Upset in England would surely work to their advantage.

Liz and her family wondered whether they would get their brother and son home.

The first major news from the south was not encouraging for such as Stanfield. Richard Cromwell, faced with a divided army, which had ruled the land for long, acted injudiciously. He announced himself to be commander-in-chief thereof, which promptly had Lambert declaring this as unsuitable, not to be accepted. The younger man then called on parliament to support him. This the members did. Then the generals set up their own council, calling it the Committee of Safety, and declared it supreme. The parliament then said that this council, or any other group of high officers of the Commonwealth army, must not meet without the new Lord Protector's permission.

Complete deadlock ensued, the army versus the legislature.

Stanfield shook his head over the entire situation. Monk had been right. This of appointing his son as his successor had been Cromwell's great mistake and folly. The Commonwealth might not survive, he feared. Richard Cromwell himself ought to have known better. After all, he had served in his father's army, knew the temper there. He had sat in two parliaments. He was no callow youth, now in his early thirties. England's fate hung in the balance.

What of Scotland's? his friends wondered. Middleton, with Charles at Breda, must be rubbing his hands in glee. Perhaps it would not be long now?

By the onset of winter there was little improvement in England, save that the army was consolidating its hold, with parliament all but powerless. John Lambert undoubtedly held most influence, more than the nominal Lord Protector. A parliament notable persuaded some of the doubting major-generals to rise against Lambert. They seized Cheshire, but were defeated at Nantwich, and the man, George Booth, confined to the Tower. Lambert to all intents ruled. Monk would be less than pleased. He held *his* army, in Scotland, poised.

Christmastide that year could not be signalised in more than token fashion, as all wondered and waited. At Ballencrieff, however, they did have something to rejoice over: the return to Scotland of Liz's brother, Lord Lintoun, from captivity in England. He had been released by the major-general who held the county of Lancashire, and who was apparently opposed to Lambert. His long captivity had been passed at Accrington, not far east of Preston where he had been taken, unlike his father who had been sent to Warwick Castle. So now he too arrived at Ballencrieff, having nowhere else to go.

Liz, rejoicing, made especial Yuletide celebration, recognising that it might well be the last such in which her ailing father would participate, in this life at least, the earl so greatly relieved by the return of his son, whom he had feared he would never see again. So there was a great gathering. James Stanfield attended, however on edge he was about the current state of affairs in the south.

That situation developed rapidly in the new year. The Committee of Safety that was, in effect, Lambert, forced Richard Cromwell to dissolve his parliament, and in its place recalled the so-called Rump Assembly which Cromwell senior had dismissed. The Rump, in its turn, thereupon formally dismissed Richard as Lord Protector, this in April. At first he resisted, but next month, finding little or no support throughout the land, he announced his abdication, and retired to his family home at Cheshunt.

Utterly confused by all this, the Scots, like a great many in England, looked northwards to Dundee, where Monk waited. What next?

Lambert, although he had been largely responsible for reinstating the Rump, now distanced himself from it, and began to act the supreme ruler of the Commonwealth.

Stanfield said that Monk, for one, would never accept that.

He was right. He received an order from the general, at Dundee, to have as many troopers as he could possibly spare to march south with him into England on New Year's Day, retaining only the very minimum required to hold Haddingtonshire secure. He was going to seek to set matters to rights in England.

Joanna told Patrick and George that the colonel was concerned that Monk might wish *him* to take part in this endeavour, which, it seemed, he had no wish to do. This interested them both. After all, Stanfield was a Roundhead senior officer. If he preferred to remain in charge at

Haddington, did that mean that he was not in favour of Monk's campaign? That he was reluctant to take up arms against some of his own countrymen? Or that he found life in Scotland to his taste?

That next Yuletide was a very different one from the last, especially at Ballencrieff, for Liz's father died just days before Christmas, so that mourning prevailed. Now her brother was Earl of Traquair, and none the better off for being so.

On the last day of 1659 Monk and a great army arrived at Haddington, on the way to Berwick-upon-Tweed, and there duly picked up most of Stanfield's men, leaving only a single troop of Ironsides behind. What orders and instructions he gave to the colonel were not revealed, but he did not command him to leave his post of governor there and accompany his army, for which all were thankful. He would bring in 1660 in better style for England, he declared. Meanwhile Scotland must remain quiescent, Morgan left in charge.

News of events in the south was slow to arrive. Would Lambert go to the length of opposing Monk in battle, his former commander? What would the Rump's attitude be? There were bound to be still quite large numbers of royalists in England. And the mass of the people themselves: how would they react to Roundhead against Roundhead?

At length rumours and questions were replaced by factual reporting. The two Commonwealth generals had indeed clashed in arms, in the English Midlands, and Lambert had been defeated. He had fled the field, whither none knew. So George Monk was now, in effect, ruler of both England and Scotland, Ireland also to be sure. He was marching on London where, it was to be assumed, the Rump parliament would welcome him.

Word came that it did, seeing him as a worthy successor to Oliver Cromwell. It would no doubt have appointed him Lord Protector, but he disclaimed any such title, even though he took over the duties and sway thereof. Parliament promptly denounced Lambert as a traitor, and indeed condemned him to death when his whereabouts could be found.

Monk took it upon himself to change this decision, stern authoritarian although he was. He ordered life imprisonment for his rival, but not in England. He would be imprisoned on the Channel Island of Guernsey – just why Guernsey was not revealed.

In Scotland all this was received with doubts. Would Monk, in total command, be any better for the northern kingdom than this Lambert, or indeed Cromwell? He had proved to be a rigorous if reasonably fair ruler. Much would depend on whom he passed the government of Scotland to, since it seemed improbable that he himself would return north, save perhaps for visits. If he left Morgan in charge, that might be none so ill, a more moderate man. But was that likely, for he was known to criticise Morgan for mildness, however able a soldier?

Was this, then, the time, the possible opportunity for the Scots to rise against the invaders? What of Glencairn? Other leaders? Crawford, Atholl, Huntly? Would Middleton, in the Netherlands, see this situation as opportunity to attack, with French help? The Auld Enemy divided, however strong a man in charge?

And then, in April, the great, the stupendous, the extraordinary tidings reached them. Monk had decided that what England required was stability, an enduring period of peace, security and undisputed central government, undeniable authority. He announced that the only sure way to secure this was the return of the monarchy. England had always been a kingdom until Cromwell came to power. Revert to this, in strength, and the people would accept it. Bring back King Charles.

If this abrupt change of direction left most folk bewildered, perhaps it ought not to have done. After all, George

Monk had been a royalist once, an officer fighting for Charles the First in the Scottish wars. In fact he had been captured, and imprisoned in the Tower for two years by Fairfax, the first of the parliamentary generals, until released by Cromwell and sent to command the army in Ireland as a notable military man. So perhaps this conversion was not so strange.

Now he dismissed the Rump, and appointed one more new parliament, which he called the Convention, which was to issue an invitation for Charles Stewart to return to his father's throne, Monk adding a personal message of urgency, and promising welcome and loyal support. He had become a royalist once again.

Scarcely believing it all, the Scots waited, almost holding their breaths.

11

Patrick asked Joanna to discover, if she could, what James Stanfield thought of all this, and what he would do now, a Commonwealth governor with the Commonwealth seemingly coming to an end. What would be his role now?

The results of her enquiries were highly interesting. The colonel had told her that if Charles was installed on the throne and assumed the rule, already being King of Scots, crowned and accepted, then there would be no place for such as himself in Haddingtonshire. But nor would former Roundhead officers be popular in royalist England. Monk might get away with it, as the main architect of the restoration of the monarchy, but the likes of himself could look for no favours, possibly indeed punishment. So why return to England? He liked Scotland and the Scots. He might well decide to stay on here. Sell his property in Yorkshire. Wife and son were not mentioned.

News thereafter came thick and fast. Charles issued a statement being called the Declaration of Breda, expressing his desire for a general amnesty for all who had supported the Commonwealth and opposed his royalist cause; also liberty of conscience and in matters of religion; an equitable settlement of political and land disputes; and, quite astonishingly, the full payment of arrears for the Roundhead army. If this was indeed an indication of the quality of the new rule-to-be, then the future looked bright for England, whatever would be the position in Scotland. But surely the royal will would be strong enough to help to ensure peace between the extreme Presbyterians and divines and the other quarrelling factions.

But would this amnesty and royal forbearance towards the former Ironsides affect Stanfield's disinclination to return to his Yorkshire?

Only a week later the word came that the Convention parliament had proclaimed Charles as king, and that he was expected to arrive in England in May, eleven years after his father's execution, and nine years after his defeat at Worcester and flight into exile. He was alleged to be extravagant, notably fond of women – he had a son by the daughter of a Welsh squire, Lucy Walters, in the Breda entourage – but friendly and easy of manner, not in the least like his late sire, who had been high-principled but stiff and unwilling to compromise. At any rate it seemed that the English people were prepared to accept him, whatever his vices and virtues, as the Scots had done, in the main, already.

On 29 May, his thirtieth birthday, Charles Stewart duly landed at Dover, to be met by a deputation from parliament, Commons and Lords, headed by none other than General George Monk, a notable and stirring occasion indeed. And, as notable, was the monarch's first act on landing on his native soil: the creation there and then of George Monk to be nothing less than a duke, the Duke of Albemarle, and also honoured as a Knight of the Garter. Charles also declared his military aide to be Earl of Middleton, and his political adviser, Edward Hyde, to be Earl of Clarendon.

After all the years of republican and Puritan alleged equality and stern government, it made a colourful start to very different times.

London, all decorated and on holiday, awaited the royal arrival.

In Scotland, General Morgan announced his loyal support for the monarchy, and an end to all actions against Commonwealth opponents. He would remain in command, however, maintaining law and order, until he might be superseded or replaced. Presumably that pronouncement applied to all governors of provinces and shires also. James Stanfield, therefore, was still in charge at Haddington, for however short a time. Patrick and George need no longer consider themselves to be captives on parole. Not that they had really felt in that state for long.

They celebrated all this great change in affairs, conditions and outlook by having a great party at Ballencrieff, the colonel present. And at last he made his announcement and decision not just privately to Joanna but publicly to them all. He was going to remain in Scotland, sell his Yorkshire properties and cloth mill, and when he was formally discharged from his duties at Haddington, commence a new life here among friends.

This declaration was greeted with warm applause by all. Although the news was not entirely unexpected, Patrick and George advanced to shake their former captor by the hand, and Liz came to give him a kiss, Helen following suit, and then Joanna shyly doing the same in front of all.

It made an occasion to be remembered.

In the event, it was quite some time before there was any really noticeable change in affairs in Scotland, save in the prevailing atmosphere of freedom and end of tension. The transformation would no doubt become very evident when the alteration in rule and authority became established, and positions therein were sought and fought for. But meantime it was peace and relief. There would be many, to be sure, who, like the young Earl of Traquair, still at Ballencrieff, wondered whether he could somehow recover his Peebles-shire lands, forfeited to the Covenanting cause. The Kirk, presumably, would not now be so powerful. And, after all, he had fought for King Charles.

Meanwhile great changes were afoot in England, needless to say. The Convention parliament was dissolved, and a new one appointed, Clarendon acting as principal or prime minister, and making sweeping alterations, including passing the Military Act, which gave the monarch complete control of the armed forces and fleets. A more spiteful gesture was the order for Oliver Cromwell's body to be disinterred from Westminster Abbey and taken to Tyburn, where criminals were executed, there the head cut off and stuck on a pole above Westminster Hall, while the rest of the corpse was buried beneath the gallows.

The Scottish situation took some time to be considered at London, in all this to-do. But towards the end of that eventful year it was attended to. The Earl of Middleton was appointed to be commander-in-chief of all forces in Scotland, made keeper and governor of Edinburgh Castle, and Lord High Commissioner to represent the throne and hold and open parliaments there, the first to be on New Year's Day, 1661. And Maitland of Lethington, second Earl of Lauderdale, captured at Worcester and for nine years prisoner in the Tower, was made Secretary of State for Scotland, and sent north with Middleton.

So at last royal rule returned to the northern kingdom. Warned, General Morgan quietly disappeared, where no one knew; and James Stanfield, like the other governors, stood down. Most, like Morgan, vanished; but the colonel marked the occasion by unobtrusively going to Edinburgh, there to buy a modest house in World's End Close off the High Street, near the Netherbow Port or Gate, to be his base meantime, although he visited Ballencrieff, Monkrigg and Gosford frequently, while he waited to see how matters developed under the new regime, hoping that the authorities would not concern themselves with such as himself, if they so much as were aware of his existence.

One of the acts of the London parliament was the implementation of Charles's promise that all forfeited estates should be restored to their rightful owners, Middleton declaring that this would be one of the first priorities of the restored Scottish parliament also. This meant that John, Earl of Traquair, would get his lands and houses back, to his relief and gratification. He would no longer be a pauper, living off his sister and her husband. As an expression of his appreciation for their kindness, he declared that, as one of the earls of Scotland, he would use his influence to protect their friend Stanfield should there be any action raised against him.

That first sitting of the Scottish parliament for long, on the first day of 1661, was held in Edinburgh Castle amid great splendour and flourish, opened by Middleton and attended as lords by both Patrick and John of Traquair, Lauderdale acting Chancellor. And among the acts passed thereat, including the restoration to their rightful owners of forfeited estates, the appointments of new officers of state and sheriffs of the counties, was the order for the Honours of Scotland, the crown, sceptre and sword, to be unearthed from their hiding-place under the floor of the Kirk of Kinneff, near Dunnottar, and brought in suitable ceremony to be installed in this Edinburgh Castle where Middleton was now keeper. That man saw to this himself, for his lands of Middleton of Fettercairn lay no great distance from Kinneff and Dunnottar. It was announced that due acknowledgement would be made of the services rendered to the nation by those responsible for the saving of the regalia from Cromwell's clutches, this minister and his wife at Kinneff, the keeper of Dunnottar Castle, and others involved.

As one of the lords of parliament, Patrick realised that he was going to be kept busy for some time with all the affairs to be seen to in the national cause, the positions to be filled, and the wrongs to be put right. George at least did not have parliamentary duties, and could get on with his sheep-rearing activities in the Lammermuirs, which he enjoyed.

No summons came for James Stanfield. He had been such a good and kindly governor for Haddingtonshire that he had no enemies there, and no charges against him were brought to the notice of the new authorities.

It was the start of a new and fulfilling era for all – not least for Helen, who declared that she was pregnant again.

Part Two

12

No problems in public matters arising for James Stanfield, he announced, early in 1661, that he was going on a visit southwards – and he stressed that it was only a visit. Since he was intending to live in Scotland, his affairs and concerns in Yorkshire had to be put in order. But he hoped that he would not be gone for long. Liz, Joanna and Helen were especially interested in this, over the question of that wife and son of his. Would he now bring them back with him?

He was gone for almost a month, and when he returned he came alone. He told his friends that he had managed to sell most of his land, and rented out the cloth mill that he had established, retaining only the manor-house for his family, this the only mention of his marital state – and it was not a subject on which they could decently question him.

With Patrick having to attend much at a very busy parliament, James spent quite a proportion of his time with George, frequently up in the Lammermuir Hills, where the latter had taken over considerably more ground for the expansion of his sheep-rearing. That range of hills was particularly suitable for sheep, especially of the black-faced type, hardy and thriving on the heathery slopes, their coarser wool in demand, notably in the Low Countries, for the manufacture of heavier cloth, blankets, cloaks, wall-hangings and curtains, even carpeting, the export of this long a source of eastern Lothian wealth. These hills covered a great area, some twenty-five miles by from eight to ten, reaching no very great heights but with many small sheltered valleys for the sheep in rough weather or snow, and rich in rough grazing, grass as well as heather.

James found it all interesting and challenging, different territory from his own Yorkshire moors and dales, but producing a harvest of wool much in demand and fetching good prices overseas. He saw George's expansion therein as wise and to be encouraged, even though the Hays of Yester, Earls of Tweeddale, and distant kin of Liz, owned much of the hills, and well recognised the value of the land, and charged accordingly for its sale.

They were discussing the finances of this with Patrick at Ballencrieff one evening, when James made his suggestion.

"See you," he said, "the price being asked for these acres of hill is none so high for the value of the grazing. And the market for the wool strong and ever growing. When I sold my Yorkshire lands I got a good price for them. I am prepared to lend you moneys, George, on easy terms, if so you would wish, to take over still more of these hills."

George eyed him, stroking his chin. "You are kind, James." They had ceased to call him colonel. "But I would be unhappy at borrowing money. Even from you. I have never done that in my life. I would not wish to be in debt to anyone. I must be content with what I have been able to buy. Who knows, if the price of the wool keeps rising, as it is doing, I may be able to buy more before over-long."

"Mmm. I understand how you feel. But it would be a pity not to be able to take advantage of the opportunities." He paused. "How say you to some sort of partnership in this, then? If I put some of *my* moneys into this of the land, and earned from it some suitable share of the gain in the wool trade? I have dealt in a different sort of wool for long."

That had George looking differently. "You would do that, James?"

"To be sure. My money might as well be earning something. I would not interfere in your sheep-rearing, but could share, in some measure, in your interest."

108

"That would be good, kind . . ."

"Not kind. To my advantage. And you, and Patrick and your good ladies, have been very kind to me."

Patrick nodded. "I say that would be an excellent move," he declared. "I wish that *I* had Lammermuir land."

"Very well. We will ride up there, one day, and survey the ground to west and south of my present holding. See what would be best to seek to buy. If so you care?"

"That would make good sense."

"I might even join you, myself, in this enterprise. In a small way," Patrick added. "I have no large moneys, but could produce *some* siller. And gain from it! And if *I*, with Liz at my side, did the bargaining with the Hays of Yester, I might possibly win a somewhat lower price for you!"

So it was agreed. Two days hence, weather permitting, they would ride up into the hills.

Picking up George at Monkrigg, the trio did ride due southwards, by the village of Gifford, near where, at Yester, the Tweeddale Hays had their usual home, although they had great lands along the river valley that gave them their title. They did not call in at Yester Castle yet, however. Patrick would see to that later. Into the foothills thereafter they entered, by the Danskine Burn and Snawdon and Darent shepherd's shieling, to commence quite steep climbing into the real heather hills now, George starting to point out the area that he already owned. His own brothers occupied the slopes, ridges and valleys eastwards to the edge of Dunbar Common, which their father had left them, *his* land beginning at what he called the Spartleton Edge, and extending south by west from there for many miles, to include the hills of Priestlaw and Penshiel, Herd Hill and Redstane Rig and Collar Law, the Faseny Water valley with the Kilpallet Heights beyond, and the Says Laws, Meikle and Little. These names scarcely registered with James Stanfield, but he did recognise the wide extent of uplands involved. He was also interested in the places his friends pointed out en route, as they rode over the braes and hollows and splashed through the burns innumerable, in necessarily round-about fashion: the former Pictish forts of Green and Black Castle, their grass-grown ramparts still very visible; the ruins of a religious hermitage and burial-place strangely situated on the summit of Priest Law; and the more distant hill of Nine Stane Rig, where still stood the standing stones of a Pictish sun-worship site, this area having been very important in the ancient days of King Loth, who gave name to Lothian, and where his daughter, the Princess Thanea, had had to act as shepherdess before giving birth, unwed, to St Kentigern, or Mungo, who had eventually founded Glasgow.

The sheep names of so many of the hills were also emphasised, such as Tuplaw, tups being rams, Rammerscales, Wether Law, wethers being second-season young rams, Ewelaw Heights, Lamb Rig, even Lammer Law and Lammermuir itself.

It was the area still further south and west which George was interested in today, however, where his land ended and there commenced what he called the Hopes, with its lochans and the hills of Harestane Law, Laurans Law, Bleak Law, Hog Hill – hogs were sheep before they had lost their first fleece – and the great Lammer Law itself, the highest point in all the Lammermuirs. Its height was not the objective, however, but its wide extent, all but a green plateau which could support hundreds of sheep, yet with its valleys of the Cowie Burn and Stobshiel behind, to offer the required shelter in bad conditions. Would the Hays be prepared to sell him this? And at what cost?

All day they rode, picking their way over the heights, disturbing grouse in large numbers and many roe-deer and a few wild goats. It was noticeable to the visitor that there were no evident boundaries marked, walls or dykes, and George had to explain that this occasioned one of the principal tasks of his shepherds, to keep his sheep from straying any distance into the neighbouring ground, a major problem.

Well pleased with what they saw, they turned back at Stobshiel's valley, to head back by Kidlaw's Pictish fort and Longnewton, and so eventually to Gifford again. George assessed that the area that he would like to purchase might well amount to some five thousand acres of hill. Would their joint moneys rise to this?

"The Hays do not seem to be using these uplands very much," Patrick said. "Few sheep on the hills. I judge that they see it as sporting land rather, good for hawking of duck from the lochans, and grouse, and deer-hunting. So they may not demand so much. If they agree to sell at all."

"Could you not allow them still to hunt and hawk there?" James wondered. "That would not greatly disturb your sheep, I think. And make them more prepared to sell."

"Aye, that is a notion!" George agreed. "I think that they do some hawking over my ground anyway, on occasion. Yes, I would so allow."

"I will put that to them. With Liz. She gets on well with them. Tweeddale is not a difficult man."

Adding up, and not allowing James to over-contribute, they arrived at a maximum price that they might offer. Patrick said that he was hopeful.

In the event, a few days later, all went well, very well. The Hays, at first chary of selling, for they were not in any way impoverished, when they heard that hawking and hunting, not only over this land but over George's territory as well, even over his brother's also, could be continued, agreed to a sale, and at a figure well below the maximum calculated.

So a sort of partnership was formed, with no legal conditions but a friendly working arrangement.

Now, the next stage would be to attend the Lammas sales, at Haddington itself, at Penicuik and in the borders, where in August the grown lambs and gimmers, young ewes that have not yet borne lambs, and tups, which the hill grazings would not support over winter, were sold off. The money saved in the land-purchase price would be very useful for this. James said that he would be interested to attend. He declared that he was going to enjoy this entire exercise and enterprise.

The trio made a round of the early autumn sales. They did best at Linton in north-western Peebles-shire, where as many as nine thousand sheep could be sold in one day, these mainly from the Moorfoot or Northwaite Hills, but some from the Pentlands, ranges extending west and south from the Lammermuirs into the main uplands of southern Scotland. Haddington's own markets were good for the sellers, but less so for buyers. The Linton sales were not so well attended, and prices consequently lower. Markets at Dunbar and Duns in the Merse also drew them. George did the bidding, after careful inspection and judging. As a result of two weeks of travelling and buying, they had purchased some fifteen hundred sheep before their allotted money began to run out. It was reckoned that, on their ground, they could run one sheep to two acres; so there was still room for expansion. The bought animals had to be herded back, slowly inevitably, to their new high pastures.

All this demanded an increase in the number of shepherds required. And it was none so easy a task to find experienced and able men prepared to change masters and homes. The shepherd's life was necessarily a distinctly lonely one, their houses apt to be placed in lofty and far-out locations, most frequently without another house in sight, and so not always popular with wives and families. Very often, in these wide and high pastures, the men themselves had to have additional remote shelters and huts, shielings, and so could frequently be away from their homes overnight. Also they had to be able to build buchts, of dry-stone construction, usually circular, as folds or pens for the sheep in sheltered areas, for dipping and shearing and treating for diseases, such as fluke and scab, afflicting the stock. So good shepherds were much sought after.

The ladies asked why women were not employed for this task. If Princess Thanea, Loth's daughter, could be a shepherdess, why not others? The men did not take this suggestion seriously it is to be feared. But Liz and Joanna did accompany them on some of their surveys and market-visiting, Helen only very occasionally, her mothering duties preventing, her daughter Beth but a few months old.

The search for shepherds went on.

Then there was the anticipated increased marketing of the wool to be thought of. Hitherto George had sold his fleeces to a merchant in Haddington. But the enterprising James pointed out that the said merchant must himself sell it all elsewhere, to make *his* living; so why not deal direct with the ultimate exporters? These were mainly based on Dunbar and Eyemouth harbours, very often being of Flemish descent, Low Countries' representatives who had come to Scotland to improve the trade long ago. The Earls of Dunbar and March, that important line of royal origin, now defunct, had instituted a great trade in Lammermuir wool, their main source of wealth, with their own fleet of ships to carry the fleeces, and the salted mutton also produced, to the Netherlands and Flanders ports, Veere in especial. This export trade still subsisted, bringing back spun and woven cloth, leather goods, pantiles and the like. So to these ports wool should go. And James Stanfield was able to negotiate improved prices for their product, having been the respected governor of these exporters, as of everybody else, during those years of occupation.

Liz declared that James was going to make them all rich.

From his house in Edinburgh that man was able to make useful contacts with the authorities in rule and law, as well as in trade, even with some of the churchmen, where his Puritan background told in his favour. But most of his time was spent in Haddingtonshire still; and more and more he tended to lodge at Gosford, with Joanna and her son, who was now a young man, rather than at Ballencrieff and Monkrigg. The pair's friendship was frank and accepted by all now, although also accepted as decorous, as far as a man's and woman's could be. He did announce however that he was looking for a house to purchase for himself in or near Haddington, and that he could by no means remain permanently a guest of other folk, however much they might esteem each other.

That first year had proved to be a busy, innovative and productive one. The next, it was hoped and anticipated, would be a profitable one.

13

The three ladies were active in helping James to find a house; and with their aid, find one he did – or at least, premises that he could make into a home. There were a few mills along the course of the River Tyne in the Haddington area, these for the grinding of meal from the fertile low grounds of the Vales of Peffer and Tyne. One of these was now abandoned, and this, oddly enough, the latest of them, yet styled the New Mills.

One day, all three ladies took him to see what they had decided was an interesting possibility, this just to the east of the town on a stretch of the river beyond the Nungait.

"This is a rather especial place, James," Liz announced. "Despite the state that it is in. Patrick and I have known of it for long. The buildings themselves are of no great concern, but you could improve them no doubt. But the land – and there is quite some land belonging – is notable indeed. It is a shame to be neglected, as it has been."

James cast his eye over the riverside and the slightly rising ground behind, braes of grass and trees which eventually rose up to Monkrigg itself.

"More than once George has said that he ought to buy this property," Helen declared. "It would make a worthy addition to Monkrigg. But, as you know, he has had other things to do with his money!"

"You have a fondness for things ancient, James," Joanna added. "This could appeal to you."

"It is historic," Liz went on. "There can be few places in the land, other than Dunfermline perhaps, where two kings have been largely reared and another born. This was part of the ground of the Countess Ada's dowry, when she married Prince Henry, Earl of Huntingdon, King David's son, who died before his father, David the First, leaving two boys who eventually succeeded him on the throne, in turn. When Ada was widowed she founded a nunnery here, on her own land. David lived largely at Roxburgh Castle near the borderline, but his grandsons, Malcolm and William, were much with their mother, for she lived at her nunnery, occupying herself with good works. So Malcolm the Fourth and William the Lion largely grew up here; and later William's own son, Alexander the Second, was born here. Ada it was who really made Haddington famous, sufficiently so for her nunnery to be styled the Lamp of Lothian."

"I have heard that term, yes. But did not know what it signified."

"It was because her nunnery and its offshoots were responsible for so much of learning and beauty and riches. This will have been built on the site of an earlier mill, run by the nuns and called, I think, Nunsyde."

"And the nunnery itself? It was nearby?"

"Yes. On the slightly higher ground yonder. Quite large ground. George would know the names of the lands, which they bear now. He has often spoken of seeking to buy them."

James nodded. "Then here, indeed, is a property that I might well purchase. If I do not seem to rob George of it . . ."

They examined the derelict mill and attached living quarters, and all agreed that it could be rebuilt and transformed into a pleasingly situated and attractive house, in addition to its historic background.

Later, George expressed himself as well content to have James as near neighbour of Monkrigg, and not concerned over the sale of the land which he was not presently in any state to buy. He informed that the names of the former nunnery lands on the higher ground, covering fully a square mile, were now Crossflatt, Adamflatt, Sprotsflatt, and Quarrellpit, Upper and Nether. And they belonged to the widow of a distant kinsman of his own, James Hepburn of Whitstoun. She would sell, almost certainly.

So James Stanfield had a target to aim at, other than sheep-rearing and wool-selling: a new house to make. He enquired of the Hepburn widow who owned most of the ground between the New Mills and Monkrigg, long little used, merely let for occasional grazing for cattle and horses, and found her willing to sell. So he bought it, and found himself laird of most of what had been the Countess Ada's dowry, given her by David the First, it much pleasing him to have such a noteworthy stake in his adopted country. Now for masons and other craftsmen, as he planned his house. Some parts of the abandoned buildings could be incorporated; in fact it was possible to use more of the mill itself rather than the miller's house; but in the main it was to be a very different and finer establishment, with outbuildings, stables and the like within a little courtyard, no castle or tower-house, more of a small hall-house. His friends vied with each other in making suggestions, especially the women needless to say.

Yuletide came and went. What would 1662 bring them?

It brought major progress in the Lammermuirs, even though they were still short of shepherds, the new sheep stock settling in well and lambing productively, the weather fairly kind. When it came to shearing, the wool crop ought to be notable indeed. George now had over three thousand sheep, apart from the lambs, and their fleeces would amount to something to boast about. But they would have to find extra shearers; their seven shepherds certainly would not be able to cope.

The building work at New Mills progressed steadily. Liz, Helen and Joanna were already collecting furnishings for it.

On the national front all went less than well. Middleton, intent on himself ruling Scotland as all but viceroy, had fallen out with the Earl of Lauderdale, the Secretary of State, and declared him "incapacitated", in other words dismissing him from office; and these two were now at loggerheads, apparently much to the displeasure of King Charles in London. But, commanding the armed forces, Middleton was in a position to have his way meantime. He had also reduced the Lindsay Earl of Crawford to this of incapacity, and *he* was very popular in Scotland, an error of judgment it was deemed. So the parliament in May, which Patrick and Traquair attended, had seen much discord, but with Middleton dominating. He had had episcopacy established in the Church, which turned many against him, and had all non-conforming clergy – which was in fact the great majority – ejected from their livings. Although an Episcopalian himself, Patrick voted against this. Not that the Act, passed, would be easy or indeed possible to enforce fully; but it was the cause of much resentment and unrest.

In England the situation appeared to be better, Charles behaving moderately, and seeking not to antagonise the various factions. He was thought himself to have Catholic leanings, but made a point of not permitting religious discrimination, being especially careful towards the former Puritans, this with Albemarle's guidance.

Then, in matters nearer home, at this beginning of May, it was time for the sheep shearing, which meant all hands to work, for clipping the wool off thousands of the creatures represented a major task, and other sheep-farmers in the hills were also looking for extra labour, so practised manpower was not readily available. Although it was scarcely lairdly toil, the three friends went up to take a hand. George had done it before, as a youth, and was able to show the others the art of it, how to take and turn the sheep over on its back, hold it still between their knees, and where to start the cutting with the shears, close but not too close as to risk cutting the skin beneath. Starting at the neck, the objective was to strip off the entire fleece in one piece, it then becoming something like a carpet, of approximately five feet square, this to be rolled up and tied as a bundle, undersides outward, densely white and oily.

Patrick and James picked up the way of it reasonably quickly, and went to work amid a great baaing, the shouts of shepherds, the barking of dogs and the strong oily smell, which George assured them would cling to them and their clothing for some time, and have their ladies commanding much washing and bathing to make them acceptable again.

The piles of cut fleeces grew and grew.

At length, weary, tired of back with the stooping position to hold the sheep firm, stinking of the oil, but well pleased with themselves, they took their leave, a lord of parliament, a former governor and a physician-laird, to the grins of their fellow-workers.

The notion of bypassing the Haddington merchant and dealing directly with the wool exporters at Dunbar proved to be very worth while. Their large supplies had to be transported, of course, this on ox-drawn waggons and pack-horses, in itself no minor matter, but the extra profits making it entirely practical. They knew that the price obtained was to a large extent dictated by what was called the Staple at Veere, a centuries-old arrangement whereby the burgomaster at that Low Countries port, the principal place of entry for wool, decided each year the moneys to be offered for the various grades, according to demand and supply. However arbitrary and antiquated a system, it was probably the fairest valuation, and acceptable, although with different kinds of fleeces much calculation was involved. Next year, undoubtedly, the rewards would be greater still.

The transporting of all that wool had cost them money, hiring carts, oxen, drivers and horses. The ever-resourceful James started to speculate as to how this might be avoided in future, or at least lessened. This River Tyne? he wondered. It was fairly wide and well-flowing, and did it not reach the sea quite near to Dunbar? Might not barges, or even some sort of rafts, serve to carry the wool at little cost? They used their rivers and canals in Yorkshire for conveying heavy or bulky goods.

George and Patrick pointed out that although the Tyne remained a placid river for the remaining ten miles to the sea, liable as it was to flash floods from the Lammermuirs in heavy rains, there was a point where it narrowed and became a linn, with broken water between higher and rocky banks some six miles eastwards, this at the little burgh of East Linton, so named, where barges and rafts would not be able to operate. Also there were fords, where the river shallowed, here and there. James did not think that fords, for horses, would obstruct rafts or flat-bottomed lighters; but admittedly linns or rapids were different . . .

They decided to make a survey of the river's length.

One day, then, through fair and fertile country, they followed the Tyne's reasonably straight course, only at two points, not far apart, noting that the lie of the land narrowed in to restrict the even flow, the fords offering no obstacle. The first, four miles from Haddington, under the heights of the isolated Traprain Law, where the Hepburn castle of Hailes took advantage of the narrows to dominate the flanking road; but here, although the river flowed more swiftly, it was not such as to debar the passage of boats. But at East Linton and Prestonkirk, two miles further, rapids and overfalls did make passage impracticable for half a mile, until at Preston Mill the Tyne became level and even again, and remained so for the remaining three miles to its estuary at the tidal sands of Tyninghame, just north of Dunbar harbour.

James declared that the only solution would be to unload the rafts – probably such would be best – and have the wool carried over the half-mile, and then relaunched at Preston Mill. It would add to the cost, but even so would greatly reduce that of using the ox-carts and pack-horses for the entire journey, as they had just done. There would be no great problem in building wooden rafts, these to be towed, roped in groups.

So proposed the innovationist, he being saluted by his friends.

The three ladies continued to show more interest in James's house than in all this of the wool, advising as to accommodation, although sometimes changing their minds, which was less helpful. The work proceeded on the whole satisfactorily.

"How will you do about the housekeeping?" Liz asked on one occasion. "You will need a woman to see to matters." That was as near as she could come to enquiring whether that wife from Yorkshire was to be brought up to take over.

"I will make some suitable arrangement," he told her, without any sign of discomfort. "Time enough for that."

Little as it satisfied them, they had to be content with that.

14

The building operations were due to be completed in the early spring; but before that took place there was upheaval in the land. The Secretary of State removed from office by Middleton, Lauderdale, had gone south to London to complain to the monarch who had appointed him; and Charles, angered, had sent for Middleton. That man had made himself very unpopular, not only by his misgovernment and by the promotion of his friends, some of them low-born, over the ruling figures of the country, but also by his riotous living excesses. Down at court he was left in no doubt as to Charles's displeasure, and was removed from office and disgraced. In fact, he was more or less sent into exile, as governor of far-away Tangier, where his military prowess might be of use.

Lauderdale returned home to resume his duties as Secretary of State, and took over as keeper of Edinburgh Castle, being honoured as an extra lord-in-waiting of the king. A sitting of the Scots parliament was called to formalise all this and rectify the wrongs committed, which took some time, Patrick being involved. He was placed in a rather strange position, for it so happened that the disgraced Middleton's wife, Grizel, daughter of Sir James Durham of Luffness, only a mile from Ballencrieff, that laird a friend of the Elibanks, had chosen to remain there with her son, Lord Clermont, and his two sisters, in her declined state. She had not been happy with her husband for some time.

The finishing of the construction of New Mills House,

and much of the furnishing thereof, was celebrated in the March of 1663 by a house-warming party, in great style, at which Liz, Helen and Joanna together acted as hostesses, and many of the county magnates and their families were invited, including Sir James Durham and his daughter, the Countess of Middleton, a situation that could not fail to arouse comment, the unfortunate lady being taken good care of by her three hostesses.

It proved to be a great occasion, and established the former governor as an accepted pillar of Lothian society and affairs, as distinct from being an invading overlord. But as well as that, it was very much a social success and enjoyed by all. It went on until the small hours, so much so that some of the guests were in no state to ride home that night, and had to be found accommodation in other than normal sleeping-quarters.

Among the many distinguished guests was Jean, Countess of Tweeddale, from Yester, who was the sister of the late second Earl of Buccleuch, who had been chief of the famous borders family of Scott, he who had died fairly recently. And she had an interesting story to tell her hostesses. Her brother, who had been fined no less than fifteen thousand pounds by Cromwell for support-ing King Charles, had left no son but two daughters. Now, in an extraordinary measure of compensation for that fine, the king was proposing that the daughter Anne should marry his, Charles's, son, James Stewart, by Lucy Walters, born in the Netherlands during the royal exile. Charles had since married Princess Catherine of Braganza, daughter of the King of Portugal, at the urgings of his mother, Queen Henrietta Maria, who had threatened to have her son's pension from the King of France, her brother, cut off if he did not do so. The impoverished Charles had felt that he had to agree. But this young James's mother, Lucy, protested that she had been quietly married to Charles at Rotterdam. Queen Henrietta had brushed that aside as unworthy and ineffective, not to be accepted; and her son had weakly given in and gone through a marriage ceremony with the princess, who was now Queen of the United Kingdom. But if he had been already wed, and the marriage not annulled nor divorced, what then? Was Catherine lawfully his wife and queen? To seek to quieten any such awkward questions Charles, fond of his son James— Lucy having died — came up with a notable device. He would have James married to Anne, Countess of Buccleuch, this lady's niece, and countess in her own right, there being no male heir, and the pair raised to the status of duke and duchess, this of Buccleuch, and of Monmouth, to permit an English link. This had been effected; so now Scotland had a Stewart and Scott royal dukedom.

Her hearers stared at her. "But . . . this is quite astonishing!" Liz said. "It, it could mean . . . ? Could this Duke James succeed to the throne one day? As Duke of Buccleuch and . . . what was the other style?"

"Monmouth. This is what I ask myself."

"Charles's Queen Catherine, if she is truly queen, has had three miscarriages. It is said that she will never bear a child. In which case . . . ?"

"There is no other heir. Save Charles's brother, another James, the Duke of York," Helen declared. "And he is a Catholic!"

"And the new duke is Protestant," the Countess Jean said. "James of York will never be accepted by Protestant England. Nor yet Scotland. Unless he changes his faith. So this James of Buccleuch could well succeed, eventually. The houses of Stewart and Scott united!"

The ladies were much intrigued, eager to tell their menfolk.

When Patrick and George and their wives eventually departed for their own homes, Joanna declared that she would stay on, to aid James feed and dispose of the unexpected overnight visitors in the morning, Gosford being the furthest away of the three establishments. Eyebrows were not raised at this.

"I think that I can serve in this sufficiently," Joanna added. "James has two maids and a manservant." This when Liz tentatively offered to help. "You are kind, but . . ."

So James and Joanna were left to cope with the situation.

The lambing season was upon them, and it proved to be highly successful, and this produced, as well as potential wealth, one more idea from James Stanfield. On the way up to Lammerlaw's heights to inspect progress, they passed, on the lower ground at Longyester and Longnewton, small flocks of the larger and white-faced Cheviot sheep grazing on these two farmeries belonging to the Hays. These already had lambs, clearly born earlier than their own blackface variety, and had different wool, closer grown and less shaggy, all but curled and of a finer fibre, not suitable for the same weaving and clothmaking as their own, but used for lighter garb and materials.

"Would it not be possible to crossbreed these Cheviot sheep with our own?" he wondered. "The offspring of such might well be valuable, no? Able to graze and survive on the hills and higher ground, but producing a larger animal and finer grade of wool for a different market. It could be profitable?"

George looked thoughtful. "I have never heard of this being done," he said. "But who knows? It might be possible."

"There are crossbreeds of sheep in Yorkshire. We call them Lonks, these, I think crosses between Shropshires and Leicesters. So different breeds can be mated and produce a mixed strain. I am not informed on such matters, but we could enquire."

"It could be worth considering, yes," Patrick agreed.

"We could ask your shepherds, George. They would know if it could be done. And if such beasts would thrive up there."

Presently ask they did, and learned that Cheviot sheep were themselves a crossbreed, thought to have been of border Leicesters and Cotswolds. The shepherds did not know whether blackface and Cheviot would produce satisfactory lambs, hardy as the one and larger with the desired finer wool. But they could try it.

So it was a project for the next breeding season. Mating would have to take place in late October for lambs to be born in March.

At clipping time thereafter their manpower was kept busy indeed, the area having to be scoured for extra shearers, the lairds again glad to take their part, for there was a real satisfaction in producing those mountains of white fleeces.

Meanwhile the raft-building process was going ahead, employing more men. It was a simple matter to construct these, requiring no special skills, and the local timber supply ample. Even though the rafts, elementary in design, of cross-barred logs, would lie low in the water, it would not signify if the lowermost fleeces got wet, the natural oil impregnating the wool rejecting water.

When it came to the day of the first shipment downriver there was much interest, even concern that all might go well. The system was for pack-horses, with long ropes, to draw strings of laden rafts behind them, led along the riverbanks, heedfully necessarily, with spurs of land, marshy patches, trees and awkward projections to be negotiated, each horse pulling four piled rafts, with each having a man at the tail of the fourth, with a rope therefrom, to ensure that the snags and obstructions were not allowed unduly to halt progress. Eight of these raft-trains were organised for that first venture, carrying large quantities of wool of considerable weight, for it was reckoned that the average cut fleece weighed up to nine pounds, and there were thousands of them. It was all a slow process inevitably, but there were no really major hold-ups, the fords providing no problems.

At East Linton the overland porterage was the crux of the matter, ox-carts waiting there to carry both wool and rafts over the difficult half-mile, local manpower recruited to help. The rafts were the greatest source of trouble, heavy, bulky and wet, to hoist on to the carts; but compared with the year before's tiresome and taxing journey it was all a great improvement. Once the rafts were relaunched and reloaded, at Preston Mill, the rest was comparatively straightforward, for the more constricted and rushing waters at the Knowes proved less of an obstacle than feared, the rafts swirling down almost over-fast and the horses attached occasioning the greatest concern.

Great was the acclaim and congratulation when at last Tyninghame and the Tyne's mouth was reached, and the accompanying horsemen could ride to Dunbar and have the fishing-boats, as already arranged, to sail the couple of miles to take over the towing process and bring rafts and cargoes to the piers for shipment.

It was all a success story indeed. The rafts, unloaded, were to be towed, not by the river but up the coast by the fishing-boats to enter the estuary of Forth and taken to be grounded and stacked for future use at the shallows of the great Aberlady Bay, less than two miles from Ballencrieff.

One more of James's projects had borne fruit.

They had bought a few Cheviot tups to test out that other proposal. How would that one work? They would have five months to wait for results.

Meantime, the lamb sales.

All this Stanfield initiative towards wealth production and local industry and employment was of especial satisfaction for Patrick Murray. For, however hospitable and open-handed were he and Liz, they were always in financial straits. That fining by the Covenanting authorities for his support of Montrose, of twenty thousand merks, or thirteen thousand three hundred and thirty-three pounds sterling, had grievously impoverished the estates of Ballencrieff and Blackbarony, and put Patrick into debt; his lands had been producing little wealth, with trade all but at a standstill during the Cromwellian occupation, and money everywhere was in short supply, yet with taxation heavy. He was, therefore, the more eager to have part in this sheep and wool development, although feeling himself to be very much the poor man of the trio he could not afford to contribute much money, despite the fact that in status he was the loftiest as a lord of parliament.

And his parliamentary duties prevented him from taking quite as active a part as did the others in all the sheep activities. That year of 1663 was a very busy one for Scotland's Three Estates of parliament, in seeking to rectify the mistakes and misdemeanours of the Middleton regime, and establishing the royalist and episcopalian role in the land. Lauderdale, as Secretary of State, was now in command, and on the whole he was effective and fair, although he had his failings. He was assisted, if that was the word, by the Leslie Earl of Rothes, appointed High Commissioner in the place of Middleton by King Charles, a rather extraordinary character however loyal a royal supporter, seldom wholly sober and with a riotous sense of humour, so very different from the stern Lauderdale. But at least he was no military dictator, and was popular with the people, much more so than was the Secretary of State. Attending the June parliament in Edinburgh, Patrick was struck, as were all others, by the opposing methods of the two supposed partners in rule, Rothes acting as the king's representative on the throne and Lauderdale as Chancellor and chairman. There was firm and decisive direction from the latter, and loud and laughing interjections from the former, although sometimes with shrewd intent. There was no doubt as to which pleased most delegates the better, even though little of the business was such as to lend itself to humorous reaction.

The first act to be proposed and passed was very significant, in that it handed over all but complete control of the realm to these two, namely the reviving of the institution known as the Lords of the Articles, which had been done away with by the Covenanters, and this endorsed by the Roundheads, the said body acting as a sort of Privy Council, and in more or less complete control over all, under the direction of the Chancellor. The method of appointing its members was odd. The churchmen, now all bishops, chose eight lords, and the lords eight bishops, and together the sixteen chose another sixteen lairds and burgesses representing the royal burghs, these all to act in the name of the Three Estates. So parliament itself need not meet over quite long periods, and the Lords of the Articles acted in its place. Thankfully Patrick was not proposed as one of the lords, although Liz's brother, Traquair, was. Officers of state were automatically included.

The next business was to have Sir Archibald Johnston of Warriston, the principal Covenanting lawyer and former Lord Clerk Register, brought before the assembly for a judicial examination. He had co-operated with Cromwell, who had actually created him a peer, as Lord Warriston, and sat in the English parliament. He had been notoriously hard on Montrose's supporters, and an ally of Argyll, indeed had been largely responsible for the heavy finings of such, including Patrick and Traquair. He it was who, at Montrose's execution, had rebuked that handsome and heroic figure for combing his hair carefully before mounting the scaffold, and had been answered thus: "My head is still my own, sir. Tonight it will be yours. Treat it then as you please!"

Needless to say, this parliament did not expend a lot of time on this sour character, so very much the reverse of the boisterous Rothes. He was found guilty of treason and condemned to be hanged at the cross of Edinburgh and his head severed from his body.

Quite a number of new appointments were then made, to fill gaps in the ruling establishment, none, to be sure, of former Covenanters. And then Lauderdale did come up with an unexpected motion, this to form a sort of replacement of the former General Assembly of the Kirk, which once had all but governed the land. It was to be composed of divines, yes – but of bishops, deans, archdeacons and university representatives. Some of the last could be Presbyterians, if so desired, but of insufficient numbers to risk diminishing the power of the episcopal clerics. This Patrick considered to be quite a statesmanlike proposal, and voted for it; but its consideration took up more time and debate than any other item before the delegates.

The last business before them was over the matter of witchcraft. The Covenanters had been very hot against alleged witches, indeed it had become almost a mania with them, and with dire consequences for many all but innocent victims; also as a means of dragging down enemies by accusing them of such. In Fife, for instance, thirty witches had been burned at the stake in one month or so. Now the matter, while still seen as a serious offence, was to be regulated and dealt with in more judicial fashion, justiciary courts set up in all areas specifically for the elimination of witchcraft and similar unnatural trespasses, and the suitable punishment of such offenders, all lords and commissioners of parliament to serve on these in their own districts and local courts. This was passed by a majority, although Patrick abstained from voting, seeing himself as having to become involved in this unpleasant and contentious task.

That concluded the business, and the session was adjourned.

Patrick told Liz, on his return, that he much preferred to be a wool trader than a lord of parliament.

15

That summer, the news from England was that the new Duke of Buccleuch and Monmouth was very popular at court, handsome, friendly and talented, much smiled on by his father. He had been appointed a general of land forces, Captain of the Life Guards, Lord Lieutenant of the East Riding of Yorkshire, and Chief Justice south of Trent, notable favours for a youth of fifteen. Of course, the wide Scott of Buccleuch lands in the borders and elsewhere were productive of wealth, even if the Monmouth ones were not, indeed of litle worth, and no doubt the king was well pleased to collect some of their revenues for himself, for he was heavily in debt, extravagant and having to support a galaxy of mistresses such as even Whitehall Palace had never before seen. Yet Charles was favoured by the people, his failings put up with, even by the legislators in what was now becoming known as the Cavalier parliament.

Despite the continuing Dutch wars, or perhaps because of them, the price of wool that year at the Staple at Veere was good, and money arriving at Dunbar and Haddington was substantial. Patrick's share of it had to be modest, of course, since he had put least into it all, but it was a help. And he continued to take an active part in the wealth-forming process, spending as much time as he could attending sales, riding the hills, seeking out and interviewing new shepherds, and the like. His lands were rich in trees, so he made himself responsible for the raft-building.

The Cheviot-blackface crossbreeding experiment proved to be very effective, and a crop of piebald-featured lambs were their reward, these having long but less shaggy coats of finer-grade wool, well able to survive on the high heather grazing. The friends would not seek to have these sheep supersede their main coarse-wool producers, the market for whose fleeces was strong; but they would provide an alternative and additional source of revenue. Thoughts of purchasing still more Lammermuir ground began to occupy their minds.

Patrick was less than delighted to receive a call to attend one of the area justiciary courts, this at Musselburgh, halfway to Edinburgh, to deal with accusations of witchcraft against two local residents, a man and a woman, thought to be not husband and wife. The charge was that this pair, from Salt Preston nearby, had a pet hare, captured somehow as a leveret, which they used to lope around neighbours' houses of a night as a kind of familiar spirit, laying curses upon them. They were accused of chanting strange songs, words unintelligible. The woman had one bloodshot eye, a recognised sign of witchery. And they behaved oddly, never attended the kirk, and gabbled in strange tongues. After one of the hare visits, to a cottage isolated from the others, a child of the family there had developed a skin rash of unknown kind. And another couple of neighbours, having reprimanded them for collecting shellfish on the shore on the Sabbath day, had been pointed at and sworn at in language unknown.

The man and woman before the justices kept silent, as witness after witness condemned them. Clearly they were highly unpopular in the district.

The provost of Musselburgh, one of the justices, declared that these two were most evidently troublesome to the community, and, it seemed, should be disposed of.

Patrick asked the pair how long they had lived at Salt Preston, and were these complaints by neighbours of long standing, or only recent? Had such charges been voiced before?

In a typical, lilting Highland voice, the man said that

they had come here only a year previously. That voice was productive of another question. Were they from the Highlands? And if so, was the strange tongue they spoke in the Gaelic?

They agreed that it was.

The Lowland suspicion of and prejudice against Highlanders were known to all. They were looked upon as barbarians, uncouth and unable to speak in a decent fashion that could be understood, an everlasting source of trouble.

"Have you been at odds with the other villagers since you came? Not liked by them, nor you liking them?"

"Och, they were not for having us, at all," Patrick was told. "They were after naming us *cearr*, the wicked ones."

"Why did you stay on here, then, where you were not welcome? Not leave?"

"It was the shellfish, just. We are shellfishers, and after catching the lobsters and the crabs. This is a good *cladach*, a good shore for it, see you. Sand and rock both." The man added something more in the Gaelic.

"They are heathen!" one of the villagers called out. "They never go to the kirk. Heathen!"

"They may well be Catholics," Patrick said. "Many Highlanders are. Are you that?" he put to the pair. "Romish Church – Catholics?"

Man and woman nodded, almost guiltily.

"That hare?" one of the justices, from Tranent, put in. "An unchancy crittur, that. Devil's work!"

"What of that, yes? I have never heard of a pet hare."

"Och, we had a snare for the rabbits, just. A *maigheach*, a hare was after getting caught in it. Dead. This small bit of a creature was there, at the side of it, just. Sitting close to its mother. Morag was not for killing the small one. She is like that, Morag. We took it. We kept it, and, och, it grew. It is *lagach*, no ill in it, at all, at all."

"It has become their familiar, my lord," the provost

134

asserted. "A hare, in a house! Right unseemly, unnatural."
This to clamant agreement of the villagers.

"Many of you will have dogs? Even cats?" Patrick put to
them. "Do you call these familiar spirits? They are animals
also. And can roam around."

There were contrary mutterings.

He went on, to the accused. "This of witchcraft. Have
you practised it ever?"

"I am not after knowing the craft, at all. We are shell and
lobster fishers. And set the snare now and then, just. What
are they, these witches being after doing, I would be
asking?"

There were shouts from the accusers and others.

"They practise sorcery and devil-worship. Do you?"

"How would we worship the devil? We are the good
Catholics. From Loch Fyne. Are we not, *a graidh*?"

The woman turned to nodded.

"Lies! Lies! All lies!" came from the listeners, or most of
them.

There were four other justices apart from Patrick, an
uneven number so that there could not be a drawn vote,
always a majority possible. One of them, from Gledsmuir,
near Haddington, raised voice, not having spoken hitherto.

"I say that this man is an accomplished liar! All reports
show him and his woman guilty. They must be found so.
And sentenced. We have spent sufficient time listening to
them. They should pay the price, as undoubted warlock
and witch. Burned at the stake!"

Cheers greeted that.

"I disagree, and strongly," Patrick declared. "Nothing
that we have heard convicts them. They are Catholics from
the Highlands, and entitled to live as they do. They are
subjects of King Charles, as are we all. I say that they must
be discharged, as not guilty."

Protest was loud.

Patrick looked at his fellow-justices, assessing them.
None was of lairdly status. All looked uncomfortable at

his statement. "Do not tell me that you, men of position and responsibility hereabouts, accept these unfounded and prejudiced accusations? Against fellow-Scots, merely because they come from the north and speak together in a different tongue?"

"The hare. And the child's skin complaint," the Tranent bailie put in.

"Sicknesses are with us at all times, without witchcraft. And a little hare saved from death by a woman's kindness? Name you these as sufficient proof of sorcery?"

Silence from his colleagues at the table. There was no doubt, of course, that the fact that Patrick was a lord, and a commissioner to parliament, had its major effect on these others, not awe exactly but inborn respect.

"I say, then, that we dismiss this charge as unworthy. Not guilty our verdict." That was a statement rather than a question.

The murmurings of the villagers went on.

Patrick raised an authoritative hand. "Silence!" he ordered. "This is a court of law." Then he changed the direction of his gesture, to point at the accused couple. "You hear? You are cleared of any guilt. You are free to go. But—I do say to you that *go* you should. Elsewhere. Leave this Salt Preston. Find you somewhere else to gather your shellfish and lobsters. There is much seaboard here in Lothian. Or over in Fife. Or go back to your Highlands. You would be wise so to do. For your neighbours here will never love you! Go, I say. And do not delay overlong." And he rose.

For the first time that day there was some agreeing reaction from the company.

The other justices rose also, the trial clearly over, however tight some lips.

Thankfully, although not showing it, Patrick departed for home.

George and James, meanwhile, had been enquiring as to the purchase of more land. They had discovered that the

Hays of Yester were not willing to sell more of their Lammermuir property, having perceived the possibility of themselves adding to their wealth by increasing its sheep stocks, hitherto of only minor significance to them. So the search must be southwards and eastwards, rather than westwards. The Lammermuir Hills extended in that direction for many more miles, so there was considerable scope for expansion. The lands thereabouts belonged to different lairds, but the two they were most concerned to deal with, both just over the Berwickshire, or the Merse, border, were mainly concerned with cattle-rearing rather than sheep, their best territory lower-lying and fertile. So they might well be prepared to part with some of their high ground, and possibly at a lower price than had been the Tweeddale Hays, again especially if the hunting and hawking was still allowed for them.

So another careful survey was conducted, of the area near and around the very isolated village of Longformacus on the Dye Water, that river the limit of their present holdings. There was still a great spread of hills south of this, between it and the tributaries of the larger Leader Water in Lauderdale, fully sixty square miles, it was reckoned. If they could buy a slice of all this, including the Wedder Lairs, Blythe Edge, the Dod, Hog Rig, and east to Harecleuch Hill, Twin Law and the two Dirrington Laws, they would have a major accession of good hill grazing of some six thousand more acres.

And as it happened, the eastern portion of this territory was owned by Helen's brother, John Swinton of that Ilk, as part of his subsidiary estate of Cranshaws; and she said that he had never been greatly interested in sheep-farming. She imagined that he would be quite prepared to sell the hill ground – although not the little Cranshaws Tower, of which he was very fond and which served as a hunting-seat. Let him continue to hawk and hunt, and she believed that he would either sell or lease them the land. The south-western section they sought belonged to Edgar of Wedderlie, an old family, the land given to their ancestor for his support of Robert the Bruce in long warfare. Patrick knew John Edgar, the laird, who was commissioner for that western area of Berwickshire, an elderly man who lived mainly at Peffermill near Edinburgh. He would probably not be averse to selling.

It all looked hopeful.

Less hopeful were the prices coming from the Low Countries for this season's wool, particularly that of the new finer grades, these all determined at Veere. Presumably it was a lack of demand for the various cloths made therefrom that caused it, and it might well be only a temporary decline, possibly caused by the continuing Dutch wars on the Continent and upsets to trade; but it was disappointing after all the friends' efforts. The coarse blackface wool held up better, but it was still down on previous years. After the success of their Cheviot cross-breeding this represented a setback.

George, who had been involved in sheep-rearing more or less all his life, as had been his father, was less concerned than was James Stanfield. Prices rose and fell, he said, shrugging it off. Patrick, with less of a stake in it all, was disappointed but not unduly worried. But James saw it as more than a disappointment, a challenge, something to be countered, not just accepted.

It was not long before he came out with his response to it. If the Flemings and Dutchmen could make wealth out of spinning and weaving *their* wool, why not do likewise and spin their own? There would be a market for the cloth in Scotland and England. Why leave it to the Netherlanders? After all, he had established a cloth mill in Yorkshire. He himself had never worked at milling, but he knew the essentials of the craft. So a mill here at Haddington, a cloth mill. By the river. He was uncertain about spinning and weaving the coarse, blackface wool. They had never worked with that in his mill, not having had that type of sheep. It might well require a different treatment. And the market for the product? But this crossbred wool . . . ?

His two friends were doubtful, to say the least. Milling! Milling wool? This was something quite beyond them. Corn mills they knew about, of course; indeed both had such on their lands, to grind their own and their tenants' grain, oats, barley and wheat. But wool? Spinning the yarn and weaving the cloth. How was this to be done? None would know how, hereabouts.

James said that he could bring up men from his old home, who had worked in his mill, to show them how. It was none so difficult a trade. There must be other cloth mills in Scotland, somewhere? They could build a mill at his house – was it not named New Mills? They had water power there to drive the wheels. New Mills indeed! Was it not a worthy venture?

Still scarcely convinced, the others wondered. But their womenfolk were much in favour. Here was something they could interest themselves in, rather than riding about the hills looking at sheep. Cloth. They knew about and could work with cloth and clothing.

James said that he would go down to the dales and find two or three men to bring up, to show them the way of it and what was needed. Learn more himself, while he was there. Haddington would gain a new handicraft and trade. Meanwhile, his friends could see to the making of new and large mill-wheels. With all the corn mills in being, there must be millwrights who could make these.

16

While Stanfield was away in England, George and Patrick made all due enquiries, however unsure they were over this new project. There would be no problem in getting the mill-wheels constructed, nor the building of the large mill premises themselves. But the actual spinning and weaving machinery was beyond local ken. Hitherto, as far as they knew, in Scotland the spinning of wool had been done mainly by women at home on spinning-wheels, and the yarn either knitted up into garments or woven on hand-looms, most of the cloth used and clothing worn being imported. They learned that there were cloth mills of a sort, on no large scale, in the west country of Renfrew and Ayrshire; but these were not great sheep-rearing areas, and the market only local.

Stonemasons and carpenters were lined up, to be ready, and timber felled and seasoned.

When James returned, he brought three men with him, all experienced, having been employed in his mill. He declared that he had already discovered a lot from them. These would be able to guide their enterprise adequately.

New Mills House was sited on the best place on the Tyne's bank for cutting the sluices or lades to lead the water to the wheels. So it was decided to build the woollen mill alongside the house, maintaining the tradition established by the Countess Ada's nuns all those centuries ago.

There was no delay in commencing construction. Patrick and George, although now interested, were not much involved in the matter at this stage, having sufficient to see to otherwhere, especially up on the hills, their new lands duly acquired from Swinton and Edgar, and the shortage of trained shepherds a continuing worry. Indeed they established what was all but a school of shepherding for young men at Johnscleuch, between Garvald and Cranshaws, convenient for their extended area.

Patrick had to attend a parliament in the late autumn, which went on longer than usual, this on account of claims being made by lords and landowners for compensation for estates which had been seized and forfeited by both the Covenanting and the Cromwellian authorities, because of support for the monarchy and Montrose. All now agreed that this was just and fair; only the treasury was all but empty, and where was the compensation to come from? The suggestion was made that, since much of the confiscated wealth had gone to the divines to build new churches and manses, increase stipends and found schools, and aid universities and places of learning, the Kirk ought to pay much back; also certain magnates, who had favoured the Covenant, especially Argyll and Loudoun, Campbells, both now dead, but their successors mulcted. This was strenuosly resisted by the bishops who, however opposed to their Presbyterian predecessors, were not willing to dispense with the revenues; and by the heirs of the said magnates. With many individual claims being put forward and argued over, and total non-co-operation coming from at least one of the Three Estates of parliament, to the delay of other necessary business, the session went on for days. Patrick soon realised that the chances of himself gaining any compensation for his own twenty thousand merks' fining were negligible, and did no more than mention it. But others were more optimistic and vocal.

When eventually he got home, it was to learn that in his absence one of the local justiciary courts had been held, at Musselburgh again, the provost presiding, and again this time dealing with witchcraft allegations. Another man and woman, from that burgh itself, had been tried and found guilty, and promptly thereafter first strangled and then their bodies burned at the stake.

Much concerned, Patrick decided that he would have to raise this matter of local courts and their prejudices at the next parliament.

The mill-building went on steadily if hardly apace, with so much to be seen to, the necessary lades and sluices dug, the machinery beginning to be installed, the outbuildings erected. There was much talk of looms, mules, wallowers, gearing, shuttles, heddles, warps and wefts, tweels, walking and fulling, a foreign language to George and Patrick. But they got the general idea. They had not realised, however, that there was more than the spinning and weaving required to make cloth. First the wool had to be graded, then scoured, that is thoroughly washed, four or five times to get rid of the natural oil. Then dried by heating. Then carded, straightening and combing of the fibres, this all before the wool reached the mules to make into yarn. So as well as the main building, with the greater and lesser water-wheels to drive the spinning and weaving machines, there had to be adjoining sheds for the scouring and drying and blending of fibres. Setting up a cloth mill was no simple and speedy task.

They wondered whether it was worth it all; but James asserted that it certainly would be. At this stage it seemed all toil and expense; but once the mill started to work and the cloths were being produced, their profits would come, and keep on coming. They would have to find marketing aid, to be sure. But he thought that would not be difficult to gain, in Edinburgh.

Once the spinning mules and looms were made and installed, their ladies seemed to find it all highly interesting, Liz and Joanna coming to inspect progress frequently, not being involved in child-minding as was Helen. They said that they would be able to help find markets for the cloth, they were sure.

Christmas and the new year came and went, with James declaring that the mill should be finished and working by the later spring, in good time for the shearing and wool-supply.

Meantime George took a special interest in the training of new shepherds at Johnscleuch, himself becoming quite expert in the process, learning details of which he had known nothing previously, such as the different qualities of wool coming from the same sheep on various parts of the body, the back, the flanks, the neck, the rump, even the tail, with the staples long and even, coarse, curled or short but finer; that the average weight of a blackface's fleece could be half as heavy again as the cheviot crossbreed's; that they should allow three acres of hill per crossbreed sheep as against two for the others. He also learned that there were sundry ills and diseases afflicting flocks, such as fluke, the most common, especially in wet seasons, this to be helped by the use of salt; scab, a contagious plague; craxy, similar to anthrax, which could be communicated to men; and louping-ill, fairly common in lambs. George passed on this information to the others.

James announced that he had found a young man, one Robert Blackwood, a member of the Merchant Company of Edinburgh, who would handle their mill's produce and advise on quality, demand and the like. He was acquainted with persons actually in the cloth and clothing trade, and importers of foreign cloth at Leith. It might well be best, in due course, to form some sort of a company to run the mill's operations effectively.

Only a small proportion of their Lammermuirs wool would be destined for the mill, the vast majority of it still to be rafted downriver to Dunbar and despatched to the Low Countries. What with the lambing, shearing, scouring and washing, rafting and handling, as well as the shepherding and milling, they were now employing quite large numbers of men, even some women for the mill, their enterprise becoming the talk of Haddington and district.

The great day came, with the mill completed, its machinery in place and tested, and all ready to put into action. It was decided to make an occasion of it and invite many to witness the start of a new departure in Haddington's ancient story. If all this was a success, who knew, others might follow suit and new mills be founded, for there was much available riverbank and water power.

Many guests arrived, including four earls: Lauderdale, the Chancellor – whose seat of Lethington bordered the Monkrigg property – Tweeddale, Traquair and Winton, the Seton chief from Seton Palace near to Cockenzie, up Forth. Other lords and lairds, Provost Davidson of Haddington and his bailies, the Reverend John Bell, minister of St Mary's, as well as humbler folk involved in the activities: shepherds, woodsmen, builders and the like. Stanfield, whose initiative this all so largely was, insisted that, in the circumstances, Patrick, as a lord of parliament, should welcome the visitors, George and himself to say a few words thereafter.

Fortunately it was reasonably good weather, and all could assemble outside the new premises to watch the commencement of proceedings before going within the mill itself to view the working operations, then inspecting the various outbuildings, the scouring-house, drying-shed, blending-room, dye-house, and storehouses.

"My lords and ladies, gentlemen, Provost Davidson and bailies, fellow-workers and friends all," Patrick began. "Today we commence an enterprise new to Lothian, possibly to most of Scotland, the spinning and weaving of our own wool into different sorts of cloth, not as we have done in the past, in cottages and the like as women's house-tasks but as it is done in other lands, in large mills and manufactories. Why should we purchase our cloth and clothing, our blankets and hangings and floor carpets from the Netherlands and elsewhere when we produce some of the best wool in Christendom, and a deal of it?

"My share in this has been the least important of the

three, my friends' much the greater, Colonel Stanfield's vision being the start of it, and Hepburn of Monkrigg, whose great sheep-runs in the Lammermuirs provide the wool, giving it all his necessary support. Much of time, labour and decision has gone into it. Now we see the start of fulfilment." He turned to James.

That man raised a hand, to gesture towards one of their people who stood some way off beside the little pond between them and the river, where the mill-lade could be dammed when necessary and the flow withheld. The handle of the wheel which lifted or lowered the dam shutter was turned, the shutter raised, and the water surged out and down the remainder of the lade, to reach the mighty mill-wheel, its force striking the blades, immediately beginning to turn that power-producing device, to a great creaking and clanking.

A cheer arose from the onlookers.

The colonel led the way inside, it making a tight squeeze for the company. With the noise and clatter of the machinery of mules and looms, he had to shout loudly to make himself heard, pointing out the various stages and processes of the work, and commending the men and women who tended them, these all looking embarrassed at this inspection.

All gazed for a while, and then were led on to the far end of the main building where samples of yarn and cloth were laid out, fine, medium and coarse, this particularly interesting the ladies present, Liz, Helen and Joanna seeking to make themselves heard now above the din and visitors' chatter.

It was with some relief for the speakers that they moved out to the subsidiary buildings which formed a courtyard, and explanations could be given and heard, with the mill-wheel's clacking less distracting. Here, after James had indicated the different premises and sheds, and the need therefor, he handed over to George, who conducted everyone into the dye-house, where the colouring pots had been laid aside and the tables spread with wines, spirits and sweetmeats for all, including the workers in the mill, the shepherds and the rest.

"Here is an end to your patient viewing," he declared. "You have seen the results of the first part of our labours. The next will make its own challenge, the producing of sundry kinds of cloth and yarn, of a quality to gain acceptance and demand, and in a quantity to make our endeavours worth the while, the marketing and selling important indeed. May all here today, and who judge our efforts to be worthy, seek to help in this, in however small measure. Robert Blackwood, of the Edinburgh Merchant Company, who is here with us, will guide us in this; but all aid will be welcome, to make our efforts known." He turned. "So now I salute Colonel James Stanfield, without whom none of this would have come about – as, I am sure, do you all."

As James waved a modestly dismissive hand, amid murmurs of agreement, the Earl of Lauderdale took it upon himself to speak, as from them all.

"Today, my friends, we have seen much to acclaim. Here is a labour that we can admire. And which we can learn from, to be sure. Three men – and one of them from south of the border – have commenced an endeavour which could be of great value, not only to themselves and their folk hereabouts, but to Scotland itself. All in this realm need cloth and clothing. Here is a start to providing it for ourselves, which will save us much of our moneys being sent overseas, to our benefit. I say, may the good work prosper, and indeed be taken up by others. I myself have lands, in especial in the borders, where the like could well be engaged in. Scotland is a land of hills, which can carry sheep. We can increase our flocks, and use the wool and mutton. I for one will not forget. I raise my goblet to those who show us the way!"

More than polite applause greeted that from the nation's High Chancellor himself.

When all the visitors had departed, Liz summed it all up. "Much of hard work, of wits as well as hands, is represented here this day, the seed now come to fullness after long sowing. The reaping of the benefit must follow. And not only for ourselves, as has been said. I do not greatly like Lauderdale, but he is powerful and does not lack wits either; a deal better as some kind of friend than an enemy! I say that we are unlikely ever to regret this day!"

The mill-lade was ordered to be blocked again. But tomorrow it would open again, and in earnest.

James, ever thinking ahead, came to the conclusion that Lauderdale's possible friendship and aid could be valuable in the enterprise, and should be actively fostered. The Chancellor, at Lethington, being the closest neighbour to George at Monkrigg, the three friends decided to go and see him there without undue delay. They were kindly enough received by the Countess Anne, and her daughter of the same name, she daughter of the first Earl of Home. She told them that her husband was gone on his governmental duties to Edinburgh, but had said that he would be home by late afternoon. So they went back to Monkrigg, to Helen and her children, until early evening, when they repaired to Lethington again, and duly found the Chancellor there, and interested to know the reason for their visit. He was not a genial man, but his wife having made them welcome enough, he accepted them civilly.

Patrick led off without undue delay. "My lord Earl," he said, "we have been encouraged by your kind remarks at the New Mills the other day, and your expressed interest in the milling and cloth-making. We would be glad to assist you if ever you did decide to have mills set up in your border lands. But meantime, perhaps you might be interested in supporting further the said work nearer at hand? Colonel Stanfield has a proposal to make."

A little doubtfully Lauderdale looked at that man.

"My lord, we are presently considering forming a company of sorts, to further this cloth-making," he said. "To aid in both the milling and the marketing. How say you to joining such company in some fashion? Not to put moneys into it, to be sure, but to have an interest. We would have you to be a stockholder in some degree, and so you would in some measure share in the profits.''

''Stockholder? Myself? Share in profits? And you say no moneys to be paid for it?''

''Your support and prestige would be sufficient, my lord. If so you wished at any time, you could purchase other shares. But that is not our intention at this present. It is to have your favour and blessing on our endeavours, which you expressed that day, and which we believe would be of advantage, not only to *our* enterprise but for others, many others, the nation at large. If this of spinning, weaving and cloth-making could be encouraged elsewhere, it would be a source of wealth and employment at present untapped. Much money leaves Scotland in this of importing cloth and clothing and woollen goods. That money could be saved, and *us* possibly doing the exporting. How say you, my lord?''

Lauderdale looked sufficiently thoughtful. ''You would have me as a member of your group? Without moneys contributed?''

''We would. Moneys would come into it, yes – but coming to you, from the holding we would allot you. In return for your support. You, as Chancellor, carry great weight in this realm. Your help would be valuable. And not only in parliament and government. Prosperity increased in the land to the advantage of all.''

''You need not speak for the proposed company, my lord Earl,'' George put in. ''But your favour would be advantageous. In especial in finding markets for our cloth. This is an essential for us, in the selling nationwide of our products. You will see that?''

''I see that you must rate my favour highly!''

''We do, yes. But at no hurt to you!'' Patrick added. ''On the contrary. No announcements need be made. But your unspoken support could greatly assist this new trade in Scotland.''

"In what way would you see it so doing?"

"For one thing, parliament could put a tax on the import of foreign cloth."

"Ha! Now I see what you are at. But such tax would have us all but bareshanked! Until enough cloth was produced to reclothe us all!"

"Only a very small tax at first. As encouragement for further mills to start up. It could be increased later, as the homespun supplies grow."

"You have been busy in more than spinning yarn, I see. Ambitious men!"

"Ambitious perhaps, my lord, but not only for ourselves," James added. "All the land could gain. How much money goes abroad each year for clothing, think you? More than can be spared."

"Perhaps. I will consider it. And inform you."

They had to be content with that. But before they took their departure, Lauderdale told them, at some length and in detail, of the career of his great-great grandfather, William Maitland of Lethington, who had been Mary, Queen of Scots' secretary and loyal supporter, and what fighting for that unfortunate monarch had cost him. Also how *his* grandfather had died at Flodden Field with James the Fourth. And another Maitland ancestor fought strongly for Robert the Bruce. This emphasis on his predecessors' influence on Scotland's story struck his hearers as somewhat significant in the circumstances. What was he seeking to prove? And would he have thought to tell them all this if he had not been favourably considering their suggestion?

They left, heartened.

Three days later a messenger arrived at Monkrigg, none other than the younger Lady Anne, the earl's only child, a young woman in her early twenties, to announce that her father would accept some stockholding in the New Mills project.

* * *

150

The milling went ahead satisfactorily, to Patrick and George's gratification, but less so to James's. He declared that, however active and productive were their mules and looms, their mill ought to be making much more cloth and serge than it was doing to make any real impact on the situation, and encourage the marketing people, and indeed parliament. They needed more machinery, and more spinners and weavers.

So orders were given for the wrights and carpenters to get busy again. And James announced that he would go south once more, to seek to enlist more experienced operators to come to Scotland, these not only to work on the new machines but to train more spinners and weavers.

Their success seemed to breed ever more effort.

While he was away, a development occurred which had nothing to do with milling or sheep-rearing but which had its effect on the area. George's far-out kinsman Sir Adam Hepburn of Humbie died, parliamentary commissioner for Haddingtonshire, Humbie an estate and village some ten miles south-west of Haddington. An elderly man, he had been a strong Covenanter, indeed former Treasurer of the Solemn League and Covenant, but less than active for some time. So the county would require a new commissioner to parliament. Patrick suggested that George should stand. Their enterprise's successes should make him a fairly popular choice for the voters.

But that man was less than eager. He had no desire to go in for politics. From what he had heard, it was not his sort of life. He had a sufficiency to see to, all his great sheep-rearing responsibilities, and a young family to bring up. Patrick could remain their parliamentarian.

But when James returned from Yorkshire, with a group of new workers, and somewhat concerned that he had had to offer them higher wages than they were paying to their local workforce to lure them northwards, which would of course require them to advance the same to their present

151

operators, he also mentioned to Joanna, whence it came to the rest of them, that his son Philip had married a local squire's daughter. He made no other family comments.

Patrick now put to him that *he* might consider standing for parliament, to fill the vacancy, and this suggestion was received more favourably than that to George. With two of the trio in the legislature, and Chancellor Lauderdale presiding, who knew what advantages might accrue?

James saw the point, Joanna and Liz encouraging him.

So his name was put forward; and with Patrick and Traquair and Tweeddale backing him, no other nominee ventured to contest it. There were not a great many voters to convince, that privilege being reserved for magnates, lairds and folk in fairly influential positions. The colonel was duly declared commissioner for the shire of Haddington, who had once governed it for Cromwell. An Englishman to sit in the Scots parliament.

That next session of parliament proved to be a notable one, and not only on account of James's installation. George took the three ladies to witness it all, to sit in the gallery of the greater hall of Edinburgh Castle on its rock-top. As usual, the Earl of Rothes, led in by the Lord Lyon King of Arms, sat on the throne as the king's representative; and Lauderdale presided and conducted affairs. He did not normally refer to the presence of individual members, but on this occasion he did.

"My lords, temporal and spiritual, commissioners of the shires and representatives of the royal burghs, at this session of parliament I greet, in your name, a new representative for the county of Haddington, a notable figure who, with my lord of Elibank and Hepburn of Monkrigg, has established a new venture for this land, a milling manufactory at Haddington, for the spinning of yarn and the weaving of cloths, serge and blankets from our own wool. This to spare us all the costs of importing so much of our clothing from the Low Countries and elsewhere, in the hope that this labour will be taken up by others, and soon be able to supply all the realm, and so greatly save us large moneys. Even be able, in time, to sell our cloth overseas, to further advantage. I shall return to this matter hereafter, for your consideration. But meanwhile I present to you Colonel Stanfield."

That man, sitting well back in the hall, rose to his feet, bowed, front, left and right, and sat down again.

There was a hoot from the throne as Rothes waved a hand. "Hear you that!" he cried. "We'll no' ken ourselves dressed so fine! A' because o' one o' the man Cromwell's sodgers!" The present monarch's grandfather, James the Sixth and First, would have approved of Leslie of Rothes.

Frowning, Lauderdale tapped with his gavel on the Chancellor's table to indicate that the assembly was now in session, and due order to be observed. "First there is the matter of the Duke of Buccleuch and Monmouth, son to King Charles. His Grace has made him commander-in-chief of the armed forces of England, and recommends that we do the same in Scotland. Is this agreed by parliament?"

There were murmurs and mutterings.

The Earl of Buchan rose. "This duke is but a youth of sixteen years," he objected. "However illustrious his birth" – and he looked around him, eyebrows raised, to emphasise the question of legitimacy or otherwise, and the position of Queen Catherine of Braganza – "I would not wish *my* men to be under the command of little more than a boy. I would defer decision."

Two or three others jumped up to second that.

"Och, he'll likely bide in London-town, the lad, and never set foot in Scotland," Rothes announced. "It is a name, just." He guffawed. "Nae hurt in it. We can still appoint our ain leaders."

That reassured the doubters, and the thing was passed.

"There is still the issue of compensation for those who were fined and their estates forfeited by the late Covenant regime," the Chancellor went on. "This has not been settled. Not a few here today are the poorer for it. But the realm's coffers are all but empty and unable to make payment. Some means of raising the moneys there must be. It is suggested that new taxes should be levied. Proposals for such are requested.''

Taxation was never a popular subject for discussion, all considering their own pockets. There was silence in the hall.

"I say proposals," Lauderdale repeated.

"The Church still has great wealth," the provost of Ayr declared. Frowns from the clerical benches.

"There is a tax on imported wines," the Bishop of Brechin said. "Could this be increased somewhat?"

More general frowning. All there found wine to their taste.

Patrick stood. "My lord Chancellor, we all have wines in our houses. And they cannot be produced in Scotland. Save for honey wine. But distilled spirits we can and do produce. Our whisky is famed. An increase in the tax on foreign spirits, then, rum, brandy and the like. Would that not serve? And increase our whisky trade."

There was some applause for that, especially from the northeners where the whisky was distilled; from churchmen also.

"I so move," Buchan declared.

"And I second," the Archbishop of Glasgow added.

"This will be insufficient to meet our needs," Lauderdale commented. "Other proposals?"

None was forthcoming.

"I will leave you time to consider this," he went on. "We shall return to it. There are appointments to be made. The Lords of the Articles recommend that Archibald Campbell, the Lord Lorn, son of the executed Marquis of Argyll, who nevertheless has loyally and strongly supported our King Charles, and was wrongly and unjustly imprisoned by the Earl of Middleton, be restored to the earldom of Argyll, rightfully his. This in recognition of his

154

good services, not least at the battles of Dunbar and Worcester. The earldom, I say, not the marquisate bestowed on his unworthy father. Is it agreed?"

None there objected. Lord Lorn's situation had generated much sympathy.

"Then there is the declared wish of the king that James Johnstone, Earl of Annandale, here present, be appointed hereditary constable of the royal castle of Lochmaben. None, I judge, will question that?"

None did.

"John Murray, Earl of Atholl, Sheriff of Fife, to be Lord Justice General, on the recommendation of the Lords of the Articles. Agreed?"

Since Lauderdale and Rothes all but controlled the Lords of the Articles, there was no objection voiced.

"Now, to revert to moneys and taxation; there is a proposal that, to encourage the manufacture of cloth and clothing in this realm, a tax should be levied on the like from other lands. I ask my lord of Elibank to speak to this."

Patrick rose. "My lord Chancellor and fellow commissioners, we who have commenced this endeavour at Haddington to use our own wool from our own sheep to make our own clothing, say that such tax on foreign cloths would be an encouragement for others to do as we are doing. At the first, only a small levy, a token as it were. Our mill, of course, cannot produce sufficient cloth, as yet, to clothe even Haddingtonshire, although we are increasing our output. But this token tax would, we judge, be effective in having others set up similar mills. There is much wool produced in Scotland, especially in the borders, and it is surely unsuitable that it all should be exported to other lands, and the cloth and serges made from it brought back, at much cost to us all. As mills are established and cloth woven, the tax could be increased. But meantime, the gesture made, as indication of parliament's support."

"Do you so move, my lord?"

"I do."

"Then I judge that there will be a worthy seconder to this motion. I call on our new commissioner for Haddingtonshire to speak on it. Colonel Stanfield."

There was a stir as James rose.

"My lord Chancellor, I, as the newest member of this assembly, am concerned that I should be sufficiently bold as to speak and second a motion on this the first day of my presence among you. I pray that you bear with me. But since I have been called upon to do so, I crave that forbearance. This of the establishment of new mills, with my friends I see as of great importance. Scotland has all the means to produce cloth and clothing. Sheep by the hundred thousand and empty hills to support more. Rivers to give water to drive the mills." He smiled. "And no lack of rain to keep the rivers running! Folk to build the mills – for there are corn mills everywhere. And able workers who can learn to tend the machines, the mules and looms. And, I swear, no lack of tailors to make the cloths into the garb which we all require. We see this as a means of bringing much wealth and prosperity to this land. And hope that you all will see it so, likewise. For too long, you . . . forgive me, *we* have been content with small spinning-wheels and hand-looms for some women in cottages. Now let us do better. As to the tax, only some small sum at first. Perhaps one quarter-merk for an ell of imported cloth. That would not add greatly to the cost of clothing meantime. But as the product grows, so increase the tax. My lord Chancellor, I second the motion."

There was even some applause, no great acclaim but enough to encourage mover and seconder.

"Before I ask if there are any contrary motions," Lauderdale said, "I would indicate that what our friend has said regarding opportunities for this of milling and increased sheep-raising in the borders, is worthy of much thought. *I* have lands along the Tweed and the Teviot rivers, and hills a-plenty for sheep. From Ersildoune and

Selkirk and Jedworth and Ancrum to Denholm and Hawick, two score of miles and more, mills could be set up. Others elsewhere could consider it likewise."

After that, when he asked whether there were any counter-motions, it would have been a determined contender who would have raised voice. None did – save Rothes.

"Yon tax," he called, "we are a' going to be the poorer, I jalouse, until the tax gets levied. For our ladies will a' be at the merchants and tailors for new gear afore the costs go up! Hech, hech – we'll a' be paupers for the next month or so!"

None saw that as a serious objection to the motion. The thing was passed.

That marked the end of the session. As members rose and exchanged impressions and chatter, Patrick was not the only one to congratulate James on his maiden speech.

When the ladies came down, with George, from the gallery, Liz it was who put the three men's thoughts into words. "Your making of Lauderdale a stockholder in the proposed New Mills company has paid its way already!" she asserted.

18

Liz was right. It was three weeks later that the Chancellor
sent a messenger to New Mills House requesting a visit to
Lethington by Stanfield, reasons not stated. Assuming
that it must have something to do with the wool trade,
his two friends agreed to accompany James the next day.

They found Lauderdale welcoming enough, in his stiff
way. He informed that he had been to London, on the
summons of King Charles, to discuss various matters, in
especial the application to Scotland of some features of the
New Conventicle Act passed by the English parliament –
this a harsh move against dissenting clergy, those who did
not accept the episcopal form of Church government.
Charles himself, who was not greatly in favour of this –
indeed alleged to be inclining towards Catholicism – had
said that parliament considered that the Scots were insufficiently strong against such backsliders and recusants,
Presbyterians, Puritans and the like. And for the sake of
harmony between his two kingdoms, urged that his representatives, Lauderdale himself and Rothes, should see
that stricter measures were imposed. Apparently Archbishop Sharp of St Andrews, the Scots Primate, had
complained to Canterbury and York. This English Conventicle Act had dismissed no fewer than eighteen hundred
ministers from their charges, and forbidden them to come
within four miles of their former parishes. Lauderdale,
scarcely a religious man, was concerned that such a decree
in Scotland could result in major upheavals, with the
episcopalian worship not nearly so strongly installed as
in England.

This was not all that he had to report. Apparently Edward Hyde, Lord Clarendon, was in disfavour, and might well fall totally from his position of authority as the king's principal adviser and chief minister. He was critical of Charles's womanising and what he called immorality, not only from the ethical point of view but because of the great cost and undue influence of his mistresses. The king was already grievously in debt, so much so that he had recently sold the English toe-hold in France, Dunkirk, for four hundred thousand pounds to his uncle King Louis. These mistresses, whom he was creating duchesses, had too much sway over the easy-going monarch, and were even gaining their own favourites positions of some authority in the land, oddly enough some in command of ships-of-war engaged in the Dutch conflict, this without naval experience. Small wonder that the warfare was not going in England's favour. Not only this, but Charles's brother and heir-apparent, James, Duke of York, had secretly married Clarendon's daughter, much to the king's disapproval.

All this, however, was not what the Chancellor had called Stanfield to hear.

"I have been considering this of establishing cloth mills on my lands, as you suggested, sir, and see it as probably worth the doing. I would be glad to have your advice on this. Where best to build. I have properties in various parts. Guidance would be wise."

"We all would be happy to aid in this I am sure, my lord. Where think you would offer best setting? In the borders? And near to sheep-country, for wool at hand."

"I have much land in the shire of Peebles. Stobo on the Tweed. Dawick. Eddleston nearby. Broughton. And further off, on the Water of Leet, in the Merse. Also Ladykirk, again on lower Tweed. And there is Whitslaid, on the Leader, in my own Lauderdale."

"Wide lands, yes. You have much choice. But as well as the rivers and the sheep, there is labour to think of. Folk to work the mills. So best near to sizeable villages or towns. I do not know the parts you mention . . ."

"I do," George put in. "In especial, the Leet Water. Swinton, where my wife is from, is on the Leet Water. And there is a village of fair size. Ladykirk is none so far from there. And the Tweed would give you good carriage, by barge, for your wool and cloth."

"All that is to be considered, yes. Water, sheep, folk and portage. The best choice, then? Would you be prepared to visit these lands with me, for my guidance?"

"To be sure," James said. "It is important to make your start in the right place. For guidance for others, it may be."

"I would go with you also, my lord," George added. "For this of the sheep. I have had much of sheep-raising to do."

"That would be of help."

Patrick saw no point in offering to accompany the others in this, but added his good wishes.

So it was arranged. Lauderdale had duties to attend to in Edinburgh and Glasgow first, but in a week's time could make a tour of inspection. While they were gone, Patrick would superintend the extensions to the New Mills and the installation of further machinery, and the rafting of wool to Dunbar. They were all becoming notable men of commerce.

The involving of Lauderdale in their activities pleased them, even though none of them found him particularly good company. But as the man who now largely ruled Scotland, his growing association could be valuable indeed.

The quite lengthy perambulation of the Maitland lands duly took place, and occupied four full days, they stopping overnight at Thirlestane Castle in Lauderdale itself, the hallhouse of Stobo in Peebleshire, and at Swinton House, where Helen's brothers were surprised to find themselves acting as host to Scotland's Lord Chancellor.

James and George were at one in advising Lauderdale

160

that the best choice to commence a cloth-milling enterprise was a site on the Leet Water, in the Merse near Leitholm, Swinton village only a mile or two away for the labour, with plenty of sheep-pasture on the flanking grassy slopes of the middle Merse for the finer grade Cheviot breed rather than the blackface, and the river smooth-flowing and not liable to spates and itself reaching Tweed near to Coldstream, convenient for Berwick. Whitslaid, on the River Leader, at the tail-end of the Lammermuirs, would have served well, but there was no sizeable community near at hand. And Stobo and Dawick on the upper Tweed were further away.

The Chancellor was well pleased, especially when he was offered the use of experienced mill-builders in due course. Although, on their travels and surveys they did come across riverside mills other than for grain, waulk mills they were called, for the scouring and washing of fleeces of Cheviot sheep, these very oily, and requiring much treatment by fuller's-herb, or soapwort, grown locally, something that George and James had not heard of. Presumably the men who built these mills could do the like for cloth ones.

Out of this association with Lauderdale, Helen became friendly with the Countess Anne and her daughter, who did not see a great deal of husband and father in his circumstances, and were glad of company. Liz and Joanna got involved in this also, and through it with the countess's Home family, which had always been in a sort of rivaly in the Merse with the Swintons – an amusing by-product of sheep and wool and milling,

That year's prices for fleeces, at Veere, were better than usual for some reason, and this helped to pay for the mill extension.

There was, however, a drawback to the said extension, in that the additional premises were now encroaching on James's house and living space and making of it a less pleasing residence, Joanna in especial not failing to remark on this. A new house, further down the river? Or purchase an existing property somewhere convenient?

It was through the Countess of Lauderdale that they heard of a possibility, Morham. This was a hamlet, with a modest hallhouse, situated only a couple of miles south of New Mills but on the other side of Tyne, and roughly the same distance from Lethington and Monkrigg. The laird, Hogg by name, had died some time before, leaving the property to an only child, a married daughter now living in Galloway, and unable to visit it frequently. She had now decided to sell it. She had been a friend of the countess's daughter.

A visit was paid over to Morham, the ladies particularly interested, and with their own ideas as to what would make a suitable home for James. They found a somewhat decayed small village, with an ancient church, strangely remote-seeming to be barely three miles from Haddington, set quite picturesquely among small braes and hillocks, with a burn winding through in its little valley. On a knoll above this was the hallhouse, set on a quite defensive position, which gave the impression of having been the site of a former fortified building, possibly a tower. The house itself was not unattractive, with pleasing views, not large but more than sufficient for James's needs, in a state of minor disrepair but basically sound enough. It had a vaulted downstairs kitchen with great arched fireplace, probably a relic of the previous structure, a hall on the first floor, with withdrawing-room off it, and six bed-chambers higher, this as much as the site would contain. On the northern, landwards side was a sloping orchard. The feminine contingent pointed out where improvements could be made, but James himself was well content with it all, and thought that he could scarcely do better and remain within easy distance of their mills. With only a single farmery attached, the price should not be unreasonable. The elderly minister of the church told them that the great John Knox had been born here – this a commendation or otherwise.

It might well be some time before a price could be agreed upon and a purchase made, with the present owner so far away; but the process should be commenced. William Hogg, the late laird, had been an advocate, a lawyer at the courts, so his daughter might have learned to bargain.

Meanwhile there was the problem of disposing profitably of the different sorts of cloth made at the New Mills. Robert Blackwood, in Edinburgh, was made responsible for this. He had unused housing, just below the city's Tron Kirk, converted into a warehouse to store the products while they awaited sale. With the second set of looms in operation, James reckoned that they would be making as much as sixty thousand ells a year, that measure, originally taken from the length of a man's arm, having become established as considerably longer, four and a half feet. So much space was required to store it all; and many merchants involved in the selling, all of whom had to make their own profit, involving higher ultimate prices than the makers would have wished. Some portion of it was exported to England; but unfortunately, under the new Navigation Act there, all trade to and from England had to be carried in English vessels, which not only angered Scots shippers but cost a lot, for their southern counterparts saw the opportunity to levy high charges, and took it. So most of the cloth and clothing had to go by waggon and pack-horse over the border. The three friends were discovering trading problems new to them. The export from Leith and Dunbar to the Baltic and Scandinavian kingdoms was developed and fostered, although the Low Countries had had all but a monopoly of this. Should one or other of them go over there, and seek to establish favourable links and terms? With his two colleagues parliamentarians, if so it would have to be George.

That autumn's markets at Haddington and the East

Linton of Prestonkirk sales of surplus lambs, hogs and gimmers, which the high hills would not support over the winter, brought in excellent revenues, these in addition to the crossbred sheep which Lauderdale bought from them to stock some of his lower pastures to produce wool for his Leet Water mill now nearing completion – so he was taking his involvement seriously.

James's share in these moneys helped in his purchase of Morham, which was able to go ahead with less bickering than might have been; and that man found himself to be a laird, as well as a parliamentary commissioner and manufacturer, all something of a change from being an Ironside colonel. Not that he was a great laird, the Morham property extending to only twelve hundred acres, but now he could pasture and breed some sheep and cattle of his own, which pleased him.

The hallhouse repairing and refurbishing occupied him also, making him a busy man indeed, although much of the interior work was superintended by the three ladies, who were determined that all should be of maximum comfort and suitable style.

The removal day, or flitting as it was termed – however inappropriate such name was for the laborious and prolonged transfer of furniture, books, clothing and gear, food, wines and the rest – was a major event, the replacing of everything thereafter being no light and simple task either, servants to be instructed, changes of mind made and agreed, James somewhat bemused by all the feminine advice.

An eventual celebration had to be held, of course, and made somewhat different from that of the New Mills House one, and the number of guests increased to include a large proportion of eastern Lothian's magnates, the Chancellor himself and his wife and daughter honouring the occasion. Lauderdale revealed that he was going to London again, to receive more royal instructions and commands, this time presumably via Anthony Ashley-

Cooper, now Earl of Shaftesbury, who had succeeded the fallen Clarendon.

That over, and James Stanfield more or less installed, as it were, George was to be despatched to Norway, Sweden, Denmark and sundry Baltic dukedoms and provinces, this on behalf of the cloth trade. He was not eager to attempt it, and he wished that he could have taken Helen with him, but she was detained with their young family ties.

George sailed from Dunbar, with a cargo of coarse wool for Veere, then to go on eastwards, this well before the winter storms period set in. It would all make quite a lengthy journey, both in distance as in duration, he feared. But he found the Dunbar shipmaster, one Peter Dalgleish, a man with whom he could get on well, which would be a help and some companionship. The voyaging would certainly make a change from raising sheep on the Lammermuirs, acting the laird and milling.

The sail down to Veere took five days, their progress not expedited by no fewer than three inspections by small English ships-of-war to ensure that their trade was not aimed at English markets, this in a Scots ship – Dalgleish used to this, however humiliating a procedure. Unloading the fleeces at Veere, they learned the current price of the wool, which this year was fair without being generous; then, with only the samples of cloths, they moved on the over six hundred miles north-eastwards for the Skagerrak, before the Kattegat and the Baltic. At least they had no English inspections to trouble them now; and the Dutch warships did not seek to interrupt them, flying as they did the blue and white saltire of Scotland.

Peter Dalgleish had been to their first stop, the capital of Norway, Oslo, now being called Christiania, before, as he had to Gothenburg in Sweden, none so far south, but had never been as far as Copenhagen in Denmark, and beyond. He was unsure as to how far into the Baltic Sea it would be worth going.

At Norse Christiania George quite quickly found a young merchant who could speak English and who, after negotiations, agreed to act interpreter for him – for he himself, like so many Scots, could only speak his own language and the French – and who also was persuaded to go on with them further, able to converse in other tongues, this a major help. George thereafter quickly learned that by cutting the price that the Low Countries traders charged for their wares, which was substantial, he could interest buyers in his own offerings, their quality being acceptable. They had decided on minimum prices before he left home, knowing the Netherlands rates; and he did not have to go nearly so low here. Well pleased, they headed on southwards to Gothenburg, where the Skagerrak began to narrow into the mouth of the Kattegat, and the famed tide races began, to keep their Peter on his mettle as the North Sea commenced to compete with the shallower Baltic.

Gothenburg was little different from Christiania as to the trading, with the Scots cloth, being so new, interesting potential buyers, and dealers quite glad to have an alternative source of trade, cheaper but of as good quality. If this continued they were going to find little difficulty in their marketing. Their interpreter helped them to list names of traders for the future.

One hundred and fifty miles down the Kattegat's turbulent waters they came to where it suddenly narrowed, at Helsingor, or Elsinore, which the English playwright had written about, Shakespeare. Here at what they were interested to learn was called the Sound, a term they used in Scotland for a narrow passage between islands, they found themselves only a few miles from both the Swedish and Danish coasts, the latter that of the island of Zealand. There was the capital city of Copenhagen, their next destination, it now rivalling Hamburg and Lübeck as the greatest trading port of all the Baltic, with the formerly all-powerful Hanseatic League weakening its grip.

Reaching this large and sprawling community, with its extensive dock area, George found the competition stiffer, the Hansa merchants themselves vying with each other to under-bid. He did not do so well, but did gain some potential orders.

He wondered whether, in these circumstances, it was worth going further southwards to the German Baltic ports of Kiel, Lübeck, Stettin and the rest, all bases of the Hansa trade. He decided to try the first, Kiel, in Schleswig-Holstein, another one hundred and fifty miles through a vast network of islands; and if this was unre-warding, to leave the others alone.

He proved to have a poor reception at Kiel. After all, the traders here were keen rivals and were already having to cope with the Dutch imports. So there was no point in proceeding onwards. He had done very well in Norway and Sweden, somewhat less so in Denmark; but it had made a hopeful beginning, and well worth the journey. Home for him.

The sail back, against prevailing westerly winds, with much tacking required, was much slower than on the outward voyage. George was thankful to see, eventually, the Craig of Bass towering ahead at the mouth of the Firth of Forth, with Dunbar's castle and harbour nearer still.

19

Lauderdale returned from London soon after George got back with, whatever other important tidings on the national front, quite dramatic news for his friends. He had taken some of the New Mills cloths to present to the king, and these had been well received, especially the finer weaves which would serve to pass on to his mistresses, an ever-growing entourage. And this, with some description of the source thereof and the enterprise, was sufficient to cause Charles to declare that this man Stanfield deserved a knighthood. Next time he, Lauderdale, came south, he should bring the colonel with him to receive the accolade.

Needless to say, Patrick and George and the ladies were delighted to hear of this notable honour, especially for a former Cromwellian officer, and the demonstration to all of the importance of their industry and efforts. Great were the congratulations.

Congratulations also were in order for Lauderdale himself, whose first mill was now completed and working. He was planning another, at Ladykirk nearer Tweed. He was seeking to buy more sheep also.

George's report on his Scandinavian travels much encouraged his partners, and the question of still more mills began to be discussed. Could cloth milling become a major Scottish industry? With the Lord Chancellor aiding them in giving a lead, who knew how widespread and important it might become, especially in the Borderland, where conditions were so favourable in rivers, communities and sheep-country.

George went to Edinburgh to report to and consult with Robert Blackwood as regards foreign marketing and pricing, and the qualities he had found to be favoured. Blackwood would pass this on to the merchants. No lack of enthusiasm resulted.

A parliament was held in late Novermber, and at it the Chancellor invited Patrick and James to expound further on their initiative, he mentioning his own involvement and progress, also the king's interest and the knighthood to emphasise it. Much debate and discussion was forthcoming with the leadership, and not a few present indicated some likelihood of doing something positive about it all, particularly the representatives of the borders area, on Tweed and Teviot, Jed and Leithen.

When the Chancellor put forward a motion that the import of foreign cloth should now be taxed, and possibly eventually be prohibited, this was passed without demur.

It was not so much at the session itself but afterwards, in personal exchanges and chat, that the Haddington pair were approached and questioned at some length and in detail, and they gained the impression that at least some of these would act. Scott and Kerr lords were especially concerned, as were the provosts of the royal burghs of Hawick and Jedburgh and Peebles. James and Patrick invited all such to visit the New Mills and hear of the lessons learned there over problems and priorities. James emphasised that they themselves still had much to learn, particularly as to the different kinds of cloth and yarn and the markets therefor, and the breeds of sheep best to produce such wool, disclaiming any suggestion that he and his friends were know-alls.

In the event they did have enquiring visitors to Haddington thereafter, who gave every indication of following up their investigations with action. Liz and Helen and Joanna had much hospitality to provide.

Meanwhile the first cargoes of cloth were despatched to Scandinavia, not all of it going from Dunbar, for the

Edinburgh merchants used Leith as port. This entailed transport of the material thither, requiring more waggons, oxen and dray-horses; so the raft-makers had to turn their hands to different constructions, and wheelwrights to making more than mill-wheels. Roadways were, in general, in poor shape, and such small improvements as were possible had to be attempted. Spin-off employment and industry were generated inevitably, all demanding the attention of the busy trio.

After Yuletide and the lambing, shearing and sales periods following, with the looms busy, word came of a disastrous fire in London, which had destroyed a large part of the inner city. Details were slow in coming, but in time they learned that no fewer than thirteen thousand houses had been destroyed, as well as many public buildings and churches, even St Paul's Cathedral ruined, fifteen city wards devastated, and two hundred thousand folk homeless. Whitehall and other palaces were not damaged apparently; but whatever the cause, consternation reigned down there. The only small consolation seemed to be that the conflagration had also cleansed the city of any lingering effects of the plague which had visited London a year or so before. Some Presbyterian divines were declaring that this was God's judgment on the proponents of episcopacy.

With the consequences of all this preoccupying king, court and government in the south, it was some time before Lauderdale received another summons from the monarch. He did not have to remind James and his friends that they were to accompany him on this occasion – at least the colonel was, and the other two were not going to miss the great day. They were able to offer the Chancellor and his aides the opportunity of sailing to the Thames in one of the Dunbar ships en route for Veere – that is, if they did not object to the oily smell of the fleeces – so much more convenient and speedy than would be the long ride down through England. This was accepted.

The weather being kind, it made a pleasing enough voyage, despite the smells. Lauderdale slept much of the way.

Their sight of inner London as they sailed up estuary and river was sufficiently eye-catching and affecting, the devastation of the great fire so widespread. With so many of the houses timber-built, unlike most of those in Scotland of stone, the ruin was dire indeed.

As their vessel turned round the great southwards bend in the river, they saw that the fire had not appeared to reach this area, their destination, with Whitehall Palace, the Houses of Parliament and Westminster seemingly intact. They docked at the busy Charing Cross pier with some difficulty, their saltire banner of no help.

It was no lengthy walk to the palace fortunately, where they had no difficulty in gaining entrance, Lauderdale being known to the guards. It proved to be a very sprawling establishment, a strange mixture of the very fine and the somewhat tawdry and delapidated, all traces of the Cromwellian period of neglect not yet erased. Courtiers abounded, all notably finely dressed, and women's presence seemed almost to predominate, presumably the king's mistresses and their lady attendants.

They were ushered into a handsome gallery, and there left to have a long wait, ignored by the many passers to and fro, mostly lofty-looking personages, chattering females and hurrying servants.

Lauderdale told the trio something of the ladies who meant so much to their monarch. The present reigning beauty was Louise de Querouaile, now Duchess of Portsmouth; but this did not mean that the others, the Duchesses of Cleveland, Richmond and Lennox, the Countesses of Ossory and Southesk, the Lady Grammont, and even the Welsh-born city girl, Nell Gwyn, were meantime banished from the palace. Charles evidently was as catholic in his affections as allegedly he was in his religious inclinations. How well they all got on together was a matter for question, but the visitors sensed no female enmity among those ladies they saw.

At length an official of some sort came to inform Lauderdale that His Majesty would see him, but apparently only himself at this stage. So the others were left alone for another lengthy wait. No refreshments were forthcoming.

When finally the same individual came to tell them, haughtily, to follow him, they were led to another wing of the establishment altogether, and taken into a most handsome but not very large apartment, where three men sat at a table drinking wine, Lauderdale one of them.

"The Scotchmen, Your Majesty," they were announced, and their conductor backed away.

The trio bowed to one who raised a languid hand, Lauderdale rising.

"These, Sire, are Colonel James Stanfield, Lord Elibank and George Hepburn of Monkrigg, partners in the colonel's undertaking."

Charles Stewart eyed them, and he had large and expressive eyes, notable in sallow features. Slender and long-legged as he lounged in his chair, he looked less than majestic, lengthy of nose and clean-shaven, not at all like his unfortunate father who at least had been handsome and proud of bearing. Patrick wondered whether this Charles took after his grandsire, with that complexion and appearance, for James the Sixth and First had been sallow, dark-eyed and ungainly, knock-kneed indeed; and although *his* mother had been Mary, Queen of Scots, his father almost certainly had been the queen's Italian secretary, David Rizzio, and not the Lord Darnley, her husband.

"So you are the cloth-makers," he said, "Strange men to be the like, a lord, a soldier and a squire. But, from what I hear, admirable. I greet you."

They all bowed again.

"What brought you to this effort, may I ask?"

Glancing at his companions, James spoke. "It was the

sheep, Your Majesty. The great numbers of sheep, pasturing on the hills near to Haddington in Lothian, high hills of heather whereon Dr Hepburn here raised long-woolled sheep in their thousands. Their wool was all sent to the Low Countries, there to be made into cloth. Then some of the cloth and clothing was brought back to where the wool came from. At a cost. This seemed to me to be . . . unfortunate. I deemed it possible, when I was stationed at Haddington, that there was no need to depend on the Netherlanders for cloth, which we could make ourselves. So . . ."

"And now you have had others to follow your lead, I understand?"

"Yes, Sire. Thanks to my Lord Elibank, who sat in parliament, the Scots parliament, interest was aroused. And my Lord Chancellor Lauderdale showed the way for others to follow."

"And you are now a member of that parliament yourself?"

"It is my great privilege, Sire."

"And you no longer send your wool to the Netherlands."

"We do, Your Grace. Some of it. Most, indeed." It was George who spoke now. "Our Lammermuir wool has in the past been from a kind of sheep that produces very coarse fibre fleeces. The outer coat, that is. Good for blankets, shawls, carpets, hangings and the like. But not for softer clothing. Now we are also raising crossbred sheep to produce finer fibres, for clothing. But my main flocks are of blackface, Sire."

"Blackface?"

"So called for their heads being black, unlike other sheep, Your Grace."

The third man at the table spoke. "Majesty, sir – Majesty! So you address the king. Grace is but for dukes and duchesses."

"In Scotland, Shaftesbury, we call the monarch Your Grace," Lauderdale said.

"You are in England now!"

Charles waved that languid hand. "It does not signify. What does, is that we hear of worthy endeavour, wealth to be made. Is there aught that we could learn here in England from all this?"

"I think not, Sire. We have woollen mills in Manchester, I have heard. We scarcely require guidance from Scotland, I think!"

Lauderdale frowned at him. "We can all learn in some matters and manners, my lord," he observed coolly.

The two earls eyed each other less than warmly, while the king smiled. Lauderdale was, after all, fifteenth Maitland of Thirlestane and Lethington, third Lord Maitland and second Earl of Lauderdale, while Shaftesbury was but newly ennobled.

"Whatever is the message for England, for Scotland I judge this venture to be good," the monarch said, with a half shrug. "Sufficiently so for me to commend it by promoting a former Roundhead colonel, who fought against my royal father, to the honourable estate of knighthood. Now you shall all witness it." And he reached for a hand-bell on the table near his goblet and rang it.

The clanging had barely died away before the door was opened and the same official who had brought the trio there came in, to bow.

"The sword," Charles said briefly.

Backing away from the presence, the man left the chamber, but almost immediately returned with a sheathed sword, which had obviously been kept ready. He drew the weapon out, and taking its pointed tip in the other hand, advanced to hold out the hilt towards the monarch, bowing once more.

The king rose, as must the other two. "Come," he summoned to James, who stepped forward. Then, "Kneel," he commanded.

The colonel sank to his knees on the carpeted floor, head bent.

In his casual fashion, Charles tapped the sword-blade first on the left shoulder, then over on the right, the steel passing only an inch or two above the lowered head.

"James Stanfield," the monarch said, "I, Charles, hereby dub thee knight, thus and thus. Be thou good and true knight until thy life's end. Arise, Sir James." And he handed the weapon back to the attendant, waved a hand, and sat down again.

James remained kneeling for a few moments, unsure, then rose and bowed. He stepped back, uncertain as to what happened next.

When nothing seemed to happen, he spoke. "I, I thank Your Majesty."

The royal hand waved again, vaguely, presumably dismissively, before it reached for the wine-goblet.

James glanced over at Lauderdale, who nodded, with a shrug, glancing towards the door.

The new knight bowed once again, and almost turned about before remembering that that was not done in the royal presence. So he backed away, and reaching his two friends, they bowed and backed also, the official with the sword now with them. Out through the open doorway they steered themselves cautiously, without any bumping or stumbling, and into the anteroom. And the door was shut behind them.

There the trio turned to stare at each other. That was it, then, that was all! Promotion for one of them to an entire new status, degree and rank, performed thus briefly, nonchalantly, scarcely to be credited. The new knight shook his head.

Patrick did the same but reached out to shake the other's hand in congratulation, as did George. There was really nothing to be said.

The official led them back to their gallery without comment.

There, left alone, they exchanged their remarks and observances on what had taken place, and all but on what had not, a sense of anticlimax upon them. But they had to recognise that, however unimpressive a performance, the reality was there, established. James was *Sir* James from now on, with all that that meant.

They waited. But no instructions were forthcoming to tell them what to do now, no return of Lauderdale, no leading them to other quarters. At length they decided that there was nothing for it but to go back to their ship, where at least they were sure of their quarters. They could not just linger in this gallery indefinitely. Lauderdale would have to find them there, at the docks.

They left Whitehall Palace without escort or any ceremony, and into the city streets.

Back at their vessel they did some more waiting, but now more at ease, in their own cabins, whatever the odour of the fleeces.

It was quite late in the evening before Lauderdale came to them, and making no apologies. He announced that he had various personages to see in the next day or two, as well as further discussions with the king. Nothing had been said apparently about quarters for the three friends at the palace; but probably this could be arranged. They would find something to do with themselves in the days that followed, no doubt.

It was George who pointed out that their ship was on its way to Veere, to unload its cargo there, before it could take them all back to Scotland. Instead of them lingering on here at Whitehall with nothing particular to do, waiting, would it not be much better for them to go on to the Netherlands and visit this Veere where the wool went, where his two companions had not been before, and which might well be of advantage as well as of interest to them, rather than idling in London? They could pick up his lordship on the way back. It would take only three or four days, he thought.

Lauderdale was quite content with this. So he left them to it.

Their shipmaster said that they would sail at first light.

*   *   *

From London to Veere was no lengthy voyage, one hundred and fifty miles it was reckoned due eastwards, a quarter of this in the Thames estuary itself, a mere day and night's sailing in a westerly wind.

This proved to be an accurate assessment, and they rounded the tip of the Walcheren peninsula of Zeeland, and turned into the Oosterschelde channel in the early forenoon of two days later, to head westwards now up the long and winding waterway which separated North and South Beveland, eventually to reach their destination just before noon.

They found Veere to be no very large port and town, considering its importance to the wool trade and to Scotland. They landed at a quay flanking the main street, and, led by their skipper who knew the place well, were conducted, in only a few hundred yards, to two fine houses standing side by side, over the doorways of which they were surprised to see the blue and white saltire banners of St Andrew of Scotland flying. These they were told were Lammeken and Oliver Houses, tall four-storeyed residences built of brick, with stepped gables, and highly ornate arches above the windows and doors. The former, they were amused to learn, having the same origin of its name as had Lammermuir, indeed having a façade depicting a lamb in stone. In this house they were introduced to the present occupant, who proved to have a good Scots name, Arnold Cunningham, although he looked Dutch enough, of ample girth and wearing the rather odd silver front-pieces which they had already noticed men wearing at their crotches, distinctly emphasising their sex.

This man, Cunningham, who it seemed was a councillor of the town and indeed deputy burgomaster, greeted the unexpected visitors in friendly fashion, speaking to them in a heavily accented but fair Scots tongue. It seemed that his great-grandfather, Thomas Cunningham, had come to Veere as a wool merchant about a century before, and bought this house. There were many other Scots families, usually now intermarried with Dutch, resident in the town, and they tended to hold privileged positions, the present burgomaster having a Scots mother, he who, on advice, settled the annual price for Scots wool, the famous Staple. They even had their own legal system, and used their own chapel in the Grote Kerk, the principal church of the town.

Offered hospitality, the trio, with their shipmaster, were then taken next door to meet Meinherr Yssewijn, the present burgomaster. He was not in, but they were welcomed by his Scots-born wife, Mariot, who offered them more refreshment, a sonsy, laughing creature. She said that her husband would be back at any moment, and demanded to hear of what went on in Scotland now that Charles Stewart had regained his father's throne. He had dwelled, during his exile, at Breda, only fifty miles to the east of Veere, in the duchy of Brabant, and was known for his fondness for ladies! Her own people came here from Hawick two generations before.

Burgomaster Yssewijn did arrive soon thereafter, a great, hearty bear of a man, who seemed pleased and interested to see them when he heard that they came from Dunbar, and promptly offered them accommodation in this his house of Oliver. They would eat, he assured them, presently, but meantime he would conduct them round the town to meet some of the councillors and merchants who dealt with their fleeces. He announced that the Lammermuir coarse wool was likely to fetch a fair price this year, the demand for good felt in especial increasing. Carpeting was also becoming more popular for flooring and not only for wall-hangings.

So they were taken off to see Veere and some of its leading citizens; apparently they ate in mid-afternoon here. They had looked for cloth mills but saw none, only many great warehouses, as well as timber-yards. Apparently the wool was only stored here before being despatched to the milling centres such as Bergen op Zoom,

Eindhoven, Antwerp, and Dordrecht in especial for the coarses fibres.

They were taken to see the sheds where the curved pantiles, made of red local clay, were cast and baked, and which would constitute the cargo and ballast for their ship on its return voyage, those pantiles which had been used for long to roof so many Scots houses and cottages.

All this was interesting but scarcely valuable for the visitors. When they went back to Oliver House for the almost over-large meal provided, they asked whether it would be possible to go and inspect actual mills where the spinning and weaving was being done, and where they might learn skills and improvements so far unknown to them? Where were the nearest such?

Burgomaster Yssewijn said that the nearest, of any size and consequence, would be at Bergen op Zoom, a score of miles to the east. If his guests so wished, he could have them taken there next day. Barges were constantly carrying the imported wool thither. They could sail in one of these, and be back the next day if desired.

This offer was gratefully accepted.

The eating and drinking, all but feasting, went on into the early evening, growing the noisier the while; clearly the Dutch had hearty appetites. Thereafter a visit was paid to the Scots chapel in the Grote Kerk, where they were shown painted wooden statuettes, set in niches, representing former councillors, merchants, dyers and cloth exporters, all from Scotland. There were portraits on the walls also, something the visitors had never seen before in a church; so the Dutch were as artistic as they were industrious, for Oliver House and Lammeken House were also well provided with pictures.

Back to bed, then, with overloaded stomachs.

In the morning, after almost as substantial a breakfast as had been their previous meal, they were taken down to a different quayside, where many great barges were lined up, bows to shore. It seemed that almost all travel in this part of the Netherlands had to be by water, with channels, canals, islands and flooded polders, all at sea level, everywhere. Their host took them to one of these heavy, wide and low-set craft, already laden and waiting for them.

They cast off forthwith, the bargemaster, who spoke no English, being instructed by Yssewijn to bring them back next day from Bergen. He and his six-man crew clearly considered the Scots to be very strange characters, eyeing them frankly, and laughing, but not unkindly.

It made an interesting journey. The barge had short masts fore and aft. Square sails were hoisted, and the westerly breeze carried them along slowly but steadily. They wondered about coming back, since the wind would be in their faces, but they saw great oars, sweeps, tied up against the masts, so presumably these would be necessary.

The flatness of the country was very much brought home to them, the travellers used to hilly landscapes, the only features here rising up to catch the eye being church towers and steeples, windmills, tight clusters of houses round islanded farms, and the occasional large mansion, none looking like castles. It made somewhat monotonous viewing, but, they recognised, represented much labour and industry over the centuries in reclaiming it all from the prevailing water. Well might this area of the Netherlands be named Zeeland, the sea having covered it all once.

The Oosterschelde reached, up that wide river they turned, now going still more slowly, with a current for their two sails to counter – but this of course would help them on their return journey. Some ten miles of this, with the river widening still more into a great basin, taking them almost two hours; and they saw ahead of them the high buildings, towers and smoke of a city, Bergen op Zoom. The bay seemed to be formed by the joining of the other river, the Weesterschelde.

They landed at larger docks and piers than at Veere. The problem of language was now very much with them, and they sought out a churchman, these always apt to be among the best linguists. The Grote Kerk here was, as ever, very obvious, and at one of its manses they found a young Calvinist divine, called Cornelius, who could speak good English. He agreed to accompany them when he heard that James was a Puritan; his two friends did not mention Episcopalians or Catholics. He knew about the wool and cloth trade, his father having run a dye-house.

He took them to this in the first place, and they were rewarded by learning of the various colouring agents that different fibres and wools required, treatment varying, and the emphasis on the necessity of having all the grease and oil removed before the dyes could colour evenly.

Nearby was a mill powered by what he called a Saxony wheel, making something they had never seen but had heard of, called at home linsey woolsy, where a mixture of wool and linen fibres, the latter made from flax, created a fine cloth. The process they took note of, recognising its possible development in Scotland.

Other mills and manufactories demonstrated techniques new to them, in mixing fibres, varying thicknesses and smoothness and blending yarn for large varieties of cloths. They were particularly interested in the felting process, especially the non-woven method, which could be very useful for their coarsest wools, this achieved by stone rollers binding the layers. Another advantageous discovery was the blending of sundry fluids to make what the Dutch called *suint*, effective in the quicker extraction of the oil from fleeces, better than anything that they had at home. The last they visited was a tapestry-weaving mill which, although rather too ambitious for them to consider meantime, they could perhaps visualise for the future.

Altogether it proved to be a most rewarding tour of inspection, well worth the making.

Next day they returned to Veere in the same barge, now laden with cloth, after spending a comfortable night in

Cornelius's manse, and making a donation to church funds.

At Veere they found their ship, with its cargo of pantiles and wines, awaiting them. They were not long in setting sail for the Thames, much pleased with their visit to the Netherlands and liking the people, friendly, hospitable and amusing.

At London they had to wait for two days, for Lauderdale had gone with King Charles to Windsor. They occupied the time by inspecting the burned-out areas, and watching the work of restoration. They also attended a session of the House of Commons where, from a gallery, they compared the English procedure with their own, and this they discussed with the Chancellor when he rejoined them and their ship.

Then it was Dunbar for them, with much to tell their womenfolk as well as their mill operators.

20

Coming back as *Sir* James made quite an impact on the community, for knighting had been a very rare event in Scotland for long, Charles keeping his distance, his father involved in Cavalier wars in England, and the Cromwellian invasion. There were baronets, of course, a hereditary title using the style of Sir, but actual knights all but non-existent. James wished that he could have made Joanna Lady Stanfield – but he already had a wife, unfortunately.

The trio found that their milling ventures had proceeded satisfactorily in their absence. They promptly got busy in translating some of their new knowledge into action, in the first instance setting up improved dye-works, and the making of the Dutch *suint* for their fulling and washing plant. Liz and Helen were eager for them to try their hands at tapestry-weaving on a large scale; but that would have to wait meantime.

They found that Robert Blackwood had managed, by using Lauderdale's known interest, to obtain a contract to provide uniforms for the new national army. There had never been a standing army in Scotland hitherto, the kings of Scots dependent on the levies of their lords, lairds and chiefs, a not altogether satisfactory situation, for these were not always made available when required, and very much tied to seasonal demands at home such as harvesting, sowing, lambing and the like. But Rothes had used his influence, backed by Charles via Lauderdale, to set up the nucleus of a permanent force such as they had in England, fairly small numbers as yet because of the expense, these not concerned with rural pursuits. But they would grow.

And they needed uniforms. They were based on the traditional Highland Watches. Blackwood had gained this contract through the Merchant Company of Edinburgh; there were really no other contenders with sufficient home-made cloth as yet, and the New Mills product was much cheaper than imported material. So it was a notable step forward as to marketing. Much red dye was required, and substantial quality of cloth called for.

This all led up to a development envisaged for some time, indeed all but instituted already in an informal fashion: the founding of a merchant company of their own, with its shareholders and directors, Lauderdale's agreed share now being formally stated. Lawmen had to be involved in this, which was expensive; but undoubtedly it would all pay in the end. Sir James would be managing director, his two friends, with Blackwood, the other directors, with Joanna's son secretary.

This was something new for the woollen trade, arousing much interest in Edinburgh, sufficiently so for another order to be forthcoming, not large but quite prestigious: uniforms for the Edinburgh Town Guard.

Liz declared that it was all due to James's knighthood.

Another session of parliament took due notice of it all, and passed further legislation to enhance the cloth industry. All imports of cloth were now to be prohibited, fines to be imposed on offenders, parliament's encouragement given to new millers, in the border areas especially, this suiting Lauderdale. And, as a direct result of the trio's visit to the Low Countries, naturalisation offered to incomers, Netherlanders and Flemings, who would further teach Scots millers, these to have full citizenship. This last the friends and Lauderdale had discussed on their way home from London, the advantages having become very apparent.

James and Patrick were now quite prominent commissioners, Haddingtonshire never before having been so much to the fore in debate.

George, although all but offered a seat for southern Lothian, from Borthwick and Gorebridge right down to Stow on the Gala Water, still would not stand for parliament, preferring his family life, his hills and his sheep.

Scotland had a notable visitor later that year, none other than the king's brother, James, Duke of York and Albany, whom Charles sent up more or less to initiate the newly formed army, and make it a royal force, he himself, it was said, having vowed never to enter Scotland again after his humiliating treatment by the Covenant divines. James Stewart was a better-looking man than his brother, three years younger, formal and somewhat humourless, but more efficient and reliable and less extravagant. His exile, on his father's downfall, had been in France, not Protestant Netherlands, where his mother the queen had brought him up more or less as a Catholic, which in England now told against him. He was an effective soldier, and had joined the French army at the age of nineteen and served in four campaigns under Marshal Turenne with courage and ability, and later had commanded the right wing of the Spanish army at the Battle of the Dunes. He was now Lord High Admiral of England, and it was at his initiative that the English fleet had siezed the Dutch colony of New Amsterdam and called it New York. Hence his suitability to send to Scotland to oversee and advise on this new army.

He came as Lauderdale's guest at Lethington, and the earl invited the three friends to meet him there.

They found James of York somewhat stiff but not off-puttingly so and, strangely, sounding interested in their wool-milling activities, asking quite detailed questions as to methods, marketing and the impact on the community and nation. The founding of the joint-stock company and its advantages had him demanding chapter and verse as it were, he never having heard of such. When Lauderdale mentioned the requirement for guarantors, such as himself, Traquair and Tweeddale, the duke surprised them all by declaring that they could add *his* name as a guarantor;

185

after all, his royal brother had thought the undertaking worthy to be honoured by the knighthood.

Needless to say, this most unexpected support from the heir-presumptive to the throne had the trio much encouraged in their efforts. Undoubtedly it would make for further mill-building activity, encouraging others. Blackwood would make good use of this.

Next day, indeed, Lauderdale brought the duke to see the New Mills. He was clearly much impressed when he was shown the twenty looms now in operation, with the extra two being made for serges. When he heard that they now employed no fewer than two hundred and thirty workers, with cottages having to be built nearby to house them, he declared that this initiative should be copied in England. Hitherto Manchester had all but a monopoly in the wool trade, with mainly imported Spanish and Cypriot wool, merino; it should be expanded elsewhere, and sheep-rearing encouraged, this also to help the rural economy, especially in the largely neglected uplands. His dukedom had large lands in Yorkshire. He would see to this, personally.

At the royal departure the friends agreed that if he outlived his brother he would probably make a better monarch than Charles, despite the problem of his leanings towards the Catholics.

It was shortly after this heartening interlude that Patrick and George became aware that James was preoccupied with some matter other than two new projects they were considering: the setting up of new looms to make superfine cloths with the admixture of linen; and machinery to spin silk stockings, these now much in demand for men as well as women, *gentlemen* that is. He did not divulge to them what was on his mind; but Joanna told Liz. His wife and son and daughter-in-law were intending to leave their Yorkshire home to come up and join him in Scotland, this presumably because of his increasing prominence, wealth and the knighthood and royal approval. It seemed that James had sent them messages, not exactly forbidding this but seeking strongly to discourage them; but Lady Stanfield, as she now was, appeared to be determined on it. Small wonder that he was preoccupied; although he had said nothing his friends had long assumed that his marriage had been all but a disaster.

Joanna was much upset.

Another marriage, hopefully to be more happy, was interesting the friends that winter. Lauderdale's daughter Anne, whom they liked, was to wed their near neighbour, the newly succeeded Hay of Yester, Earl of Tweeddale, and great was the stir in Haddingtonshire, its two greatest families uniting. And it was a love-match, not just a suitable landed arrangement, as were so many marriages among the noble houses, so there was much rejoicing. Only, at the king's and his brother's suggestion, the wedding was to take place at Highgate, in London, where James of York had a palace, so that all could be honoured by the attendance of the monarch and his heir-presumptive, this an indication of the appreciation of the services of Lauderdale – however inconvenient for the two lovers. But it was in the nature of a royal command.

So a preliminary celebration was held at Lethington before the long journey down to London. The young people had to recognise that there were some disadvantages in being the objects of royal favour.

It was not long after the return of the newly-weds from England that James's fears were substantiated. In early March, Lady Stanfield, her son Philip and his young wife Margaret arrived by coach from Yorkshire at the house of Morham, announcing that they had come to stay. James broke the news to his friends next day, tight-lipped.

"Here is a sorry matter," he announced. "You may think me unkind, lacking in due care, in my duty to wife and son. But I have for long found them . . . averse. Mary was my father's choice for me, rather than my own. I was wed before coming of age, she a neighbour's daughter whom I knew but scarcely loved. I quickly learned the mistake of it. Perhaps I did not try sufficiently to make a success of the marriage, but she was . . . difficult. I chose, instead, to become a soldier. My uncle was in the parliamentary army against King Charles – our family was Puritan – and he gained me a lieutenancy therein. So I saw but little of Mary, and what I did I did not favour. So it may be that the fault was mine. And when she bore a son, I admit to wondering whether the child was mine. Blame me if you will. But the boy grew up with no love for me, nor I for him. It makes a sorry tale, I admit. But there it is. And now . . ."

They shook their heads over it all. What was there to say?

"Mary now sees me as a man of consequence, with moneys, and a knighthood, worthy to be with. Lady Stanfield! I begin to regret the knighthood. And she has already begun to change all at Morham. All Joanna's good arrangings . . ."

"You are master there still, James," Patrick said. "Show it. You, a colonel of Ironsides, who controlled a regiment and governed a county, control your wife and son. And, if so you wish, after a little time, send them back to Yorkshire."

"I can scarcely do that. She *is* my wife, Philip my son. If they wish to stay with me here, how can I dismiss them?"

"If you show them that they are not welcome, and you provide for them elsewhere, and where they have lived all these years, could they refuse?" George put to him. "You are a man of authority. Make that clear to them."

"Would *you* send your family away? If you were not at one with them?"

The other two exchanged questioning glances, unable to conceive the situation with their own happy marriages.

"Perhaps they will themselves choose to go," was the

best that George could say. "When they perceive that they are not wanted. That you do not make them part of your life here."

"When it is known that I have a wife and son with me now, they will be invited to houses. I cannot announce to all that I find them a trial . . ."

His friends saw that.

"Joanna . . . ?" Patrick wondered.

"Aye, well may you ask! I know not what to do there. *She* means much to me . . ."

James was in no hurry for the others to meet the newcomers; and they did not visit Morham House meantime. But some two weeks later the Tweeddales held a party at Yester Castle, and Lady Stanfield, son and daughter-in-law were invited along with James, as were Patrick and George with their wives, also Joanna. So all met.

And it very promptly became clear to most there present why James Stanfield had for so long lived apart from his wife and son. Mary Stanfield was quite a striking-looking woman, in a rather masculine fashion, but with what Liz described later as the eyes of a shrew, penetrating, critical, demanding, to match the loudness of her voice and her assertiveness. And Philip was very much her son, pleased with himself, arrogant of bearing and quickly distinguishing himself by drinking too much and revealing the effects thereof. His wife appeared to be a quiet, withdrawn girl, as well she might in that company.

Undoubtedly descriptions of this would be all around the county without delay.

"What are we to do about this?" Liz wondered, with Helen, as they left the party. "We cannot completely ignore the woman, refuse ever to visit Morham. We want to see much of James. We cannot always invite him to our houses without his wife."

"I suppose that we must invite her to visit, at least once. And if we do not get on, as seems likely, not ask her back," Helen said. "We do not need to have that puppy of a son!"

Joanna remained very silent.

At least Mary Stanfield and Philip did not trouble them at the New Mills, keeping their distance, no doubt judging such links with trade and industry as beneath their dignity as landed folk.

Actually the trio themselves were not having to spend so much time at the mills now, for they had appointed a very effective manager there, one Humphrey Spurway, a Yorkshireman who had trained at Manchester and was a recognised expert in cloth manufacture. They paid him well, gave him shares in the company, and were able to leave most of the mill-running to him.

At the next quarterly company meeting, it was announced that one year's turnover had amounted to no less than £55,823, with costs of £38,900, producing a profit of £16,923, a notable achievement. Even Lauderdale was impressed.

Helen was the first to invite Mary Stanfield and son to Monkrigg, close neighbours as they now were. The visit could hardly be called a success, but with the young family present and lively, and the Elibanks helping – Joanna not invited, judiciously – the less than welcome guests were kept approximately in their places, even though Mary made it obvious that she resented much of their hosts' attentions being paid to her daughter-in-law. Duty was done.

The friends had an upset shortly thereafter. One of their own shareholders in a small way, a cloth-dealer and member of Edinburgh's Merchant Company, was discovered to have imported secretly quite a quantity of foreign cloth, contrary to parliament's orders. Nothing would do but that he must be prosecuted therefor, an example to be made. He was duly tried, found guilty, and fined four hundred pounds, and the cloth itself ordered to be burned by the public hangman. This seemed a somewhat extreme punishment to the three friends, as to others; but it might help to prevent further such offences.

Lauderdale sought aid in finding an efficient and reliable manager, such as Spurway, to oversee his mills, since he could by no means do so adequately himself. For, apart from his duties in governing Scotland, with Rothes, he was being required to spend an ever increasing proportion of his time in London. The king had largely fallen out with his parliament there, over his extravagances and constant calls for moneys, his mistresses particularly costing him dear, his court the most expensive that the land had ever known. So he was seeking to rule the country without parliament, and had appointed what amounted to a five-man government. This was becoming known as the Cabal – cabals being small secret societies – and it so happened that the five lords involved had names that could be ordered to form the letters of that word. These were Clifford, Arlington, Buckingham, Ashley-Cooper (that was Shaftesbury) and Lauderdale himself. So that man was now helping to rule England as well as Scotland, an extraordinary situation. His wife and daughter saw little of him.

And England was proving more difficult to govern than was the northern kingdom. Charles had made what he intended was a secret alliance with France, winning a pension thereby from Louis the Fourteenth, as he had done when exiled Prince of Wales in Breda; this greatly offended not only the parliament when it leaked out, but much of the Protestant population, who now were beginning to believe that their monarch was turning towards Catholicism, like his brother York, and, of course, his wife Catherine of Portugal, and indeed most of his mistresses. Shaftesbury, who was a strong Protestant – he had fought under Cromwell – was now proposing that the Duke of Buccleuch and Monmouth, Protestant himself, should be acknowledged as legitimate, and made heir to the throne in place of York, a situation which would make the position of Queen Catherine extraordinary indeed, if not impossible to be maintained. That poor woman had produced no offspring, and was quite overshadowed at court by all the other and better-looking women, so Shaftesbury suggested that she could be dispensed with. But Charles himself was said to be against this, for Catherine had brought him large possessions in India, including Bombay, colonised by the Portuguese, and contributing some of the wealth he so badly needed, this as part of her dowry. Protestant England's allegiance to its monarch was much strained, and the Cabal's task was no easy one. So Lauderdale became all but resident in London, and Rothes was more or less left to rule Scotland. That man also preferred to do this with as little aid from parliament as was possible, so Patrick and James were but little called upon in that respect at least.

But they had a sufficiency to keep them busy otherwise. They were, in effect, seeking to make the Borderland the main weaving area of Scotland, especially the towns of Hawick, Selkirk, Galashiels and Peebles, to rival Manchester in the south; and in consequence greatly increased sheep-rearing was required. George took on responsibility for this, his task to convince landowners that their hills should be used for the pasture of flocks instead of just occasional hunting and hawking over.

The trio had become ambassadors for trade, industry and employment and the better use of land.

21

Involvement in all this was not helped, for James Stanfield, by the activities of his son. Philip was rapidly making
a name for himself, much otherwise from that of his father.
Apart from frequently getting drunk and misbehaving
himself socially, he drew attention on a wider front. At
a church service at Morham he jumped up and abused the
minister, the Reverend John Bell, this before all, declaring
him a clown and a hypocrite, to the shame and wrath of Sir
James. And when his father dragged him outside, there
and then, shouted that he was being persecuted all the time
by this man, cursing him. His mother preserved stiff
features in the pew, and the daughter-in-law shed silent
tears.

The next evening the young man went into his father's
kitchen and ordered the servants there to join him in
drinking downfall and confusion to the king, the Pope
and Chancellor Lauderdale. A maid ran upstairs to inform
Sir James, who had to come and remove his son. This sort
of behaviour went on and greatly worried his sire; and
more than worried him because of its unseemliness, for he
revealed to his friends that he had had to pay already no
less than five thousand merks of debts which Philip had
run up.

At length James decided to get rid of the young man, at
least temporarily, by sending him to St Andrews University, where it was ordered that he would be put under
strict discipline. His education had admittedly been somewhat neglected.

Relief at Morham meantime.

With Lauderdale in London and Rothes supreme in Scotland, the former chose the Earl of Tweeddale to be his representative and lieutenant to try to keep the latter in some sort of order, for, despite the king's friendship with that man, a fellow-roysterer and womaniser, Lauderdale did not greatly approve of him nor entirely trust him. And Tweeddale now being close to the trio, not only in his residence at Yester and the Lammermuir sheep-raising, but over the cloth industry of which he had perceived the opportunities for his Tweedside properties, was establishing mills there. So the friends found themselves in some measure involved in national affairs, otherwise than by their industry, through this connection, even although there were little or no parliamentary calls upon them. They did not want to get wrong with Rothes, however, and had to tread somewhat warily in this respect, for whatever Lauderdale's opinion of him he was in a very strong position as Lord President of the Council, Lord Privy Seal, High Treasurer and commander-in-chief of this new Scots army. Moreover, his niece was the Duchess of Buccleuch and Monmouth, and one of his two daughters married to Montrose's son, the second marquis.

Problems could follow in the wake of becoming fairly influential in affairs.

Compared with the situation in England, Scotland was relatively peaceful. But there was still discontent in both realms in matters of religion. Charles the First's imposition of episcopalianism on the Scots Church, so strongly Presbyterian, still rankled. And although his son was less interested in such, the bishops still held sway – one of the reasons why Rothes was dispensing with parliamentary sittings, for the said bishops had seats therein. And Archbishop Sharp of St Andrews, the Primate, was less than moderate or tactful, and highly unpopular with most Scots. Lauderdale sent word to Tweeddale to keep an eye on him, as well as on Rothes – both enemies of each other incidentally. With George a Catholic, James a Puritan and Patrick an Episcopalian, the friends certainly did not want to get involved in religious disputes, and told Tweeddale so.

That England was not immune from such became very evident that summer. James, Duke of York finally made his position clear by announcing his commitment to the Roman Catholic Church – which had the archbishops and prelates railing against him and declaring that he was quite unfit to be the heir to the throne, and Defender of the Faith of their Protestant realm. This forced Charles to announce that his brother must continue to accept the Anglican sacraments and take communion and attend episcopalian worship frequently, and his two daughters to be reared as Protestants. This contented nobody. The move to make Monmouth, as he was now being described in the south, omitting the Buccleuch as Scotch and unpronounceable, the heir-presumptive, grew.

In Scotland, oddly enough, the unpopular, all but despised bishops were less difficult, and held in less awe and watchfulness than were the dedicated and stern Presbyterian and Covenant divines. None so long before, an assembly of the latter, at St Andrews, had announced authoritatively that all persons who could not recite the Apostles' Creed, the Lord's Prayer and the Ten Commandments were to be debarred from matrimony and other rights; and that the Doxology was not to be used. Magistrates and bailies were to be instructed to send offenders to prison, or chain them in irons in public places, employers to chastise their servants for using profane language, and stools of repentance were to be set up in every kirk. The new bishops, on the other hand, made no such demands on the populace, although they were being called "the Pope's harbingers" and the "servants of the Roman beast", and as such were execrated. However, they made no effort, save in Sharp's speeches, to alter the Kirk's harsh rules, however much they scoffed at them, their regime superficial, almost casual; indeed it was suggested by their Presbyterian opponents that many of them were themselves unable to recite the said Creed and Commandments, for undoubtedly some were of little or no education, religious or otherwise, winning their appointments by or through powerful friends or by payment of money. There was little or no attempt to interfere with what might be termed the courts of the Kirk Sessions and Presbyteries, so long as their own Diocesan and Provincial Synods issued all authoritative statements and dispensed patronage, and had the support of the Privy Council in London, with orders from the monarchy. It all made a sorry, indeed ridiculous situation for Christ's religion of faith, hope and love in Scotland. But it did not result in war or state persecution, with Rothes more or less ignoring both sides, and determined to keep Archbishop Sharp in his place.

Thus it was, at least, until that November, when the situation became changed, with a new arrival from the south. He was, however, no southerner, although called the Muscovy General, but came from the west of Lothian, General Thomas Dalyell of the Binns, near to Linlithgow. He came, at the Cabal's direction – presumably Lauderdale outvoted thereon, for this was not like his policies – to impose episcopal rule in Scotland, in practice rather than just in name, and to strengthen Archbishop Sharp's hand. He was a notable and effective soldier who had learned his trade in the Russian wars, where ruthlessness was the rule. Many in Scotland were disconcerted by his arrival, for he was to take over the command of their new army from Rothes.

Muscovy Tam, as he was known, did not take long to demonstrate his authority and ability, and he started to do so much too near home for the trio at Haddington, or for Tweeddale. He announced, from Edinburgh, that the bishops had the rule in all Church matters, and that anyone who did not abide by their orders and regulations would be guilty, not only of sacrilege and impiety but of treason against the monarchy, and would be treated accordingly, and put down without mercy – this in despite of Rothes with all his high offices. And he emphasised his message with the arrival of a regiment of trained dragoons from England to toughen and lead the Scots soldiery just in case they were less enthusiastic.

This declaration, needless to say, aroused uproar in Scotland, with the Covenanting divines leading the denunciations and urging all good and true worshippers of God to rise against the wicked newcomers and agents of Satan, and to take to arms if necessary to protect the faith.

All over the land the Presbyterians and Covenanters rose to the call in furious clamour and fist-shaking. Suddenly all was changed on the national scene, Rothes apparently helpless, however angered.

So there were gatherings of militant faithful near and far, to meet the challenge, in their thousands, however unprovided with weapons other than sickles and axes and clubs, some near enough to Haddington and Edinburgh and Linlithgow itself, to make clear to this emissary from London, Lothian laird as he might be, that he was to be sent back where he came from, if not deservedly slain in the process. Loyalty to the restored monarchy sank to its lowest.

The three friends feared the worst, and with their military experience dreaded the outcome, untrained and all but unarmed multitudes facing professional cavalrymen. It did not sound like Charles Stewart's decision and policy, any more than Lauderdale's.

Roused folk from Haddingtonshire and the rest of Lothian flocked to the Edinburgh area to make clear their wrath. The trio felt almost like joining them, to contribute some veteran leadership, but recognised that this was not the way forward, although many of their own mill workers were joining the would-be fighters.

They heard that the combatants were gathering at the Burgh Muir of Edinburgh, the traditional assembly-point for Scottish armies, but no suitable place for a battle, especially against mounted opponents, and so close to where Dalyell would be likely to be marshalling his own forces. But it seemed that there were at least some cooler heads among the enthusiasts, for a move was made to where the dragoons and horse-soldiers would be less advantageously placed, this on the slopes of the Pentland Hills none so far off, where uneven ground, outcropping rocks, burn-channels and marshy land would much hamper cavalry. There, as Bruce and Wallace had taught their fellow-countrymen, and Montrose more recently demonstrated, they could use the terrain to fight for them. General Dalyell had raised the Royal Scots Greys, one of the finest regiments of the royal army, but even he would find the Pentlands off-putting.

That man was, of course, watching all from Edinburgh Castle, and no doubt determined to make an example of these rebels, as he called them, for all others to see.

That first evening, so as not to be observed by the general's scouts, the Covenanters moved south-westerly in the November dark, and got as far as Colinton, where they settled for the rest of the night in the local church graveyard, here to wait for reinforcements coming from the west to join them, of which they had had word. They posted watchers to look for and lead in the newcomers, of which no great numbers arrived. And at first light they all headed for the nearby hills, now about nine hundred strong.

Dalyell's scouts were equally active however, and did not fail to locate their targets. So the cavalry was on the move also, and they moved much more swiftly than did the footmen.

The Covenanters did manage to reach the hillsides just ahead of their foes, on rocky ground below the peak called Allermuir, one of the major summits, and here, a little way up, they turned to face the challenge, ministers with them calling down the wrath of the Almighty on the enemy. But Dalyell, despite outnumbering them by at least three to one, perceived that the terrain was very unfavourable for horses, and his men were unused to fighting on foot. He deployed his force in a long line, and waited, but sent a troop westwards to seek access to the upper slopes where the ground was less broken and rock-strewn, and where these might get over and up and so move behind the enemy.

Seeing this last, the Covenant leaders recognised the danger, and took the decision to move also, and in the opposite, easterly direction, for it so happened that the next hill in the chain was Caerketton, notable as the most steep and scree-sided of all the range, where no horsemen, however determined, would be able to ride, even men on foot, like themselves, stumbling and having to pick their way.

The general turned his long line eastwards also, to maintain the threat.

So the two forces moved on parallel. But presently Dalyell sent another troop on ahead, obviously to prospect the ground beyond, where they might be able to find grassy slopes for cavalry to climb, a worry again for the footmen. Those who came from the Edinburgh area knew that after Caerketton the hills became much less steep and stony, and moreover swung round southwards in a great bend. Possibly horsemen could make use of these. Yet they themselves could scarcely remain standing on this steep craggy hill, with the risk of the two enemy detachments getting up on to the higher ground at their backs and dismounting to descend upon them.

So it meant on and on, to round that shoulder of the eastermost hill, at what indeed was known as Hillend, and so southwards towards the opening of the deep and major valley of Glencorse, still with General Tam shadowing them.

Worried that the first detachment of troopers could get over the topmost Pentland ridge and down this glen upon them, the Covenanters sought to cross the valley before this could happen, and get up on to the next major summit, named Turnhouse Hill, beyond, where again there was somewhat broken ground which might favour them, and with the long series of lofty heights ahead, ever southwards. It was their hope that this delaying strategy would allow reinforcements to reach them from the west where it was known that the faithful were assembling in large numbers. They had, indeed, expected to be joined by a force from north-east Lanarkshire before ever they left Colinton; there were hosts rising all over the land. If they could avoid actual battle until some numbers of these arrived . . .

They did get across this glen of the Corse Burn and were climbing the slopes beyond when, ahead of them, they saw horsemen on a minor grassy ridge – so there evidently was ground possible for horses there. This alarming recognition forced them to turn right-handed and climb. A large slantwise hollow, a corrie, lay between them and that ridge. This could be a grave danger and must be avoided.

A danger it was proved to be, for soon they saw Dalyell's main force moving up into it, not in the centre but on the flank nearest them. This compelled them to turn and climb higher still; that is, until there, on the topmost skyline, they saw more mounted figures, no doubt that first detachment sent westwards and now having circled round over the intervening high ground behind them.

So it was confrontation, an end to stalling and avoiding and manoeuvring. If they were to turn back now, these topmost troopers would be able to charge down on them on this smoother stretch. Ahead was the main enemy force. And half right the other detachment. They were caught on this lip of the corrie. Nothing for it but to stand and fight – and hope!

Their leaders chose what they judged was the best spot they could see, to form up into a tight circle, this with those with scythes and staves on the perimeter, weapons pointing outwards as some sort of threat to horses, those with

axes, clubs and dirks behind, some men with knives
kneeling at the front, to slash up at horses' bellies. It
was the best they could do.

What happened thereafter was all but predictable, despite the divines' assurance that God on high was with
them. The horsemen came upon them in their hundreds,
since only such numbers could engage the circle at one
time, while the others waited their turn, troop after troop,
these protected by steel helmets and breastplates, armed
with long lances and swords, to wheel round and round the
tight formation, thrusting, slicing and slaying, their comrades waiting to replace them in attack. It could not last; no
battle, more of a massacre. The Covenanters sought to
fight, but were scarcely able to do so in their circumstances, and died bravely. Before long escape did become
the priority for many, although this was not easy since they
could be chased by the large numbers of troopers waiting
more or less idle.

Disaster. The corrie was called Rullion Green.

Word of it all reached Haddington in due course, told by
some of the mill-hands who had managed to make their
escape. How many had been slain was guesswork, possibly
one-third of the host, including some divines.

Reports that followed were more detailed and coherent.
Dalyell, now being termed Bluidy Tam, further demonstrated his Russian training. Many captives were executed,
some tortured first, ten Edinburgh victims hung on one
single gibbet. Others were deliberately sent under trooper
guards to their own homes, to be hanged at their house
doors in front of their wives and families. All who survived
this were promptly shipped off to Barbados as slaves for
the sugar plantations.

Scotland seethed as possibly seldom before. Everywhere
men vented their fury. The Kirk preached fire and vengeance from every pulpit. Even some of the bishops
protested at the barbarity, although not Sharp. In the
south-west especially, Dumfries-shire, Galloway and Ayr-

shire, hosts rose in such arms as could be contrived. At
Brig of Doon, in their area, a group of soldiery was
attacked and defeated, the victors marching on to Lanark,
where the Covenant was renewed, to fierce acclaim.

The friends were appalled. Here was shame, wickedness
and sheerest folly also, the reverse of all good and fair and
wise government. Here were they, a Puritan, an Episcopalian and a Catholic, working to create industry, employment and prosperity in the land; and this was London's
policy, allegedly in the name of religion! Was the monarch
behind it? Surely not. Was Lauderdale, a Presbyterian
himself? Equally unlikely. The Cabal, then, without the L.
Fools, and worse. Something must be done. Rothes
seemed to be helpless, with this Dalyell in command of
the army. Was there anything that reasonable and honest
men could do? Parliament? Scotland's parliament was
there to govern. But it now seldom met. Themselves,
two of them were commissioners, members. And Lauderdale was the Chancellor, and friendly towards them. A call,
an urgent call to Lauderdale for parliament to act. One of
them or two, presumably Patrick and George, could sail
down to London . . .

22

The pair did not have so to do. Lauderdale himself arrived back in Scotland, it seemed at the urgent behest of Rothes. Hearing that he was at Lethington, the trio wasted no time in seeking him there.

They found John Maitland an angry man, almost as upset about the situation as they were themselves.

"Think you that I am a witless idiot!" he demanded, on their protests. "It is my sorrow that I have to seem to work with those fools, Shaftesbury, Clifford and the rest, men blind to what should be evident, blind to justice, wisdom and statecraft. To them, Scotland is but a far-off place of all but savages, disturbers of the peace, who must be taught by whatever means is necessary that London's will has to prevail. *I* am one against four. And they have many who support them, in order to gain positions of power and privilege."

"But – the king?" Patrick asked. "Charles, what of him? He is no fool. Surely he knows better? His grandsire was King of Scots before he moved south. Charles is a Stewart. And King James was no bishops' man."

"It is said that he has vowed never to return to Scotland again, after the way the ministers treated him," George added. "Can he be so against his Scotland?"

"He does not love the Covenanters, no," Lauderdale agreed. "But he is not a harsh man. He is ever at odds with his English parliament, which refuses him moneys. They claim that he is extravagant – as he is. His women cost him dear. But there are worse failings in a king."

"It was not Charles who sent up Dalyell?"

"No. That was Shaftesbury and Buckingham. I was much against it, for the man has the reputation for cruelty, however good a general. But I was outvoted."

"So now what?" James wondered. "Can you get rid of him?"

"That is what I have come back to gain, if I can. Parliament's authority to send him back. Rothes, I say, has been remiss in not calling sittings of parliament."

"There will be outright civil war in Scotland if the Muscovy Beast is not sent away," Patrick said. "It is none so far off that now. What of parliament?"

"Aye, only parliament can order it, I judge. *I* cannot."

"This of Rothes and parliaments. He mislikes having all these bishops sitting in it, as of right."

"But there are not enough of them to outvote the rest." That was George.

"No. But they have undue influence. On account of their ability to promote their supporters to strong positions, and to the holding of properties which they took over from the outed ministers of the Kirk. That gives them undue power."

"What, then?" James argued. "Would not many who oppose the bishops, which represents the great majority in the land, surely, but do not always attend sittings, lords in especial, and having to come from afar, come now if it were known that this parliament was called to get rid of Dalyell? Would not that bring them?"

"That is my hope. Time must be given, therefore, that all may learn, and sieze the opportunity. The long-standing forty days' notice ought to be sufficient. But . . ."

The notice of this assembly was indeed issued promptly, far and wide, and no secret made of the parliament's objective.

Archbishop Sharp quickly made his own announcements. He declared that even moderate Presbyterianism could not be consistent with the king's interests – he who himself had been a Presbyterian divine. He denounced the leading Covenant ministers, Guthrie, Gillespie and Rutherford, as wicked and pernicious protesters and deceivers of the people, and went so far as to say that the Earl of Lauderdale was now offering allegiance to the Episcopal Church and Liturgy, having attended services in the court chapel at Whitehall with loud Amens. He also demonstrated his own influence by announcing that he was recommending the Reverend Robert Baillie, a former Covenanting minister, to be the new Principal of Glasgow University, indication of the value of supporting an archbishop. A state of war was now in evidence between him and Lauderdale and Rothes, as the nation waited for its long-delayed parliament. Dalyell meantime was busy with his hangings and banishings.

Lauderdale, with his seat of Lethington, at least spared Haddingtonshire the general's attentions.

The parliament met at last, in Edinburgh Castle, and was attended by almost a record turn-out, all factions concerned to have their fullest representation, this of course including the bishops. George, Helen, Liz and Joanna were in the crowded gallery watching, but Lady Stanfield was not present.

An interesting start, surprising for many, was the Lord Lyon King of Arms' announcement that His Grace the King had reversed the roles of the Earls of Rothes and Lauderdale, the latter now being Lord High Commissioner, as representing the crown, and the former as Chancellor to conduct the business. Eyebrows were raised, for this was some sort of demotion for Rothes. But at least these two were known to be equally against the bishops.

Lauderdale then greeted all, in the name of the monarch, and declared that His Grace was concerned over the recent troubles and bloodshed in Scotland, and was determined that there should be an end to this, and peace prevail in his northern kingdom. There was much business to occupy this parliament, which almost certainly would take more

205

than the one day. But the first priority was this of peace and harmony being restored. He called upon the Lord Chancellor to initiate the proceedings with that concern.

Rothes was nothing loth, whatever his feelings about no longer being High Commissioner. He announced that His Grace's wishes for peace and an end to fighting and savagery would undoubtedly be echoed by most there present, and that he, Rothes, advocated a motion condemning the actions of the armed forces, with the aid of English dragoons under General Dalyell, in taking armed action against loyal Presbyterian subjects of the king, and outrageously treating the survivors of battle. He proposed . . .

He got no further, his voice drowned by the loud cheering of the great majority in the hall. He allowed this to continue for quite some time, shouts, accusations and demands intermingled, before he tapped his gavel for order and silence. Then he called upon one of the commissioners to put forward a motion to bring into effect the king's and the nation's wishes.

Men jumped to their feet throughout the assembly, hands raised. Rothes, smoothing his chin, pointed to one of these at the front of the earls' benches, the elderly Cunningham, Earl of Glencairn, a former Chancellor, this undoubtedly arranged beforehand.

"My lord Chancellor, I, Glencairn, move that this parliament condemns the wicked assaults on the freedom of so many in this nation to worship God as they wish, this at the decision of English leaders to send troops up to Scotland. And the appointment of General Thomas Dalyell as commander of the Scottish forces. Also the said general's attacks on members and supporters of the Kirk in armed conflict, with the shameful hangings and slayings of survivors. And I move that the said General Dalyell be prevented from using any further such malice to our fellow-countrymen by sending him back to London and those who despatched him here. I so move."

Cries of agreement from all around greeted that.

"Is that motion seconded?" Rothes asked.

Seconders innumerable rose, and the Chancellor did not trouble to select any one individual.

"Is there any contrary motion?" he demanded.

Archbishop James Sharp rose from the clerics' benches. "I move that the motion be rejected," he announced. "I say . . ." He got no further before his voice was lost in the outcry.

Rothes again permitted the clamour to go on and on, before holding up his hand for quiet. "This is a parliament not a fairground!" he declared. "All relevant representations must be made and heard. The vote decides, not shoutings. My lord Archbishop . . . ?"

That heavy-jowled and portly man repeated, "I move rejection of the motion. The episcopal form of worship is by law established as the national Church of this land, and I speak as its representative. In worship, as in all else, discipline must be maintained . . ."

Again Rothes had to raise hand and gavel for quiet.

"If men rise in arms against the Church they must be taught their fault. General Dalyell did no more than his duty in so teaching these dissenters. The necessary lesson had to be given, to prevent other such risings of the disaffected . . ."

This time, when the speaker's words were lost in the hubbub, Rothes turned to look at Lauderdale, shrugging.

From the throne that man rose, and was able to gain approximate quiet. "If this unseemly din does not cease, I will have no option but to adjourn this session," he declared. "Order must prevail if the parliament's decisions are to be valid. Motions for and against must be heard and voted upon." He turned. "Are you finished, my lord Archbishop?"

"I move, my lord, that the motion be rejected. As is my right."

"And is *your* motion seconded?"

"I second," Archbishop Burnet of Glasgow said, to murmurs of agreement from the other prelates and a few of their supporters throughout the hall – but only a few.

"Then I call a vote. For and against the first motion of my lord of Glencairn." The Chancellor did not add that it was scarcely necessary.

Normally the vote on the counter-motion was counted first, but with fully three-quarters of those in favour already on their feet and shouting for Glencairn, there was little point in going through the counting process. The decision was obvious to all.

"I declare the motion carried and by a large majority," Rothes tried to announce, but could not be heard in the uproar.

The hall seethed, mainly in triumph but with some anger among it. There was much gesticulation, fist-shaking and back-slapping. Some pointing also, at the bishops' benches, and this last had the effect of causing some of the prelates to hurry from the hall.

In recognition of it all, and its effect on the further deliberations, Lauderdale had one of the Lord Lyon's adherents blow a blast of his trumpet, and in the brief subsequent hush he declared that he was adjourning the session for one hour. Business would resume thereafter. Then he left the throne.

Patrick and James made their way through the excited, chattering crowd to climb to the gallery, where George and the ladies expressed their own satisfaction in the situation, Liz wanting to know what would happen now, not in the resumed parliamentary debate but on the national scene. How would Dalyell take this?

None could answer that with any confidence. But surely the will of the Scots parliament must prevail in Scotland. The fact that the general was himself a Scots laird did rather complicate the issue.

When, after the interval, the session was resumed, it was

noticeable that almost half of the former attendance had absented itself, some of the bishops included. Clearly that vote had been the reason for the large turn-out, and now many felt that duty was done, and celebration or otherwise elsewhere the order of the day.

Lauderdale, as he reopened debate, did announce that General Dalyell would be officially informed of the decision and ordered to return to London, relinquishing his command, and to take his dragoons regiment with him – this to more cheers. Then he handed over to the Chancellor again, to proceed with the agenda.

The first item thereon had some relevance to what had gone before. It was concerned with the restoration to their parishes of many of the so-called "outed" nonconformist ministers who had been dismissed by the archbishops. Needless to say this was strongly resisted by Sharp, Burnet and others, but they were unable to carry the day. Hay, Earl of Tweeddale, who had been primed by Lauderdale, proposed that an Act of Indulgence be passed, reinstating the said divines, or such as so desired and had not pursued other activities. Many had even founded new congregations which worshipped in various locations other than churches, barns and houses, often out of doors on hillsides and moorlands where they could escape persecution, these now being named conventicles, this especially in the south-west.

This over, the less controversial but necessary normal business of parliament was commenced, imposition of new taxation, appointments to offices, reports by county and burgh commissioners, trade terms – on this occasion, nothing on the cloth industry – and the like, all of which took considerable time. By no means finished with these, Lauderdale presently adjourned the meeting until the morrow, to the relief of most, especially those up in the gallery, and all could leave.

Next day they learned that Dalyell had been promptly informed of his dismissal, and had as promptly refused to accept it, declaring that his appointment had been made in the king's name, and until the king himself withdrew it, he remained in command of the Scots army. This announcement, of course, created major upset and confusion, in parliament and nation, but also among the armed forces themselves, for most of the soldiery were good and loyal Scots, and prepared to abide by their parliament's decision. So there was chaos in the ranks. The general consequently withdrew to his estate of the Binns, some eighteen miles west of Edinburgh, with the English dragoons, and there remained: an extraordinary situation indeed.

How to get rid of Bluidy Tam, force out of the question? Lauderdale discussed this with the three friends as they rode back to Haddington. It seemed that there was nothing for it but for him to go back to London to try to exert pressure. The Cabal, who had sent the man up here, almost certainly would not order him back. So only Charles could do that. He, Lauderdale, must try to convince the monarch that this was necessary, none so easy probably with a king who resented the treatment he had received at the hands of the Covenanters, and was by no means happy about his northern realm; and moreover was head of the Episcopal Church of England.

Had his brother James of York been on the throne, an acknowledged Catholic, things might have been different, George observed.

James Stanfield made a suggestion. Suppose King Charles was to declare himself head, sovereign, of the Episcopal Church in Scotland, as he was in England? This had never been done before. No one would be in a position to deny it, least of all Sharp and the other bishops. If this was effected, in his office of Lord High Commissioner, representing the crown, would not that put his lordship in a position to all but dominate the prelates? It might not get rid of Dalyell, but it would help to restrain the archbishops, and, a Presbyterian himself, lessen the conflict between the two contending factions of God's Church.

That was worth thinking over. They all wished Lauderdale well on his difficult mission. The trio saw themselves as now getting involved in more than the wool and cloth trade . . .

23

While Lauderdale was gone, James had a further upset over his son Philip. That unruly young man was expelled from St Andrews University and sent home. He had, during a church service, not only interrupted the sermon with cursings but thrown something at the preacher when rebuked. His father was dismayed and humiliated. What had he done to deserve a son like this? And what to do with the offender now?

George suggested sending him up into the Lammermuirs to aid the shepherds. It was heather-burning time, and the sheep had to be herded and kept well clear of the burning, demanding much watching and attention. He might, with his fiery temperament, quite enjoy the actual burning process and keeping the fires under control.

His father doubted whether Philip would go, and if he went, stay. Or do what he was told by the shepherds.

Patrick proposed that he should be sent back to Yorkshire, in theory to take charge of the small mill there, however unpopular he might be with the present manager and workers. Some feeling of authority might possibly help his behaviour. He did not add that it might be beneficial to send his mother back with him. And, of course, the young wife, poor creature.

It was decided to try the heather-burning first. George would take him up, and give him into the charge of the head shepherd.

Lauderdale arrived back sooner than expected from London. And he came with surprising and excellent news. He had persuaded the king to recall Dalyell, dismissing him from the position of commander-in-chief in Scotland. Not only that, but he was going to appoint his brother, James, Duke of York, to replace him in charge of the Scots armed forces. He was already Lord High Admiral of the United Kingdom; now he would act general as well. He would dwell in Scotland, as all but viceroy; but he would not replace Lauderdale as High Commissioner to parliament.

This greatly cheered his hearers and, when it was known, the nation at large, if not the prelacy. The duke was well regarded, despite his Catholic leanings, a steady and reliable character; and his position as heir to the throne made him almost unchallengeable. The Muscovy Beast could not contest his authority.

Lauderdale also announced that he had obtained Charles's consent to be named Head of the Episcopal Church in Scotland. He would call a parliament to confirm this new situation, and to assure the commissioners that the effect would be favourable to the Presbyterian cause, with himself as the monarch's official representative.

Altogether, developments were seen as advantageous for the great majority, and the earl much praised.

The parliament that followed in due course made this very evident, passing the Assertory Act as it was called, establishing the king as head of the Episcopalian Church, as he was in England, the bishops in no position to oppose it, whatever powers it conferred on the High Commissioner to use against them. Representatives of the Presbyterians and Covenanters declared that *their* Kirk had no other head but Jesus Christ; but this did not prevent them from agreeing to the Act.

The parliament also passed a motion to welcome officially the Duke of York's coming as commander-in-chief, and a committee was appointed to arrange an official reception at the border. Patrick and James were there and then nominated to attend at this, the duke being known to favour their enterprise.

All awaited the great day, General Dalyell no doubt with very mixed feelings.

Word came that the Duke of York was setting out for Scotland, and urgent were the preparations made to greet him at Berwick-upon-Tweed, Lauderdale and Rothes to head the large company, even the new Archbishop of Glasgow, a worthy and moderate prelate, to be one of the welcomers. Patrick and James, as commissioners, joined the company at Haddington, and took George along with them. Over two hundred of the great company rode southwards, and being joined by others from the Merse and Middle March as they went, Hepburns, Homes, Kerrs, Swintons and the like.

By Colbrandspath, Pease Dean and Ayton they went. With the Duke of York known as the reason for their visit, they had no difficulty in gaining acceptance at English-held Berwick overnight. The duke was reported to be at Newcastle-upon-Tyne. Some actually spent the night in Berwick Castle, but that was for the most lofty. The trio found quarters at an inn.

In the morning they all lined up at the north end of the Berwick bridge over the Tweed to wait, no fewer than nine earls, lords innumerable, and divines such as Rutherford and Cargill. In mid-forenoon they saw a small company approaching, and were presuming that this could be only an advance-party coming to prepare the way for the duke, but were surprised to see, on nearer convergence, that this included His Highness himself, however modestly escorted.

The meeting was warm, even though York was not a demonstrative character, and especially so for the Haddington trio, for when the duke saw them among the crowd he came over to greet them personally, emphasising before all his approval of their activities. They were suitably gratified.

Heading back for Holyroodhouse at Edinburgh, they got as far as Hailes Castle, the Bothwell seat, most of the company having to pass the night at Prestonkirk nearby. In the morning the friends dropped off at Haddington, and in view of the especial notice that the duke had taken of them, felt bound to go and pay final respects before leaving. York took leave of them there in most friendly fashion, and announced that he would not be long in coming to the New Mills to see progress and developments, and hear of extensions of the industry.

In the meantime, James was preoccupied with the Philip situation. The heather-burning, which Philip seemed to have enjoyed, was over, and actual shepherding did not appeal to him. So he was back at Morham, and showing no signs of reformation. His father was anxious that he should not misbehave himself while York was nearby and was likely to hear of it. In consequence he sent his son off to Yorkshire, in theory to manage the little mill there, which sounded like some approval, and the young man went unprotesting, not taking his wife with him. His mother also remained at Morham, where she might be in a position to act hostess to the Duke of York.

In only three days they heard at Haddington that York had summoned Dalyell to his presence at Holyrood, and there the offending general informed of the royal will, replacement by the duke, and a return ordered to London forthwith. Also of the king's displeasure over the methods taken against his Presbyterian subjects. Bluidy Tam had reportedly heard all this expressionless, and departed for the Binns, not long delaying in departing for the south with his dragoons. So that unhappy interlude was over, with esteem for York soaring.

His next act was to arrange a review of the Scots armed forces, no very large assembly as they constituted, on the Burgh Muir of Edinburgh where, attended by many of the highest in the land, he addressed the troops, or as many as could hear him, emphasising the royal goodwill towards all Scots subjects, Presbyterian, Episcopalian, Catholic and others alike, and distress at the recent violence and per-

215

secutions by Dalyell, with assurances that there should be no more of this. He then inspected the turn-out, troop by troop, and ended up by riding at their head down to the city, where at Edinburgh Castle gunfire boomed out to celebrate the commencement of a new regime in Scotland.

The Haddington friends were not involved in all this, but heard of it with much approval, as did most Scots folk.

James Stewart did come to Haddington, to stay a few nights at Lethington with Lauderdale, and visited the New Mills. He was much interested in the progress made, especially in the new installations for weaving finer cloths and non-woollen materials, declaring this to be something that he could have copied in his Yorkshire lands and elsewhere. Lauderdale, who came with him, said that he was considering similar ventures in his own new borders mills, and foresaw this Haddington initiative eventually turning Scotland, at least in the Lowlands, into a major cloth-making country, to its great advantage. He mentioned the Hawick development in particular, and there how the Scott of Buccleuch family, who owned much of the land, had seen the opportunity for advantage and profit, and were encouraging the establishment of new mills. This still further interested York, for of course his nephew Monmouth was now also Duke of Buccleuch. He would be well pleased to see what was being done there, and to report to Charles. So Lauderdale offered to take him down to Teviotdale and the Middle March in general, with the duke saying that the three friends ought to accompany them, since it was through their example that it all had taken place.

The excursion was arranged for two days hence.

So a fair-sized party rode with the heir to the throne south-westwards. They climbed over the Soutra pass, where York was shown the great hospital-complex site, the first such in all Scotland, where his far-back ancestor, William the Lion, had encouraged Augustinian monks to provide the extraordinary range of facilities for the sick and infirm, the needy and the dying and for travellers on this, one of the main highways into Scotland from the south; of this he had never before heard. Then on down Lauderdale itself, with a brief call at Thirlstane Castle, the Maitland seat there, before reaching the town of Lauder, a royal burgh, so created by the aforementioned King William, and famous as the place where the then Earl of Angus, Bell-the-Cat as he was known, hanged James the Third's favourites over the side of Lauder Bridge, this before that feeble monarch's eyes. This was pointed out, also the notably named streets of Upper and Under Backsides, and the new parish church Lauderdale was building therein, as evidence of his devotion to the Presbyterian cause.

From Lauder they headed slightly westwards and through the Allan Water valley among more hills, this on the bridle-path which the monks of Melrose Abbey had used to link with the Soutra hospice, to pass the unusual situation of three small castles owned by different lairds, all within hailing distance of each other, Hillslap, Colmslie and Langshaw. Admittedly their respective lands stretched away in different directions, but the three fortalices' reasons for being where they were almost certainly derived from the opportunity this gave them to impose tolls on users of the road after the land passed from monkish hands at the Reformation. That profitable privilege of baronial rights no longer continued.

Reaching the Tweed at Melrose, its great abbey so long a target of invading English, and now ruinous, they turned upriver, the duke much interested in all that he saw; and there was much to see. Where the Ettrick Water joined the larger river, they turned up this to reach Selkirk, on the edge of the great Ettrick Forest, in the past haunt of outlaws and broken men, where King David the First, of all but sacred memory, had built his first abbey, and then oddly transferred it to Kelso, to be near his favoured seat of Roxburgh Castle, the only known such removal of a great sanctuary in all the land. At Selkirk they paid a brief visit to a mill being built by one of the Scott of Buccleuch family for cloth manufacture, forerunner of those they were to see working at Hawick a dozen miles further south.

It had been quite a lengthy ride, and Hawick was still some distance ahead, so Lauderdale had sent a messenger forward to inform Scott of Ashkirk and Sinton that the party would spend the night at his house of Ashkirk. He was, with his cousin Scott of Branxholme, one of the cloth mill entrepreneurs at Hawick. He proved glad to welcome them, especially the duke, however flustered was his good lady at this unexpected invasion. York made an un-demanding guest however. Patrick, George and James were not alone in finding him good company in a quiet way, easy to get on with despite his royal blood, easier indeed than was Lauderdale.

In the morning their host conducted them over more hills, insufficiently sheep-strewn George suggested, to the Teviot valley and Hawick town, this the scene of the most enterprising developments in the new cloth-making in-dustry, not only the Scotts engaged in it but Douglases and Turnbulls.

They spent a busy and rewarding day inspecting the mills, the owners being proud to show the duke and the High Commissioner over, with James Stanfield's advice especially sought, needless to say, over improvements and innovations. They heard that further mills were proposed on Teviot-side. Hawick folk were going to have to become inured to the clack-clack noise of water-driven mill-wheels by the dozen.

That night they spent at Branxholme Castle three miles upriver, the large and quite famous house of a senior line of the ducal family of Buccleuch, the lord of which had led in this of the mill-founding. There was much discussion that evening over extensions of the trade, recruiting labour, different types and qualities of cloth, and the important matter of marketing, George again emphasising that the local uplands could carry more sheep than were to be seen, and the advisability of crossbreeds, James advocating crosses for blackface with English Leicester, Cotswold and Welsh mountain-lonk, as well as Cheviot. It surprised them all that the Duke of York should be so obviously interested, he emphasising the value of the mutton produced, and enquiring about methods of preserving the meat by smoking and salting.

A return next day was made, by a different route, to Haddington, all much encouraged.

Before he left them, James Stewart told the friends that he planned a token of his own and his royal brother's appreciation of all their remarkable efforts in the cause of local and national prosperity and wellbeing. It should be rewarded, and would be, despite their modest head-shaking.

24

The departure of Dalyell, the coming of the Duke of York, his assumption of the position of commander-in-chief of the Scots forces, with proposals for the better and more useful employment of the soldiery, possible increase in numbers and, to be sure, the payment thereof and their positioning throughout the land to help establish central authority, called for a parliament session, it seemed. This was arranged for November.

The duke had taken up residence in Holyroodhouse, and the friends and their ladies were invited there on the evening before the parliament, Joanna included. James was continuing to see her, in discreet fashion, although never in the company of his wife.

The next day the commissioners and spectators in the gallery at Edinburgh Castle noted something not seen since queen-consorts had sat alongside their husbands at opening ceremonies. Next to the thronelike seat where the Lord High Commissioner was to preside another chair was now placed. Clearly this was because of the heir to the throne's presence in Scotland, and presumably his attendance at this session. Some wondered which of the chairs he would occupy.

When the officers of state, the earls, lords temporal and spiritual and then the Chancellor, Rothes, had filed in, the Lord Lyon King of Arms made his announcement.

"His Grace, Charles, King of Scots, is represented by his Lord High Commissioner, the Earl of Lauderdale, and also by His Royal Highness James, Duke of York." This to a flourish of trumpets. It was the former who came in first,

220

followed by the duke, Lauderdale who went to sit on the throne, the other at his side, all noted.

Opening the proceedings, the High Commissioner announced that they all were greatly privileged in having here with them, on this occasion, their sovereign-lord's brother and heir to the throne, High Admiral, and commander of His Grace's forces in Scotland. He came to defend all loyal subjects of whatever creed and conviction, and to preserve the peace of the realm, so recently and shamefully shattered by General Dalyell. His Royal Highness was concerned also with the prosperity of the land, and had demonstrated this by his recent visits to areas of new industrial activity. He called upon all to welcome His Highness.

Cheering and a standing ovation followed.

The duke rose, bowed all around, and sat again. Lauderdale indicated to Rothes the Chancellor to commence the business.

The subject of the armed forces, the principal concern of this parliament, went ahead forthwith, the general conception agreed without controversy, the details as to numbers, locations for troops, particularly in the Highlands, and costs producing considerable debate, and the uses to which idle soldiery could be put, Scotland quite unused to having a standing army, the lords' tenants and supporters and workers, with the chiefs' clansmen, producing the forces. The thought of paying troopers to do nothing more with their time was obnoxious to most, and with the peace of the realm now being ordered from on high the military ought to earn their wages in useful fashion. Much was the debate on this, some of the suggestions made scarcely practical nor even suitable. And there was the question of horse or foot, cavalry or infantry. Payment: where was that to come from?

All this took considerable time, and the Lords of the Articles were given instructions to deal with the different aspects of the implementation, in consultation with the new commander-in-chief. What that man thought of his first experience of a Scots parliament was not to be known.

At length, Lauderdale turned to York.

The duke stood, to say that he had listened to all with much interest and no little understanding, recognising the problems and requirements. The parliament would not find him difficult to work with in this matter, he assured. Then, pausing, he declared that he had an announcement to make on a quite different subject.

"My lords and commissioners," he went on, with a wave of his hand. "I have been particularly concerned, for some time now, with the very worthy and profitable industry established at Haddington in this Lothian, and thereafter elsewhere in Scotland, this of the setting up of woollen mills to spin yarns and weave cloths, and so to use the much wool produced in your hills and moorlands, instead of selling it overseas and then buying back the various cloths, clothing, carpets, blankets and the like, this a project of great value, as all must recognise. It must be further advanced to the benefit of all, in wealth, paid labour and the weal of communities. Also, with it, the increase of sheep-rearing on empty lands. All this you know well."

He paused again, and went on. "What I am concerned with here, as is my royal brother, is that the three good men who are responsible for this great work and advantage should be seen to be acknowledged as the benefactors that they are to this nation, and in some measure to England also, for their endeavour has not gone unnoticed there, especially in my own Yorkshire and in Lancashire. I now make it known that these three, the Lord Elibank, Sir James Stanfield and Hepburn of Monkrigg, are herewith appointed by the king's Majesty founders of a royal commission and association to further the industry, trade and welfare of this land, under the style of the Royal Society of Industry. They are entitled to use the Royal Arms of Scotland, by appointment, with powers to use crown lands and privileges in their ongoing efforts for the good of the kingdom. And the three named to be permitted to quarter the said arms on their shields. Moreover they are to be known as Companions of the Order of Acclaim . . ."

Cheers rang out, but York raised a hand. "I call on the three companions of the order named to stand, for all to greet them."

Lauderdale pointed out that Hepburn of Monkrigg was up in the gallery with the women, and that man was waved down to the floor of the hall amid more cheering. He went to stand beside Stanfield at the county commissioners' benches.

Never had the like been seen at a parliament before.

Distinctly embarrassed, however pleasured, the honoured ones bowed and murmured and shook heads.

"Hail the Companions of Acclaim!" York called.

The ovation went on, many leaving their places to come and shake hands with the trio, all standing apart as they were, higher-pitched female cries from up in the gallery mingling in the applause. Uncertain what to do now, Patrick and James resumed their seats, and George, hesitating, disappeared upstairs again.

Rothes, adding his congratulations, resumed his conducting of the remaining business as York sat down.

The session over, and the new Companions of the Order of Acclaim still being congratulated, they were told by the Lord Lyon that they were invited, with their womenfolk, to Holyroodhouse again. So it was down from the castle, and along the mile-long spine of the strangely sited city, with the ground sloping down quite steeply on either side, by the Lawnmarket into the High Street, past the High Kirk of St Giles and the Tron to the Canongate, this before the Reformation a separate burgh under the Church, with its own tolbooth and hospices, to the Abbey of the Holy Rood now turned into a royal palace.

They did not go alone, for not a few of the most lofty of the kingdom apparently were to be fellow-guests. They made quite a procession of it, the trio all but bewildered by their strange, indeed unique elevation and consequent prominence, wondering just what it all really meant and presaged, and what this new Society of Industry was to be able to do. None there could tell them.

At the palace they found quite a banquet awaiting them in the lesser hall, long tables in two ranks spread for many. Up on the dais at the far end were two smaller tables instead of the usual one. Two of the Lord Lyon's heralds were already there, and busied themselves ushering guests into their places, after necessary ablutions, precedence in rank not being overlooked. The Haddington six were allotted a side table in an alcove under the minstrels' galley, from which soft music was being relayed — this distinct from the rest, which had them wondering anew.

When all were seated and wine brought for them, amid much buzz of talk, Lyon appeared on the dais, to announce the entry of His Royal Highness and their lordships the Earls of Lauderdale and Rothes, with their ladies; York had not as yet brought up his duchess from London. The music had ceased.

All stood as the five came through the doorway at the back of the dais, the duke waving for the guests to sit again. He himself did not sit however, but came to the front of the dais platform to address the company.

"It is my pleasure to welcome all here on this especial occasion," he said. "We come to celebrate something new in this realm, or in any realm I would judge. That is the formation of a Royal Society of Industry, as announced in parliament. This is a step towards further prosperity, worthy employment and profit in this kingdom. Since the demise of Holy Church, which formerly led and produced the labour, works and wealth of the realms, such good leadership has been lacking. This I need not tell you, lords and landowners seeing themselves as above such mundane matters."

He smiled, waving a hand at all, to take any sting out of his words, he a known Catholic.

"This has been a loss, not only in Scotland, the present Church authorities not deeming this their responsibility!" Again a slight pause and smile, this reflected on many hearers' faces. No prelates were there present.

"But now, happily, the way has been shown towards a renewal and advancement of such wealth-making and praiseworthy activity. Industry is becoming accepted again as valuable, indeed necessary for the better wellbeing of all. This development is to be encouraged. And who has led the way in this advancement but the three most industrious and far-seeing venturers whom I have installed as Companions of the Order of Acclaim. I further name them to be an example to all. And urge them, and as many others as may be, to work on to further the establishment of industries, not only of wool-spinning and cloth-making and the like, but of many other products which we all require and have at present to be bought from other lands. This is the new society's aim and objective. It is to be no mere association of well-wishers but an active force to advance the land's industrious abilities and possibilities. You have merchant companies and trade guilds. Why not a Society of Industry? The need is there. Here is the start of it."

Turning, he pointed towards that alcove.

"I call upon the three Companions of Acclaim to come up to this table here, with their ladies, in token of their achievement and in anticipation of their ongoing good works."

With applause from the company, the little group from Haddington rose, eyeing each other, and self-consciously made their way forward to the dais, while at a signal from Lyon the music resumed from the gallery above. York himself came to assist the ladies up the steps and on to the dais, and conducted them to the other, empty, table thereon.

When all six were seated, he smiled briefly on them; and, despite his normal rather serious expression, he could have a warm smile. Then he went back to his own place at the main table.

"Enough of words," he declared. "Let us celebrate in more enjoyable fashion." He took and raised his glass, turning to eye the six, bowed, and gestured for all others to drink. He sat down.

Patrick, George and James drew breath but sat, silent. What was there to say? Had it not all been said, and by the heir to the throne? The past had been praised, the present was theirs, and the future beckoned . . .

EPILOGUE

The future held no lack of incident, changes and challenge, as the future is ever apt to do, good, bad and indifferent, for the friends and for others. The Industrial Revolution was not yet, but a start was made. The cloth-milling flourished and other manufactures developed, including shipbuilding for the increased exports, iron-founding for making the necessary machinery, tanneries and leather-works to use the hides, oil extraction and more. Stanfield introduced English glass-makers. And sailcloth factories were established.

On what could be called the political front, matters went less well. The increasing attacks of Dutch warships on English trading vessels necessitated the Duke of York's presence in the south as Lord Admiral to take charge of the English fleet; and he won the sea battle of Southwold Bay, with other successes. His eventual return to Scotland was brief and less happy and productive of popularity, for he was sent to help put down the increasingly militant Cov-enanters who had risen in arms to defeat Graham of Claverhouse who was now leading the armed forces. Civil war developed, and York and Lauderdale, now created duke thereof, were given the task of bringing the religious extremists to heel, in a sorry chapter in Scotland's story.

Charles the Second died in 1685, and his brother duly became James the Seventh and Second. But he would not give up his convictions on finding himself nominal Head of the Church of England and Defender of the Faith. In a century of religious intolerance, he was driven from the throne, and the succession of his daughters Mary and Anne established the Protestant regime for henceforth. His son, another James, did in due course seek to regain the throne, without success, and his grandson, Prince Charles Edward, fought gallantly in support, but to no avail. The House of Stewart fell after three hundred years.

Catholic, Protestant, Episcopalian, Puritan, Presbyterian and Covenanter negated their Christ's teaching of love; but it survived, a lesson to be learned by men made in the image of the caring God.

Distresses and disasters were not confined to the nominally religious. Despite the successes of their industrial initiatives, James Stanfield, for one, was not spared grievous hurt, indeed tragedy. His son, no reformed character, returned to Scotland, and misbehaved more shamefully than ever, causing his father dire trouble, Philip quite out of control. Out of his ongoing affliction and despair, in November 1687 James's body was found in the shallows of the River Tyne, near to the New Mills. At first it was thought that he had committed suicide because of his unhappiness over his son. Philip and his mother had the body hastily buried; but when it was discovered that Lady Stanfield had previously prepared grave-clothes for her husband, suspicions were aroused. The body was exhumed and examined, and it was found that James had been strangled before being put in the river. Philip was arrested, tried, found guilty of murder, and hanged at the Cross of Edinburgh, his tongue cut out for cursing his father, his right hand severed for parricide, his head detached and exhibited at the East Port of Haddington, and the remainder of his body hung in chains between Edinburgh and Leith. His mother disappeared, presumably back to England.

So extraordinary was the end of an extraordinary man.

No such disaster assailed his sorrowing friends.

So much for acclaim.

NIGEL TRANTER

THE END OF THE LINE

The dawn of the 15th century and Scotland was plunged
into chaos. With the new king, Robert III, ailing and weak,
his younger brother, the Earl of Fife, seized his chance to
become Regent and Governor of the realm.

Sent to London to appease the English king, George the
Cospatrick, 10th Earl of Dunbar and March, forged a
lasting friendship with Richard II's cousin, Henry of Bo-
lingbroke, who was to become King Henry IV of England.

On Henry's accession to the throne, a remarkable situation
arose. Robert III's wife asked Earl Cospatrick to use his
influence with the English king in order to avert civil war.
And so it was that Cospatrick found himself seeking help
from the Auld Enemy to right affairs in Scotland.

But Cospatrick's links with the Plantagenets gave rise to
wild accusations, and in due course his son, George, Master
of Dunbar, was destined to pay the price of his father's
alleged treachery. Would the 11th Cospatrick be the last of
his line?

HODDER AND STOUGHTON PAPERBACKS

NIGEL TRANTER

COURTING FAVOUR

Younger son of the ninth Earl of Dunbar and March, John Cospatrick expected to inherit neither title nor estate. But when his mother, the formidable Black Agnes, bequeathed him the earldom of Moray in the far north of Scotland, John was to find himself unexpectedly elevated to become the King's lieutenant and arbiter up in those unruly parts.

At the age of twenty-two, with no experience in such matters, John was to prove himself a skilled diplomat. But his greatest test as envoy and negotiator came when the new King, Robert the Second, sent him to England to win over John of Gaunt and attempt to end years of cross-border warfare by entering into a formal treaty of peace and accord with England and an alliance with France.

HODDER AND STOUGHTON PAPERBACKS

NIGEL TRANTER

THE ADMIRAL

Determined to avenge his father, slain by English privateers off the coast of the Isle of May, Andrew Wood's national renown as a fearless pirate-slayer brought him to the attention of King James III.

Eventually promoted to become Baron of Largo and Lord High Admiral of Scotland, Wood's bold defence of Scottish waters was to incur the wrath of King Henry VII of England. Wood was now in great danger.

In his own inimitable style, Nigel Tranter tells the incredible story of how this humble laird from Largoshire became Scotland's most famous sailor and one of the king's most valued officers-of-state: a skilled negotiator who greatly aided his nation's cause at a time of international unrest.

HODDER AND STOUGHTON PAPERBACKS

A selection of bestsellers from Hodder & Stoughton

The Admiral	Nigel Tranter	0 340 77015 5	£6.99	☐
The End of the Line	Nigel Tranter	0 340 73928 2	£6.99	☐
Courting Favour	Nigel Tranter	0 340 73926 6	£6.99	☐
The Bruce Trilogy	Nigel Tranter	0 340 37186 2	£12.99	☐
Flowers of Chivalry	Nigel Tranter	0 340 52028 0	£5.99	☐

All Hodder & Stoughton books are available at your local bookshop or newsagent, or can be ordered direct from the publisher. Just tick the titles you want and fill in the form below. Prices and availability subject to change without notice.

Hodder & Stoughton Books, Cash Sales Department, Bookpoint, 39 Milton Park, Abingdon, OXON, OX14 4TD, UK. E-mail address: orders@book-point.co.uk. If you have a credit card you may order by telephone – (01235) 400414.

Please enclose a cheque or postal order made payable to Bookpoint Ltd to the value of the cover price and allow the following for postage and packing:
UK & BFPO: £1.00 for the first book, 50p for the second book and 30p for each additional book ordered up to a maximum charge of £3.00.
OVERSEAS & EIRE: £2.00 for the first book, £1.00 for the second book and 50p for each additional book.

Name ....

Address ....

....

....

If you would prefer to pay by credit card, please complete:
Please debit my Visa / Access / Diner's Club / American Express (delete as applicable) card no:

Signature ....

Expiry Date ....

If you would NOT like to receive further information on our products please tick the box. ☐